Reflections

in My

Tea

Sandra Porter

authorHOUSE®

Portions of this book are based on truth. However, other portions are strictly fictional. With the exception of publicly known figures, any resemblance to actual events or locales or persons, living or dead, is coincidental.

If you purchase this book without a cover you should be aware that this book may have been stolen property and reported as "unsold and destroyed" to the publisher. In such case, neither the author nor the publisher has received any payment for this "stripped book."

No part of this book may be reproduced or transmitted in any form or by any means, electronic or mechanical, including photocopying, recording, or by any information storage and retrieval system, without permission in writing from the author.

Cover designed by: Sandra Porter

AuthorHouse™
1663 Liberty Drive, Suite 200
Bloomington, IN 47403
www.authorhouse.com
Phone: 1-800-839-8640

ACCLAIM FOR
Reflections in My Tea

An alluring tapestry of characters and scenes that leave
you whistling for your own dream.
—Dr. Timothy Askew, English Professor Clark Atlanta
University, adjunct professor Spelman College and author
of *Lord, Lead Me Down The Abbeville Road*

Expect the unexpected—Humorous!
Morally inspiring! Realistic! Great for all audiences! A
good read for the family!
—Deidre Pearson

Intriguing, unpredictable, colorful
—DaNita McClain, Spelman College

Dedicated

to my

Loving Grandmother

Acknowledgments

I just couldn't let some things go by unnoticed. This book just would not have been complete without thanking those who played a role in one way or another:

Thanks to the One who has made this possible, who gave me the flow of words to write. *Thank you, Lord.*

To my Spiritual Advisor, who has given me courage to continue. I am still amazed to have walked through this door of opportunity. This exploration has led me from one melody to another—a medley to treasure. The pages just keep right on turning.

Thanks to my mother for listening. Once again, we have chatted and laughed about the contents of this book no matter what time it was. You were ready to listen to whatever lyric was playing. I hope the beat was worth listening to. You are a lady of inspiration.

Thanks to my pastor and his wife (*you sure know how to move a book!*—smile), and to the members of my church, both locally and nationally, for supporting me along the journey.

A shout out of thanks goes out to my family and friends, also. You have been there for me as relatives and friends who care. You never let me forget my mission by asking, "*When is the next release?*"

I also wish to thank, Windy Goodloe, as editor of this book. Your comments and expertise are greatly appreciated.

You have been *great* to work with. And, thank you, Seretha Young, who volunteered to edit, but was unable. Time has been limited for you and I am grateful for your contribution… *you are wonderful.*

Thanks to each author and reviewer for your reviews. Your excitement escalated my adrenaline even more to get the next book of the series published.

And I can't forget the bookstores for shelving my book: Acts Christian Bookstore, Borders, Medu Bookstore, Nubian Bookstore and Spelman College Bookstore. *Thank you.*

Thank you, Kerry-Dean Nugent and Elizabeth Alexander, for sharing your comments. Wondering what the next beat will be? Keep reading because even I am in suspense and just as inquisitive as you are. I never know what river of information will be given to me next. Just as everyone else, I am looking to the next release of this series.

Last, but not least, I would like to thank all my readers everywhere for your support and for your interest in reading my second novel—*Reflections in My Tea.* Enjoy!

TABLE OF CONTENTS

…let the beat begin…

CLASSIC

Classics are noteworthy,
of highest quality and class,
submerging in value,
as years passed.

Life is like classical music,
keynotes ringing up the scale,
dramatizing,
skipping down the scale,
something to remember,
thundering notes in wide degrees,
fingers dribbling minors with a breeze,
a serenade that won't leave,
spoken words,
colored sleeves.

Tunes of priceless memories,
are classics and rarities,
filled with stories of an open book,
EKG'n the heat of the past,
a thump'n beat,
drifting in its quality,
glissando!—a spiraling rendition,
birthing colors of life.

… classics never lose their beauty.

Chapter 1

DEVIN

Where is this place? It's dark, foggy, and strange. I wonder around not knowing where I'm going. My heartbeat is ticking faster than normal. Why? Even my skin is tightening and flinching. My eyes scroll up and down and around. Nothing. Just spooky. Not at all entertaining for my taste. All sorts of thoughts cram my brain. I twitch from the stillness, but for what? Why am I feeling this way? I don't even know how I got here. Out of nowhere, a strong wind swirls in front of me, as if it should have had some visible form. It continues past me, mounting up the fear. This is the one time that I would have hopped on the back of Mr. and Mrs. Tomahawk's horse. It would not have mattered if they had multicolored feathers wrapped around their cranium because it is time to start whistling in the wind on another level. Without delay, I hopscotch around and take off running, blazing in the dark. Ahead, there is no place to run for cover; I just run, running faster than my globe. It can't keep up. My footsteps are countless. What am I running from? Suspense is brewing. Not only am I running a marathon, but I am running on a merry-go-round. Adrenaline is fierce. My motor skills are in overdrive. Thoughts do not cease. They bounce around like ticking bombs. After building up enough steam, they, too, go running and leave their neighbor behind—my brain. In front of me, a faint noise wavers in the air. I stop. What on earth *is that? Whatever it is, it is very far away…so far away that I can hear myself breathe. The creepy sound becomes louder and louder like iron bars shaking and trying to get out of some type of contraption. It rocks with rhythm—a sound sending chills to the bone. I take one step…two…a third step, which increases by the seconds. Changing lanes, I turn to head in the same direction as before. Off again, I go. Suddenly, the noise ceases. I stop for the second time. It is silent. My eyes are wide, staring in the dark. There are times I forget to swallow. I am reluctant to breathe out of fear. Briefly, I glance toward my burning feet, which should have been roasting on fire from the relay. One shoelace is loose. With speed, I bend down to tie it before I trip and fall. As I stand, a pulse of urgency rushes through my veins, knocking on my door to flee at any moment. I can't help mumbling the timely words that shake the gate of my mouth, "One, two, buckle my shoes…three, four, money poured." And, at that moment, it does just that; it pours! One-dollar bills are floating everywhere. I just stand there and watch as George Washington flips over and over. Is this a joke? My eyes roll. The bills are glowing, beaming down on me. "BAM!" a deafening noise sounds off, overshadowing what is raining around me. My head turns, but I don't see anything. I whip my head back around. My feet feel plastered from the sudden trauma. Swaying my body from side to side helps to strike a match under my shoes. The RPM of my engine is ready for takeoff. Strangely, I still cannot move. I am a sitting duck that can't fly South from the cold. Out of nowhere, Mr. and Mrs. Tomahawk appear and throw up a peace sign. My eyebrows join with confusion, but I am relieved. At this point, it doesn't matter. I hop on one of their horses, and we ride into the night.*

The phone rang.

My body awakened with a strong jolt. My eyes raced open. "Whew!" I instantly sat up, out of a weird dream, gasping for air. My chest felt like a beating drum—heartbeat was rapid. *"What was that?!"* I asked myself out loud. Sweat rolled down the sides of my face. My head throbbed with intensity.

The phone rang again.

I stared at it, caught between a nightmare and reality. My bed had taken a beating. Half the sheet, designed with leaves and trees, was on the floor dangling from one foot. Trying to recollect, I took a deep breath.

The phone was ringing, repeatedly.

After a few seconds, I finally turned toward the nightstand to pick up the receiver. "*Hello,*" I said brief, but hoarse, "*Devin speaking.*" My throat was very dry.

"*Heyyyy, Devin, my man is back in town,*" a male's voice said excitedly.

For a moment, my brain tried to skip tracks but was still a little suppressed. "Is that you, Jarvis?"

"Of course, it's me. Bruh, you don't sound too good. *Are you all right?*"

I sighed with relief. "Yes, I'm alright but, *brother,*" shaking my head, "*I had the strangest dream.*" From the sudden interruption, residual of terror was all in my voice.

"I can tell. Do you have a clue what it meant?"

"Not sure. It didn't make sense."

"Usually, that's how it is."

I took another look around where I lay, and snickered, calming down, "Let me rephrase that…it was *waaay* out there."

"Well, maybe you'll figure it out later."

"I doubt it. But, *what's on your mind?*"

"Around noon, I'm heading to the café. I'm calling to see if you would like to meet me there for brunch."

"What time is it?" I asked.

Jarvis paused. "It's about 10:30."

"Sure."

"Meet me at 1 o'clock."

"I'll see you in a few."

Driving along the streets of Southern California, again, was refreshing. It was no different; but, at the same time, this place felt as though I was scanning its scenery for the very first time. It was great to be back home after a long and exciting, two-month gospel tour. If my vocals ever needed a rest, it was now. They had been stretched high and low, deep and wide, reaching every note imaginable. Now that I'm home, I'm back with family and friends and that comical dog, Jordache.

As I peeked above the rim of my shades, I scoped plazas, office buildings, theatres, grocery stores, and cars of all makes zoom by. This place was all too familiar, and the popularity of beautifying the city was worth admiring. Spring, my favorite time of year, was near. The turning of the season was gorgeous—bright, sunny, and suntanning warm. I welcomed any sunshine I could get. Even the high-rise buildings seemed to have their own conversation with nature as the sun rose. Its brightness can't be hidden after each quiet, lonely night of darkness. Most mornings shed their awakening purpose of beauty with stillness and contentment, revealing the atmosphere's colorful sunrays. Mother Nature's job is not complete without showering her sheer nutrients upon every shrub, flower, and tree. They're exuberant. The palm trees were profuse in stature and well baked in color. The greenery almost appeared fake because of their unique and luxurious shapes, which were designed by artistic hands. Routinely, her full-time job tic-tocks around the clock until the blackness of the galaxy vanishes, after nightly hiding behind the face of the moon. She nurtures the earth again, drying its mist for another clear and sunny day.

My eyes squinted against the brilliant sunlight as I looked toward the green street sign for confirmation that my turn was coming up. As usual, traffic was thick on a Friday afternoon. It was lunchtime for many people who seemed to be enjoying what sunny California had to offer. The crowds of people seemed extra energetic. Many would say, "Thank

God, it's Friday." They made the best of the beginning of the weekend.

I parked next to Jarvis's car. When I turned the motor off, my cell phone rang. I flipped the phone piece up. "Hello, Devin speaking."

"Good afternoon, Devin." It was a voice to remember. She was a special friend from North Carolina who cared about life and the people she knew. She even went over and beyond to help those she didn't even know.

My lips expanded into a grin. "Good afternoon, Faith," I said in a voice an octave higher than normal to humor her.

We laughed.

Before she could respond, I asked, "And how are you?" I rested my elbow on the armrest.

"Fine, Devin, and you?"

"Doing great *now*." She knew I had no problem making that known to her.

"I see," she said. "Hopefully, you'll feel the same way tomorrow."

"What's significant about tomorrow?" I asked staring, caught between seeing a mysterious shadow that was gone in a split second and the drum roll of Faith's statement.

"My plane lands at LAX before continuing on to Sacramento tomorrow morning."

Forgetting everything else, I sat straight up. "What time?" The phone was plastered to my ear.

"It arrives at 11 o'clock."

"Would you like to have lunch?"

"*Sure.*"

"What time does your flight leave heading for Sacramento?"

"Two o'clock."

Pulling out my notepad and pen, I wrote down the information. "I can meet you there."

"Sounds good," she said. "I have a full day ahead of me, but, before getting out, I just wanted to make a quick call and fill you in on my plans. It's going to be a busy one."

"I understand. Tomorrow at 11 o'clock, right?"

"Yes, I'll see you then."

"All right. Have a nice day."

"You as well, Devin."

After releasing the line, it took a few seconds to remember why I had parked here. *Oh yeah*, I hopped out the suburban. I grabbed my keys and hurriedly followed a group of people who were about to enter the café.

Timing was perfect. A waitress was escorting Jarvis to a table with a window view.

I followed them, trailing not far behind. As I approached the table, he looked up and then beamed.

"Good to see you, man," I said gleefully, extending my hand as I sat across from him.

"Likewise, bruh."

The waitress promptly asked, "Would you both like something to drink?"

Jarvis spoke up. "Yes, water would be fine."

"I'll have water, too, and could you please add a cup of hot, smooth tea."

"*Wait a minute*," her eyes squinted. "*Aren't you*—"

Grinning, I replied, "Yes, I am Devin Fairchild." Watching her try to calculate who she thought I could be, was amusing.

She extended her arm to shake my hand. "My pleasure," she beamed.

"Mine, as well."

Not to waste anymore time, she asked, "Would you both like to order now?"

"Can you give us a few minutes?" Jarvis asked.

"Sure," she said, and went to help another customer.

It seemed as though I had not seen Jarvis *in a long time.* He had not changed. Maintaining his weight and athletic physique was a priority. The only difference, being 6'6" tall and fair-skinned, was his bald chin. The unveiling of his youth was apparent, which complimented his enveloped eyes and clean-cut hair. Now, on the other hand, I had gained several pounds. Even though slim for 6'4", I had padding room to pack additional pounds. Constantly being on the road left no room for exercising. With time on my hands, I planned to resume my routine and get back on track.

We were glad to meet again, brother to brother, friend to friend. Resuming where we left off, Jarvis said lively, "*I see you couldn't stay away.*"

"Well, friend, it was nice, but I'm glad to be back."

Jarvis chuckled and laid his menu down. "I know that's right!"

I shook my head, grinning, laying my menu down, too. "*Maaan*, I have to get back into the swing of things again and lose some *weight.*"

"The weight, Devin, doesn't look bad. It would be different if you were much heavier."

"Oh, you think so?" I chuckled.

"Sure," he said, "other than that, you're still tall, you haven't lost your hair; it's still jet black with some waves. And you haven't lost any building blocks."

I quietly laughed. "My *what*, man?"

"Building blocks," he said lowly, now finding a little humor in his own comment. While motioning his hand, he clarified his statement, "Building blocks as in muscles."

Smiling while nodding, I replied, "I knew what you meant. Never heard it put that way. That sounds more like something I would say, man, not you."

"You have a point. That's something, only *you* would say because, *brutha*, you come up with some good ones."

My hand rose like a stop sign. "I surrender...no comment."

We laughed picking up our menus, realizing that before long the waitress would return. We took a minute to decide on our order again.

The smells of various foods danced in the air. I couldn't tell what the aroma was. It smelled like a combination of hot foods glazed with sweet carnations. We were trapped by the scents, which created a volcano of hunger pains. We shifted our attention toward a waitress walking by. She carried an armload of platters that almost caused the volcano in my stomach to rupture. They were smells to savor.

Out of nowhere, our waitress appeared and served us drinks. She flipped out her pad and pen and took our orders. "I'll be back shortly," she said.

As she turned and walked away, Jarvis laid his menu down. "Well, I know you must've enjoyed your trip. You have to fill me in. You've been out of town for some time. I know you have more to say besides what you have already told me when you called while out-of-town." His eyes were locked with anticipation.

Before speaking, I reached for my glass of water and drank a few swallows. Then, I moved my tea in front of me. There were packs of sugar at the corner of the table neatly lined in a caddy. I ripped a few open and tilted the white granules into the hot, fuming tea and answered, "Yes, there is much to be said." I picked up a spoon and stirred. "It all seems like a dream now." The tea looked like a sea of water that had formed into a funnel, resembling the eye of a hurricane. Bubbles appeared then vanished.

He chuckled. "Wait a minute, bruh," he seemed to have recalled something. "Let's back up for a second since you just mentioned the word 'dream.' "

"I'm listening."

Jarvis tilted his head, puzzled. "Tell me something."

"Sure, what is it?"

"You just triggered our phone conversation this morning. What's going on with you? *You know...the dream.*"

Clueless, my eyebrows raised. "I don't know," I shook my head. I noticed a waitress seat a man on the other side of the café. "I felt like I was strapped part of the time and didn't have much control. *Say amen*, if you know what I'm talking about."

"Amen, amen, my brother," Jarvis said humorously.

We both chuckled.

I thought, *Yep…we're back into our chitchat mode.* Obviously, he'd had some nightmares of his own.

The conversation was becoming intriguing. "You know," I tilted my head with wonder. "It's baffling when your brain decides it wants to do sideshows while you're asleep."

"I know what you mean, Devin, when you mentioned not having much control. Your reflexes probably couldn't strike a match fast enough. It's good you didn't trip up on Godzilla beating on his chest, *bruh*."

My eyes slid to the upper corner of my brain where clues for answers rained on the lobe that held vital information.

"Devin," Jarvis stared, "you look like you're in deep thought."

My mind felt like it turned a flip and rolled back to a horrifying incident of the past. Actually, it turned out to be the funniest thing I had ever experienced before it was all over. *"Incredible,"* I shook my head until I laughed out. The hilarious event was fresh in my mind, like it had happened yesterday. I looked at Jarvis and asked, "Man, are you ready for *this one*?"

"It's *that* serious?" he asked.

"That's an understatement."

"Umph," I heard him say lowly.

I couldn't help but drop my head toward my chest with my hand plastered to my forehead, laughing again, and shaking my head, too. *Who would ever believe it?* The thought zipped across my mind.

"Let's hear it and don't stop until you're finished. I'm usually the one who's longwinded," he reminded me.

My head bobbed up and down in agreement, "Yes, brutha, you *are* longwinded."

"Devin, your time has come."

We chuckled.

First, I wanted to sip some tea. I couldn't resist its glorious scent that had skated into my nostrils, but it was still too hot. I put the mug back down on the table and stared at the substance. The lens of my brain became a reflector of light. I began to consume myself into the chain of events that had been buried. My eyes were still, concentrating, and all else around became a blur while staring down at my outline wavering as a branded seal. The silhouette looked like a figure of my imagination as I began to tell the story. "Years ago, when I was young, the State Fair came into town. It was a yearly event that gave kids the rush of their lives. Back then, that was the talk of the town. No one dared go alone because of scare tactics. Usually, kids went in groups or pairs. The neighborhood kids were extremely excited and wanted me to go along with them. Being young, my grandparents were not too keen on me going without an adult to supervise us that they knew. They were protective. Although both were always busy and had something to do, that particular Saturday, my grandmother volunteered to take me. I was just glad to go at all.

We walked around the fairground watching people win and lose games. Some walked away disappointed and some walked away happy, winning stuffed animals as their prize. There were clowns standing isolated, wearing colorful Afro wigs with a psychedelic, one-piece jumpsuit on resembling airbags. And, their shoes looked like canoes...size 20. I always wondered who was behind the mask. Their faces reminded me of a coconut cream pie with three walnut halves and a carrot. Usually, they were juggling balls in the air.

The highlight, so it seemed, was the Kiddyland rides to the Glass House, Revolving Tunnel, Haunted House, Roller Coaster, and the Ferris Wheel. Some rides were adrenaline-pumpers, which was not my type of joyride. On numerous rides, at times, the people's vibrations from screaming carried like airwaves at various velocities. Onlookers were not quite so daring, including me. Eventually, boredom set in.

Finally, I spotted a tent that had a colorful drawing on it of Tarzan woman and a gorilla in a jungle. Broadcasters drew large crowds sparking everyone's curiosity. There were PA systems in and outside the tent with surround sound, and it was loud with intensity. I wondered what warranted all the attention. It was like rolls of a drumbeat. Whoever came up with that sideshow *knew* what he was doing; we were caught in a net of suspense. Magnetized, we walked inside. Of course, when I had looked at my grandmother, she was somewhat reluctant for some reason. Her shiny, sparkling, prescription glasses revealed whatever reaction she tried to hide; her eyes were larger than before.

Ahead, we saw a stage with Jungle Woman inside of a large iron cage. There were no chairs to sit and watch; this observation required standing. Actually, we had front-row seats without anything to sit on and it wasn't long before there was no more standing room left. It was packed. The crowd was smart to stand behind us; we didn't know what *we were in for.* I heard about it but didn't believe it because it sounded too superstitious.

Suddenly, a dynamic voice pierced through the speakers and began his introduction. We were standing at the edge of the stage watching the mysterious onset. For some reason, I turned and noticed that the entrance of the tent was securely closed. At this point, my ears felt as though they had drooped. I had a feeling we made a serious mistake. The setup was an interesting exhibit, which appeared fake, but it was *very real.* Eventually, Tarzan woman turned into a full-grown goooooorilla! *Unbelievable. This entire forthcoming demonstration blinded the audience in disbelief.*

She began as a longhaired woman with black hair, dressed in a mini, one-piece, leopard dress with a jagged hem—without tiger. As minutes dwindled, her transformation from woman to gorilla turned gruesome, as thick strands of hair grew from the root of her smooth, tanned skin. *This presentation* was becoming more and more baffling by the second. The strong voice narrating the transformation grew dynamically convincing, saying, '*She's changing…she's changing….*' It was apparent that he had engineered many of these haunting expeditions and was thoroughly trained. Before long, she had brown, werewolf hair all over her body. I couldn't tell you where her leopard dress went; I guess she busted out of it. She, it, or what no longer resembled a woman. Its feet grew as large as Big Foot's, and its eyes changed from soft to beastly.

Once the transfiguration was complete, Kongo began rocking the locked-down cage back and forth uncontrollably. The beast started losing its mind and became irritated. I was wondering how this monstrous creature was going to get out because the bars were thick and appeared very well secured. On second thought…seeing the *rage*…the gorilla was capable of *anything*.

Warning and caution brewed in the air. The man's voice over the PA system got louder and louder increasing the drama. By this time, I was transfixed. The cage rocked fiercely. I observed with confusion and felt a rush of urgency to vacate the place. Hair on the beast was rising like a porcupine. I felt a sting coming on. The terror was electrifying, and then with so much force, the door of the cage landed on the platform of the stage *right in front of my eyes*, with a loud thump. Godzilla jumped out the cage and *roared with thunder, beating its chest.* It was *HUGE, like 10-feet tall.* I was facing this gorilla at arm's length, *BUT NOT FOR LONG.* The beat of time couldn't tick fast enough! I turned to the side where my grandmother stood but she was long gone—without *me.* *What!* the thought pounded. I was the one who had jetlag. When I turned completely around to escape from getting mauled, a stampede had erupted. Some of the audience had already fallen on the ground screaming, and some were laughing in disbelief at what was happening. My feet turned into rockets. I hopped and leaped, hurdling above the crowd to escape. What was once a two-lane entrance had turned into one-lane traffic. From that point, it was a straight shot. Fleeing into the sunshine never looked so good. I had tunnel vision and didn't look back to see if *King Kong* was on my heels or not. *The combustion in my feet was on fire, blaaaaazing.*

After I had run so far, I stopped to catch my breath. An alarm set off in my head, *MY GRANDMOTHER! WHERE IS SHE?!* My heart pounded with horror. In a panic, I took off running, again, looking for her. Surprisingly, coming around some corner, there she was, running toward me, wiping balls of sweat from her face. She was *WIDE-EYED.* Her glasses were still sparkling with her purse dangling on her arm, never letting up from patting her face with a handkerchief, rapidly. Her response was, *'DID YOU SEE THAT?!'* Instantly, from the comedy of her reaction, I broke down laughing in hysterics. She wasn't the only one who had wiped her face behind Kongo. I remember now that someone told me that a preacher witnessed this same exhibition, and that this gorilla sent him away running like lightning, too, in a *suit and tie* on a warm day. This man was stocky and tall in stature and always gave me the impression that nothing scared him. I was told that his response was, *'GLORY BE TO JESUS, DID YOU SEE THAT?!'* Putting both scenes together was a serious explosion for me. From all the laughing and gagging, and nearly loosing my strength and balance, she could no longer resist. She broke down laughing, too. Then, something else *hit* me. All that was running through my mind, at that moment, over and over, was, *Umph, she really left me.* Not only that, but I asked myself, *When did she sprint getting around all those people?* These thoughts just kept etching and circling around in my head; I couldn't believe it. She had to be burning up running in Arizona's heat with what she had on and wearing *support stockings, too.* Of course, we were whipped; we left.

When we returned home, all that my grandfather said after hearing our story was, *'You expect me to believe that?'* He chuckled, dismissing what sounded fabricated, enjoying his sautéed neckbones."

After sharing my experience with Jarvis, my eyes sharpened, still staring down at my tea, which had turned cold. The steamy aroma no longer alerted me of its existence. How much time had passed was questionable, especially when I looked up and now saw Freddie the Teddy sitting in front of me. "Teddy," I grinned, wondering how long he had been sitting there, "how's it going, man?" His nickname never grew old. He was the same Teddy now as he was years ago. He had a voice, deep as bass, at 5'5" tall that caused people to take instant notice. The contrast of his personality and style was definitely striking. As much as we have had the opportunity of working together, over the years, that always struck a funny bone.

He smiled with question marks dancing in his eyes. "Great!" he answered. "Maybe I should be asking *you* that question."

I chuckled seeing the humor in his statement. Apparently, he had heard part of my story. "Teddy, how much did you hear?"

"Enough to know that you almost came face-to-face with Kongo." As striking as that sounded, we both broke down laughing. "No wonder Jarvis tipped out when you got to the part about your grandmother making a mad dash and splitting the scene without you. Sounds like you were hurt behind that."

"Back then, I was. It's a good thing she did, though, because, *maaaaaan*, I don't know—" Our attention was diverted.

Jarvis returned. He sat across from me, next to Freddie and reached for his glass of water.

Freddie and I were quiet.

Jarvis looked at me after swallowing some H_2O and said, "Devin," he said as he shook his head on the brink of laughter, "that's a classic, *brutha*."

"I know. That's *some* connection—the dream and Tarzan woman. After all these years..."

"That would be hard for anyone to forget."

"Your grandmother is *certainly* a classic," Freddie commented. "I would like to *meet her, man*."

"So would I," Jarvis joined him. "She has to be special."

"She is," I told them picturing her in my mind.

"You go, grandmother," Freddie cheered for her. "One other thing."

"What's that?" I asked.

"Something just occurred to me," Freddie wondered.

"Which is?"

Amused, his curiosity was burning. "Was she running at full speed in a full-length dress?" His head was tilted for verification.

My expression must have said it all. "Yes, she was."

Tactfully, we lost it as we clearly visualized this scene.

When we calmed down, Jarvis cupped his forehead. Then he looked at me glassy-eyed and said, "Devin... *brother*...by the time you got to your grandmother vacating the scene, I had to leave out. I couldn't take it any more. That's *toooooo funny*. I have to hear the rest of that later."

"Yeah," Freddie chimed in, "you have to fill me in on that story because I missed part of it." He was on the edge of upscaling his tone of voice to laugh again, but he kept his composure.

We weren't trying to be on display, so we kept our reactions to a minimum in public.

"By the way, *what is that you were drinking*?" Jarvis asked.

All eyes were on me.

I chuckled. "Tea."

"You called it something else," he reminded me.

"Oh, yeah. Smooth tea."

"I'll remember that," he grinned.

The waitress returned with our food and took Freddie's order.

Glancing toward the other side of the café, the same man that I noticed earlier was leaving. He wore a hat that covered part of his face. *Umph, he looks so familiar.* The thought bogged my mind. *The shadow…who is he?*

... this beat is one to remember...

TIC TOC

A clock tic tocks,
the pendulum rocks,
the hand spins,
the unknown to mend,
time as its lens.

Time ticks away,
night and day,
year after year,
strapped in gear,
for the midnight clear,
towards the approaching hour,
waiting to blossom,
as a flower,
what time it is.

The dance of time,
ballets gracefully,
the seconds of time,
as a ballerina,
just waiting to bow.

… what color is the eye of time?

Chapter 2

DEVIN

The next day at 10:50 a.m., I was standing at the gate that Faith would be walking through at any moment. As soon as I sat in the waiting area, the door opened.

Minutes later, passengers were coming in droves, greeting family, relatives, and friends.

My eyes darted with speed until I finally saw Faith approaching the entryway. We smiled as our eyes met. I met her, gleefully, with open arms. *"Hey, Faith."*

"Hello, Devin," she responded lively, as her smile grew wider. "How are you?" She brought sunshine and spring with her.

Our conversation from yesterday was still fresh on my mind as I rehashed a thought, "I'm great!"

She must've remembered those words because she slightly laughed as we left. I joined in her spirit of laughter just the same.

As we walked to find a place to get comfortable, I took note of my observation of her. There's something a little different. She had lost weight since I had seen her last. Being slender and 5'8" tall, matched her characteristics perfectly. Her hair was dark brown and had well surpassed her shoulders, giving her even more height than before. She was always stylish and up-to-date. Her maple-syrup skin was clear as cellophane wrap, blending perfectly with her pearly-white teeth. Looking at her countenance, her facial features were soft and memorable; her light brown, caring eyes seemed to speak without words. She had the right ingredients and utensils that made up a good woman.

The airport was crowded—packed like sardines. In some areas, there was not a lot of room between each person. You could definitely tell who the passengers were. Travelers walked with a purpose and with increasing speed to catch their flight. It was obvious that those who were not on a time schedule coasted. We went with the flow of traffic until we found the perfect spot to chill.

There was much to say since we had last spoken. We were overdue; it was time to pay our bills. I was looking at her searching eyes when she asked with concern, "How is everyone?"

"They're all doing fine, and occasionally, have asked about you."

"Have they? I haven't seen them in some time, although, I have kept in touch with Camille and Carla."

"Yes. They're anxious to see you again. Do you think you'll be coming back to our neck of the woods in the near future?"

She nodded. "Yes. I plan to fly to Atlanta from Sacramento tomorrow and from there, I'll be back—"

I interjected. "Hopefully, for more than a two or three-hour layover."

She was tickled by my comment and replied, "That is my plan. I will be back in Los Angeles for a few days before going back home."

"*Hooray*," I clowned. "During your visit, maybe we can have dinner, or maybe—" I paused to build up her curiosity.

She was puzzled. "Or, maybe, *what?*"

My head shifted as I pictured the thought. I hunched and replied, "*Maybeeee*, I'll see you on the pew."

She had to chuckle at that one herself. Her words were, "Not so long ago, your life was restructured and beautifully painted. We know who the Artist is." She was reliving the conversations we had during the time I was laid-off over a year ago. Faith and Jarvis both helped me to survive when I had lost all hope. Now, that seemed so long ago.

"Umph," now in a daze, "sure does and I'm enjoying the colors of life. My way of thinking was reengineered from rags to riches."

"That's a good way of putting it. How much wealthier can one get?"

The subject matter was becoming delicate. "One thing is for sure, I was healthier after that. It's amazing how the eye of time flashes its beautiful eyelashes when a change comes."

Faith lightly nodded with a soft smile.

My response flowed right along with hers.

We conversed on powerful matters until it was time for her to catch her next flight.

By the time I reached the escalator to get to the lower level, my fireside chat with Faith rekindled. My flight was en route to another world to recap our conversation. I was so absorbed in my thoughts that my surroundings became nothing but a blur. Even the surround sound that filtered into my eardrums was muted. It felt as though I was wearing an earpiece completely turned off.

When I had reached the bottom of the escalator, my balance was suddenly jarred as two kids tried to hurry past me and onto the platform. "Sorry, sir," they said.

"No problem."

Toward the left, I noticed a group of teenagers who were whispering and looking my way. "Isn't that Devin Fairchild, the gospel singer?" one almost shouted excitedly.

Their eyes were glued on me as they tried to figure out if I was really who they thought. Half of my face was hidden under my baseball cap.

Simultaneously, I nodded and smiled. I touched the bib of my cap to confirm their curiosity.

"I knew that was him," one teen said as he nudged his friend.

Glancing past them, a figure riding up the escalator caught my attention. Stretching my neck to see if I recognized the person was difficult. There were too many people blocking my view. For sure, that same hat from the café yesterday alerted me like red flashing lights. It stood out above the crowd. I changed course and stepped onto the escalators riding back up to the second level to find the mystery man. *He looks so familiar. Who is he?* Robotically, my neck continued to stretch at angles around and above the crowds to keep him in my view.

A group of people decided to walk up along the side of the escalator to reach the top since it was moving at a snail's pace.

Distracted, a young lady lightly brushed my arm while passing and said, "Excuse me, sir."

"Sure," I moved out of her way. For a second, I forgot why I was going up instead of down from the sudden interruption. Refocusing my attention to spot the man in the black hat again was like finding a pin in a haystack.

As he reached the top of the escalator, his hat vanished.

My fingers were tapping the handrail. I was only halfway up. Anticipation held its breath.

When I finally reached the top, I walked swiftly, trying to catch up and trail this unknown person. Walking the same direction that I previously left was like a maze. I passed so many people. Stretching to see through my binoculars for a strenuous length of time, caused my eyes to start barking for relief. My eyes twitched, expanded, and bounced until they slowed their intensity, but my pace never changed.

My trance was broken when someone called me from the side. "Devin!" a female's voice said. The voice sounded very familiar.

With quickness, I turned my head to the side to see who it was. "Camille!" I smiled.

She was alone. "Hello, maestro," she responded cheerfully.

Being surrounded by so many people, I was glad to see someone I knew. Of course, my expedition ended. There was no way *now* I could catch the person I was following. Letting it go was probably the best thing.

My train of thought shifted. "Hello, Miss C, how are you?"

"I'm fine, and yourself?"

"*I'm great*," I said, repeating the same words not long ago. Although, it was the truth. I couldn't complain as I reflected back, in a flash, on my past compared to how far I had come.

Camille's cell phone rang. "Excuse me for a moment." She opened her purse and scrambled for the device.

"Take your time."

She flipped open the lid of the miniature toy. "I won't be long."

We stood to the side to keep from blocking traffic.

At that moment, I turned my head and watched the planes land through the crystal glass. I was captivated by the enormous-sized objects. They have always appeared as though they controlled their own legs by the time they landed. I enjoyed watching as they skated smoothly up the runway.

I felt a tap on the shoulder. Turning back around, Camille said, putting her cell phone back in her handbag, "Thank you for waiting."

"Sure."

"By the way," she lit up, "I happened to see Faith right before she caught her flight."

A smile unhid itself from behind the drapes of my lips. "Did you?"

"Yes, she looks great!"

"She does. I thought so, too."

Before she said anything further, she looked past me and smiled. "Devin, I would like for you to meet someone."

Turning around, my smile felt like it was trying to dismantle itself out of disbelief. I saw what Jarvis had been talking about.

"Charla, this is Devin Fairchild." Realizing how surprised I was, Camille then said facing me, "This is my twin sister. She was just returning from the powder room."

My lips quivered. A slight cough was all I could do to keep from snickering. "Excuse me, ladies." The film scrolled before my eyes, again, from listening to Jarvis's experience some time ago. They entertained him by using the same words—"powder room" as they called it. Sounds outdated, but very appropriate. They had to wonder what humored me but that had to remain hidden between Jarvis and me.

Being courteous, I extended my hand. "It's a pleasure to meet you, Charla."

They were identical just as Jarvis had described them. I was glad that this wasn't a stage play. So far, I have yet to meet identical twins at the same exact moment. Usually I meet one and get surprised by the other. Meeting mirror images has been interesting and quite entertaining from my experience.

A warm smile spread across her face, glowing. "My pleasure, too."

Camille spoke again, "Charla, Devin is a very good friend of Jarvis'. You might as well say they're brothers."

A light bulb went off. "Oh, yes," she said, not thinking, "I remember you talking about them both." Then she looked at me. "Camille had nothing but good things to say."

"Yes," Camille verified. "For one thing, I let her know that you both work very well as a team."

Charla added, "A sincere friendship is hard to find."

"I agree, Charla," was my response. "That's my buddy. Camille's right. He's like a brother."

With excitement, Camille then said, "Charla was stopping through overnight."

"Oh, good. It's nice for family to drop in for a visit."

"I'm all for that," they both said.

"Maybe, we'll see you more often," I pitched in.

"Hopefully, my schedule will allow me more time in the future."

"You're not a stranger; we're all family."

She appreciated the comment. "Thank you, Devin. That was kind."

"You're welcome, my sister."

Camille glanced at her watch. "Devin, we must get going," she said. "As always, it's good to see you."

"Good to see you, also."

Smiling, they both flagged their hands and went on their way.

Once I was on the main highway, I called Jarvis.

He answered in a hurried tone, "This is Jarvis."

"*Heyyyyy,* Jarvis," I said with rhythm, "how you doing?"

"Fabulous," he quickly replied, "and yourself?"

"Doing well. Sounds like you have things to do and places to go."

"I'm on another call, bruh. I'll get back with you once I wrap it up."

"All right."

"On second thought, stop by if you have time. I have something to tell you that may interest you."

"Sounds good, man. I'm on my way."

… this beat is getting suspenseful…

CHANGE

Change brings awareness to life,
an awakening of the old and new,
old things recycled,
new things introduced,
shifting faces,
going places.

Time draws as an architect,
what comes to pass,
sketched artistically into reality,
shadows to shades,
milestones are made,
a clock as its marker,
drafting the future,
blossoming until the sounds of chimes,
fine art is hard to find.

With life comes change,
time is its hourglass,
no movement,
no improvements,
no direction,
no progression,
no transcription,
no description,
no matter what time it is,
change will play tunes,
an orchestration.

… sculptures of life color their face with time.

Chapter 3

DEVIN

I couldn't imagine what Jarvis wanted to tell me; but, from the sound of it, the news may have been worth my while. After ringing the doorbell once, he opened the door with his cell phone clutched to his ear. He motioned for me to come in.

I sat on the sofa and was drawn into the movie *The Color Purple*, a story that had pockets of humor, and many scenes of sadness. The movie caused me to wonder about the condition of relationships during the early 20th century. The setting alone would send anyone into a trance. It's amazing to see just how inconvenient it was for some people back in those days compared to lifestyles today. They made do with what they had. Some may have wished things were different, but, at the same time, they appeared satisfied.

In this day and time, the thought of riding a horse, a mule, or even a wagon in the city, 24/7, as the only means of transportation would be like watching a ringside circus. That's not the norm for a city boy or girl. However, that may be different in tucked away, wide open territory that's not well-known or a place of interest for most of the population. Some places are isolated from the rest of the world. However, that may be different for a small town.

Nowadays, there are paved roads, streetlights, plazas, malls, nicely built homes, and a vast variety of automobiles to choose from; not to mention, no one has to boil water on wood stoves. That's just the tip of the iceberg. *Hmmm, things sure have changed.* Change tooted its horn over time and continued to bring awareness to life. *How can we live without it?*

I even thought about sanctuaries. Churches were captivating. Songs moaned from deep within souls were penetrating, as fans in hands swayed in rhythm to cool down the burn of the furnace in the heart. When the pace picked up, it was *clap-slappin' good.* It was good that institutions existed to help moralize, restore, rejuvenate, and revive needy hearts, reaching out to help maintain one's spiritual health and sanity. Reinforcements secured by Padlock paid off. Over time, institutions moved from outdoors to storefronts to small buildings to larger ones, and for some, to mega churches. The gospel never changes, but the genetics of other elements cannot develop without the nucleus of change. Its dynamics were mechanically needed and played a significant role. Change is the engine toward progression. Magnetically drawn to the future, how can it generate without destiny and how can destiny survive without the past? How can it deliver without a vehicle and move without an engine? Like a car, most likely, broken down until it's repaired.

During a commercial, Jarvis returned. *"Heyyy, Devin,"* he said, as if glad to have company. He clipped his cell phone to his belt.

I shook his hand. "What's going on, Jarvis?" He was clean and sporty in his penny loafers and creased jeans with a coordinating Daniel Cremieux shirt on. "Something must have transpired since yesterday."

His head bobbed. "Yes, it has. Your name is buzzing. My phone has been ringin' and singin'."

"Oh, yeah," I said with a slight chuckle. I wondered who had been inquiring.

"Actually, two businesses called requesting your vocals in *two days.*"

My voice went up a notch, too. "*In two days?*"

"It's your call because I had not, personally, initiated this. What do you think? I thought you would want a break in-between events and I didn't know what your plans were on such short notice."

"Well, *it was* a thought," my eyebrows joined, interested in hearing more information. "What are the specifics, man?"

"You may find this a little hard to believe."

The crevices in my forehead released. "Why is that?"

He laughed slightly from the frozen stare and said, "The first business that called is requesting you to sing at a hospital."

I fell back on the sofa in hysterics.

Jarvis chuckled but didn't find it as humorous as I did.

"Are you kiddin' me?" I found it to be unbelievable.

"No, I'm not," he responded. "Quite frankly, I'm rather impressed with that one."

According to the way I was feeling at the time, the idea felt like a bombshell. "How so?" My thought process had retired for the day. Apparently, I wasn't thinking straight.

Jarvis expressed, "During my past experience, I have never encountered this type of request. Although, giving back is the key. That's what your sole purpose is, isn't it? Think about it for a second."

"Man, it's hard after trying to hunt down a ghost today."

Jarvis froze in his seat. An instant shot of adrenaline tipped him right on over into disbelief. The shift in conversation caught him off guard. *"A WHAT?!"*

The words tumbled from my mouth, "A ghost."

He stared blankly. "A ghost?" he repeated, stunned. He tried to completely digest what I had said, but it didn't quite filter fast enough. When it finally sunk in, I guess that was the last straw for him. In an outburst, he laughed.

Watching him took the cake. I couldn't take it any mo'...I joined him.

Jarvis gagged like he was suffocating until he ran out of gas. "Umph, Umph, Umph," he stood up wondering, then asked, "Did you make that one up? I never heard of anyone chasing *Casper. Usually, Casper is chasing them.*" He was just as mystified as I was.

"On a serious note, I didn't make that one up. Obviously, as you can see, a good laugh is what I needed after following someone I don't even know or recognize."

"Oooooooooh," he sat with his mouth opened. Almost whispering, he said softly, "You were actually following someone?"

"Of course. A man in a black hat," I replied.

"Whew!" he sounded off. "That's a good one. I was beginning to wonder, if, maybe, you had been working too hard, or watching too many cartoons."

I snickered. "*Cartoons.* I haven't watched cartoons *in years,*" I let him know. Then, I shifted the conversation, again, "But anyway, singing at the hospital is not a bad idea. My sole purpose for singing is giving, and helping others is what it's all about."

Jarvis clapped. "*Alllllll right. Now, we're thinking.* But tell me more about the mystery man while it's fresh on your mind. We'll come back to this later. What brought all this on?"

"When we were having brunch at the café yesterday, that's when I first noticed the guy. And then today, I spotted him again." I went on to explain part of the details at the airport.

"That's mind boggling when you can't put the pieces together."

"I know," in deep thought, "and I just can't seem to quite place him. If his hat wasn't hiding part of his face, I could have gotten a better view. Both times, part of his face was also hidden because of the angle."

Then Jarvis asked, "What made you end the hunt?"

"Oh, boy," I said, remembering another interesting segment.

By this time, Jarvis was sitting on the edge of his seat. "It's that serious, huh?"

"You ready for this?" I grinned.

"Sure. Tell it."

"I saw Cinderella and Derella today, man."

Jarvis stood up and laughed out. "Don't tell me...you met one and were electrocuted, as you call it, by the other one."

From his animation, I had to laugh, too. "You got it!" It never failed.

"You finally met *Sister and Sistah*."

"Yep! My entire expression was dismantled."

"I know it was."

"Tell me this, brother. Why some sisters do that? We never meet them at the same exact time."

"You ought to be used to it by now," Jarvis said.

"No," shaking my head, "*never.*"

"I agree on that one, Devin. After awhile, you wonder if another one will pop up."

"But, you know...if we saw twins walk up at the same time, it probably wouldn't make things any better."

"It doesn't really matter, does it? If they're identical, it's still confusing."

I couldn't deny that. "You have a point. All I can say is play it off the best you can because from my past experience, it has been challenging for me."

"It *has* been interesting," he clasped his hands together, ready to change the subject. "First, Devin, after all that, I need something to drink before we discuss anything further about the trip. Would you like something, too?"

I stood to stretch my legs. It felt as though I had been sitting in the same spot for hours. "That sounds like a winner, my friend."

"What would you like?"

"Water is fine."

"You sure?" he asked, wondering if I'd rather have something else that had some kick to it, especially after all the laughing and animation we just went through. "I have Dr. Pepper, Pepsi, RC, punch, and some orange juice."

"I'll stick with water for now," I answered.

"Water coming up."

As I sat back down, our discussion sunk in. Singing at a hospital never made headlines in my mind. The thought of it now glittered.

Hearing footsteps, Jarvis returned with speed and said, "An impromptu trip to Atlanta should be interesting." He handed me a glass of water.

The name of that city got my immediate attention. *"Atlanta?"* I grinned.

"Yes, my brother, the state that is known as the peach state," he replied enthusiastically.

"What hospital?" was my next question. I drank a few swallows of water then placed the glass on the table in front of me.

Jarvis opened his Pepsi. "Crawford Long." He took a sip and added, "Heard it's a nice facility."

"Do you have any idea what prompted this request?"

"They're having a special program and you were nominated."

I was bewildered. *"Nominated? How do you get nominated at a hospital?"*

Jarvis chuckled. "Your guess is as good as mine. I'm sure we'll find out. There's something else."

"What's that?"

"The entire band is not needed…just Teddy and yourself."

"Oh, really?" my eyebrows rose with surprise. "That's interesting."

"Yep, it's going to be a great program."

Dismissing business #1, it was time to move on to requestor #2. "And, who is the next runner-up?"

"There's a gospel concert at the Fox Theatre that takes place on Monday also. One group, for some reason, had to cancel. So, being in this emergency situation, the manager of the group called and wanted to know if you would like to fill in as a replacement."

"The Fox Theatre...*sounds good, too.*"

"Keep in mind that today is Saturday, and it would be a push to do both."

"Definitely."

"Which would you rather attend?"

"That's a good one," I said, debating. I wanted to make a good decision. "I'm leaning more toward the hospital."

"It's your call," Jarvis said as he waited.

"I believe that would be a better choice at this particular time; besides, I'm looking forward to this one."

"So am I," he turned up his soda, again, to take another swallow, and then decided to say something else. "I'll give you all the other details tonight."

"Sounds good," I replied, leaning forward, to pick up my glass.

"*You know, Devin*, we've had *maaaaaany* conversations in the past."

"We sure have," I agreed, trying to remember which one stood out above the rest, but each topic was just as interesting as the other. Since the subject of helping others was part of the current topic of discussion, it brought back memories.

Jarvis rolled back in time. "Helping others reminds me of a lifeguard." That was one of our famous headlines but he never did elaborate on it. His way of thinking usually fascinated me.

I was fishing for clues to his comment but my fishing line was not long enough. For clarity, I asked, "In what way?" Although a nice ring, somehow, I just couldn't quite make the connection.

Concentrating on his thought, he answered, "To sum it up, lifeguards help rescue when in distress, and in our situation back then, help came from different directions. We were sinking but were rescued. Eventually things fell right into place. We both can bear witness to that."

"Isn't that the truth," I said, glad to be away from the unemployment line. I've had my share of counting pennies but it took me a long ways when I didn't have anything else.

"Interruptions in life, sometimes bring uncertainty along with it."

"The intruder will knock the wind out of a person with stress."

"Absolutely, and will win if you let it. You used the right noun—*a prime suspect*. I like that."

I chuckled, remembering my own battles. "There were times when I felt tense, frustrated, and heated."

"You found a defense, right?" Jarvis asked.

"Yes. It was faith, man. How can I forget?"

"We survived."

"Sure did."

"We scoped it and choked it for the results we wanted. With patience, we beat it. The lifeguard of faith, hope, and patience was just too much for the intruder. It had to *surrender*."

The funniest scene rolled before my eyes. "*Brother*, I have never heard a lifeguard yell at an intruder, 'PUT YOUR HANDS UP!'" As long as we had been handcuffed with stress, that was just *too hard* to pass up.

We chuckled.

"Well," Jarvis wiped his misty eyes, "enough is enough. It was just a temporary setback."

Thumbs up, I replied, "It was rough, but…you're right!"

"Look at it this way…it was time for change. No matter what you try to do," Jarvis said, making another point, "it's unstoppable."

"It's definitely an awakening."

"We accepted that and moved on, which took us to higher heights."

"Change can be a good thing. Without it, there's no progress."

"I agree."

"You know, Devin," he glanced at me and smiled, "because of the change, we had to go through the process of melting down."

Puzzled, my response was, "Melting down? I've never heard that before."

"It's like this," he geared himself to explain. "Melting down is like a cycle. We actually needed some downtime to let our old routine drip away from our thoughts, and focus on a new one and make it happen. Sometimes, that can be a slow process. In a nutshell, we had to condition our minds to be successful with a new career."

"I hadn't thought of it that way. More like an interim."

"Exactly! Everyone doesn't have downtime. They go from one job to the next without a break in-between. But someone who has been laid-off will definitely experience a meltdown period, whether it's a short or long period of time. During that phase, even though it can be rough, it's a good time to take advantage of what they have been missing."

"To be frank, Jarvis, I'm glad of the change. I don't miss the factory; it was hot in that place."

"I know; it was time. Once we were reconditioned by being treated with the chemicals of change, our minds were transfigured. That's the second process. We revised our status and have been enjoying it."

"I know that's right. As I have said, giving and helping others is what it's about. That's important."

"*Amen to that*," Jarvis sealed the conversation.

Scoping around, I noticed that Jarvis's dog had not made her grand entrance. My eyes went on a massive dog hunt. This is one dog that could do standup comedy without training. I don't know who was more comical, Sable or Jordache. Usually, there was hardly ever a dull moment around those two. They were a pair that no one would ever forget.

He noticed and said, "You must be looking for Sable. She's outdoors in the back."

With a slight chuckle, my comment was, "Oh," the dog hunt ceased, "I was wondering if she was nearby. How is she?"

He grinned. "She's doing well. I have to give it to her...she's a good watchdog."

"That's what you need."

"That's what we all need," Jarvis revamped that statement.

"Absolutely," I said.

"By the way, I have to drop by and see how my buddy, Jordache, is doing."

"She's doing well, too."

"Good."

At that moment, Jarvis stood. "Excuse me for a minute; I'm going to go and put this can in the trash. I might as well take your glass, too, while I'm at it."

I handed it to him. "Thanks, man."

"No problem." As he walked to the kitchen, my eyes roamed toward the television to watch whatever was on. I didn't know if the same movie was still airing or not. A commercial was on, so, I flipped to my own mental channel and journeyed back down memory lane as Faith resurfaced. It occurred to me that she'd be flying to Atlanta, herself, tomorrow. *What a coincidence*, I thought. She'd be surprised to hear of my sudden change of plans.

Jarvis returned looking toward the television. "Anything interesting playing?" He sat down, ready to relax.

Powering down my own cable lines of thinking, I replied, "I'm not sure. *The Color Purple* was on earlier."

"Before I do anything else, I need to relax and think about something else for a few before getting into high gear. From that point on, we'll be riding on skates to get out-of-town."

"Yeah, and that won't be long."

His eyebrows suddenly joined. "Humph," something dawned on him, "I haven't seen *that movie* in a *looong time.*"

"Those words are timely because a *looong time ago* is right. That movie looked like it had been filmed way back in the late 1800s. That's something how showbiz can fool the mind."

Jarvis nodded. "It was filmed during the 20th century, *waaaaaay* down south. As a matter-of-fact, that movie was filmed in Georgia."

"That's what I've heard. There are some interesting movies that are educating in some way or another."

"Yes, there are and *packed with history.*"

"I've even had the opportunity to listen to others speak of their past or of someone they knew."

"Have you?" Jarvis asked curiously.

"Sure," I said, ready to light the coal, "*I'll take you there.*"

We laughed.

He sat up straight. "Go ahead, brother, who have you been listening to?"

That moment triggered one of the most old-time trophies of fame in my book of records. "A beau-ti-ful lady, my brother," the words tumbled out distinctively. Pulling out what had been shelved as history to the forefront, intrigued me now just as when I heard it the very first time.

Jarvis didn't say a word. He braced himself for the ride with both hands resting on the armrest as if ready for takeoff and repeated, "A beautiful lady." It seemed that he was trying to visualize the mystery person with a name, description, or anything he could grasp. Then he asked,

"Who is she and where did you meet her?" His curiosity was sweltering.

"During a tour, while in Phoenix, I had the opportunity to meet Ms.—" I went blank because this lady had an extremely long string of names. My brain was skipping and trying to put them all in a row.

"Mssssssssss," Jarvis said, trying to help me out, but he didn't have a clue.

"Oh yeah," the string of names fell into place, after silently going up the alphabet tree, "I remember. Now listen to this...*carefully*."

"I'm listening."

"Her name is...Ms. PeggyAnn Floyce Catherine IdellaDean Malone."

Jarvis's eyes grew. *"How many names is that?!"* He tried to repeat it, but dropped off somewhere along the line.

Chuckling, I said, "Seven, my friend."

He stared as if he had lost his way around town. He began mumbling; I couldn't understand a word he was saying.

"You all right?"

"Trying to figure that one out," he mumbled, again, now swaying his finger from side-to-side looking for a logical answer. "Maybe her name represents something."

I shrugged. "Maybe."

Another question hit him. "How did you even get close to remembering all those names?"

"Trust me, I wrote them down and tried to memorize them. As time went by, I hadn't thought about it since I last saw her, so I had to pull-up some alphabets."

Jarvis chuckled. "I can understand. You stumbled for a second there, but you did well. This is getting interesting. Continue," he listened.

As I moved along, my windshield wipers flashed, staring ahead. "Ms. Malone is a senior citizen at about 4'11" tall and very sharp. I didn't ask her age, but she stood out as a precious antique loaded with knowledge and history."

"*Well*," tilting his head to estimate her age, "that's enough to give me some idea or a ballpark figure. I'm curious to know where she's from."

"She and her family moved from Seminole County in Oklahoma."

"Seminole County?" he questioned for more details. "Where is this place in Oklahoma or what city is it closest to?"

"Shaunee. She said that was a major spot for shopping back then."

"Humph, I'm not familiar with that place."

"Neither am I. Have you heard of Earlsboro?"

"That rings a bell," Jarvis replied.

"That's where she worshipped."

"Oh…she worshipped there as a lamb."

I grinned. "Yeah, man." His gospel juice was starting to kick in. "It was interesting to learn of the three main churches she and those she knew attended, which were not very far apart. One was called *CME*…one was called *AME*…and the other was a Baptist Church."

Jarvis asked inquisitively, "I know about AME, but what does CME stand for?"

Knowing what I was about to say next would be even more interesting, I looked at him and answered, "Back then, CME stood for 'Colored Methodist Episcopal,' which was later changed to Christian Methodist Episcopal."

Suddenly, Jarvis's cell phone started playing music, which diverted our attention. He unclipped his phone from his belt. When he saw the number, he looked at me and said, "Excuse me, bruh, this is a call from Atlanta requesting your presence."

To give him privacy to do business, I stood to make an exit. Flagging my hand, I politely said, "I'm gone."

He followed me to the door as I pulled out my keys from my pocket and said, "We must continue that conversation later. That's quite interesting. I'll call you later to fill you in about the trip."

"All right. I'll talk to you in a few."

… hmmm, some interesting keynotes…

HISTORY

History is a record of past events and times,
something valuable,
of days—months—years gone by,
calculations,
notations,
shaping the course of the future.

History plays many songs,
keynotes ringing out a rhythm so strong,
looking back,
replaying the facts,
the tunes of change,
remembering the torch of flames,
purple melodies,
a ribbon of trophies,
without the past,
there is no history!

History in life is no myth,
they're noted for surprisin' twists,
opening blinds of closed eyes,
of the past gone by,
fulfilling decrees,
called "destiny,"
unlocked by the hand of the Key,
dancing to the tempo of liberty.

… eventually, history will sing and chant.

Chapter 4

DEVIN

As interesting as it was, Freddie and I didn't have a clue what to expect from our impromptu engagement on Monday. We brushed up on several songs. A quick rehearsal did not require much attention since we had just come off the road. Freddie and I had worked together over the years in the music industry, which made things a lot easier for us both. He knew my style and I knew his. Our taste for lyrics and music was compatible and we played our roles to the max. Freddie's schedule with the television series, *Unforgettable*, had worked well in conjunction to going on the road with me. Currently, he was not sure if or when the new season would kickoff shooting new episodes. He was just going with the flow until further notice. So was I, hoping that he could continue to play for me.

Jarvis still had his rhythm, too. He was dynamic in his role as an event planner. He spearheaded our purpose and accomplished what Freddie and I had never done—taken us to the next level. Never had I thought when I first met him, that he had so much talent. He later owned his own company and was a good businessman in more ways than one. It never crossed my mind that we all, someday, would be working together for a worthy cause. *You never know why paths cross*, I thought.

Meeting his cousin, Joy, was an eye opener. She was the connector of our success by the wreath of her mouth. Trying to uncoil what she said, at times, was baffling, but the mystery of it all turned into a good thing. She was a smart and intelligent young girl for her age.

And Jarvis's uncle, Carlton, put the icing on the cake signing me up for a 1-year contract with his business— Gospel Child Record Label Company. I chuckled, as I drove into the parking structure of the airport, reliving the moments when Jarvis first introduced this company to me and how I actually sat there talking with the owner the same evening. He was fast as a rocket with his drive; he was on a mission with a vision. By the time it was all said and done, my mind was limping. Although I was elated, I signed a contract with mismatched socks on from the whiplash. Everything happened so quickly. Working with them both and with Freddie and the band was beyond my imagination. Now, a year later, we were still standing tall.

After putting my vehicle in park, I spotted Jarvis walking with his luggage headed in my direction. I turned off the ignition and got out of the suburban.

He smiled as I waved.

Without delay, I reached for my travel bags and met him. "Hey, Jarvis," I grinned, speaking above normal because of the loud noise. Airplanes blasted off and car doors closed and sounded like a snap contraption as passengers were dropped off. Every now and then, we heard horns blow from passing vehicles. Cars, buses, and trucks were backed up from one side of the airport to the other. It was a serious parking lot of built-up traffic. Brakes were squealing, people were talking, and engines were revving to move on to their next destination.

"Devin, the man, how are you?"

"Doing well. I guess I should be asking *you* that question. You had so much to do to prepare for this trip."

He nodded, fluently. *"Fantastic.* I was able to get enough rest."

"That's good."

Jarvis glanced my way. "Are you and Teddy ready for tomorrow?"

"Yep," I said quickly. "We rehearsed a little this morning."

"Well, it doesn't take much for you both…you're good."

"Thanks for the compliment."

"Sure," he looked at his watch. "We have one hour to catch the 3 o'clock flight."

By the time we reached the gate, Freddie was already waiting. We arrived just in time. The gate agent had started boarding the plane. We gave her our tickets and were off to Atlanta.

Comfortably, we had been flying for a couple hours. The ride was smooth, as we flew at full speed. It was fascinating to experience the journey, viewing a small fraction of the universe. Gliding above the earth and watching the slideshow presentation of white clouds of puff smoke was exhilarating. The soft overlay partly covered the light blue sky. The sun intermittently shone between the peepholes to get another glimpse of creation before hiding behind the clouds again.

Hopping from one state to the next reminded me of a time capsule compared to days of driving. Flying in a mechanical bird was a trip into isolation, covered by the umbrella of the universe. Between the earth and its lid was the runway of freedom. There was no hustle and bustle to deal with there. With jets streaming that high above in altitude, the planes were the only birds flying, and big bird was carrying a heavy load, filled to capacity.

The plane was engulfed with chatter and laughter. Some passengers filled their time with iPODs, laptops,

CD players, or inserting earplugs to watch a good movie. Routinely, flight attendants made their rounds to serve snacks and drinks. It was going to be a long ride.

Each of us requested refreshments.

Jarvis opened his drink. He remembered something while I sat between them. "Devin, the story you was sharing with me yesterday about Ms. Peggy, I believe her name—"

I smoothly cut in. "You mean, Ms. PeggyAnn?"

"Yes," he replied. "Bruh, tell me more about her. That was interesting." Jarvis then looked at Freddie and asked, "Did you meet Ms. PeggyAnn, too, while you were in Arizona?"

Freddie leaned slightly forward to respond. "No, I hadn't," he shook his head, "although, I heard Devin mention her name before. He was about to fill me in while we were in Phoenix, but we were interrupted. We never had the opportunity to come back to that topic."

"I was enthralled by just the little that I heard," Jarvis let him know.

A grin of sunshine swept across Freddie's face. "*If it's anything like that gorilla story,*" he said, and chuckled, "this plane may go down." He opened his soda and poured it in a cup of ice.

Jarvis became glassy-eyed. "I gotcha. If everyone on this plane heard that...umph," he glanced at me, "this aircraft probably couldn't withstand it. *Remember?* I had to walk out."

I resisted an urge to laugh. "No, Teddy, it's not like that at all."

"I want to live, man," Freddie the Teddy said, finally getting a chance to sip on his crystal clear 7UP.

Our response was, "I know that's right."

"On a serious note, Teddy. It's just the opposite," Jarvis told him. "This lady, Ms. PeggyAnn, seems to be quite a lady. I think you'll be just as interested as I was."

Agreeing, I said, "That's how I felt when she shared her story."

Freddie asked anxiously, "What's her age, Devin?"

"Jarvis asked the same question before, but like I told him, I don't know. She's a senior citizen." I filled him in up to where I stopped yesterday while telling Jarvis the same story. When I mentioned the one church that he was not familiar with, question marks covered his face.

Freddie lightly scratched the crown of his head. *"What year was that?"*

They both appeared hypnotized and mystified.

My mind churned. "Hmmm," remembering what she had shared, "that was in the...1920s." Since all my notes were at home, I had to recapture as much as I could from the scribbles of my mental pad.

For confirmation, Freddie asked, "And this was in Earlsboro, Oklahoma?"

"Yes," I answered, "that's where she worshipped and Seminole County, Oklahoma is where she lived."

Jarvis joined in the questioning. "From what you can remember, what was Seminole County like? Just the name of that place makes me wonder."

"How so?" I asked.

"Sounds *quite* country."

"You're about right," I nodded. "She said that it was a rural area."

"I thought so," Jarvis said, as he got more involved.

"Let me talk a little bit and try to tell you both what I remember," I said, wanting to trim down the quiz session and preferably summarize some of Ms. PeggyAnn's story.

"We're listening, bruh, to whatever history you can share."

Drinking another splash of water helped to release the pressure in my ears from the altitude. I again took the floor and continued. "Some of the other things she mentioned were eye-openers. She lived on a farm with horses, mules, cows, chickens, roosters, and a dog. Neighbors lived anywhere from 1 ½ to 3 blocks away. Distance was not an obstacle; it was the norm. Town was about five miles away.

Of course, there were no streetlights or paved roads. As for food, they grew most of their own. They lived without the convenience of a refrigerator, so milk and other items were kept cool outdoors in an underground cellar. This is where they also stored their meat whenever a hog was killed."

"Umph," Jarvis broke in and derailed my train of thought, "no refrigerator! Outdoors...inside the earth!"

"Yep," I verified, "that's *a lot of legwork* for some poultry, man."

Freddie's eyes smiled through the glass of his pupils. "It's quite interesting that you mentioned that. People worked and labored hard back then. Some things you just don't hear too much about unless you are fortunate to talk with someone who was a witness, *or*, who is very educated about their ancestors, *or*, who is a history scholar."

"No, you don't," I agreed. "How often do you hear the word 'cellar?' "

"Very seldom," they answered in rhythm.

"Something else occurred to me."

"What's that?" asked Jarvis.

"I guess that's what you call a detached home back then," I joked.

He chuckled. "Unlikely, but *good point*—an underground meat house. *Imagine that.* I thought cellars were mainly used to escape from tornados."

"So did I."

"You do what you have to do as long as it's legal and the right thing to do," Jarvis added. "Maybe refrigerators *were invented* already, but they had to make do."

"Right!" Freddie and I both agreed.

The stewardess came back around. She smiled and said, "Is there anything else I can get for you, gentlemen?"

We shook our heads.

"No, thank you, we're fine," Jarvis acknowledged her out of courtesy.

Getting back to the subject, I then said, "Taking this further, she said that she walked to school five miles each way, even in the winter. When the weather was extremely bad, they were taken to school in a Model-T Ford."

"*A Ford*," Jarvis couldn't believe it. "They go waaay back. I had no idea Ford existed that many years ago."

"Neither did I," Freddie let it sink in. "Umph, that's unreal. Ford has some good cars, though. In case you didn't know, the Taurus is rated five stars for crash safety."

"Oh, yeah," I said, somewhat surprised.

"Yes," he answered, sure of himself. "Ford has prevented a lot of life-threatening injuries."

"That's good to know," Jarvis notated in his mind for future reference.

"Although," I continued, "Ms. PeggyAnn had other means of transportation, too."

Jarvis and Freddie stared wondering what other transportation could possibly supersede riding in a Ford.

Jarvis then stated, "We know she walked and we know about the Ford. What other transportation, especially back then?"

Looking straight ahead, my answer was, "A horse and a wagon." This topic of discussion was entertaining. The conversation was rocking back and forth between the three of us.

"*Of course,*" Jarvis smiled. "*Well, that's a lot better than walking.*"

"Isn't that the truth?" Freddie gave his stamp of approval.

"That much walking sounds painful." I couldn't imagine.

"It probably does now because we're adults," Jarvis commented, to refresh my memory, "but kids can run and walk for a long time before they pass out. That all depends on the age."

Freddie chuckled. "I agree. By the time we reached high school, walking 10 miles, round trip everyday, didn't even reach our vocabulary."

"Clearly, that means," Jarvis paused, "we must be thankful for what we have. Things are so modernized now and so much has been forgotten. Back in those days, things were different from the way people live now. It's interesting how two worlds have joined together."

Puzzled, I asked, "What two worlds?"

"The world of history and the world of the present have joined."

I sat up and listened just as Freddie had. I felt a lecture coming on.

"Umph," Freddie mumbled.

Jarvis opened his hands like fans to display his thoughts. They ran deep. "History is sooooo wide and broad that neither I nor you can tell it all. We have to remember the torch of flames and treasure the ribbon of trophies."

Freddie chuckled. "*I like that*, but don't have a clue," he shook his head, "what it means."

What Jarvis said detonated into a million pieces. "Man, that's explosive! Explain that," I laughed smoothly. Our computer brains exploded right into chaos. My ears burned, out of curiosity, to hear what he would say next.

"Let me explain it this way," he went on. "You already know of the present because we live in the present."

"Um hm," I shifted my head to glance at him, again, straining not to miss a word.

Freddie probably felt as I did from the surge of confusion, which had thrown us into shock. We were definitely in pursuit of knowing what was making him tick.

"Since history is broad and wide, many people are to be commended for whatever their purpose was. Thank goodness for historical figures like George Washington Carver, who invented many necessities but only had three patents. He felt that his other inventions should be shared freely."

"That was generous," I said.

"Yes, it was."

"What were his inventions?"

"His creations were shampoo, bleach, chili sauce, flour, instant coffee, mayonnaise, meal, sugar, wood stains, buttermilk, cheese, shaving cream, shoe polish, linoleum, paint, and much more. In demand, each is widely used around the globe. He shifted faces, going places. *Umph*," he seemed to have thought of something else that had not dawned on him before, "*he was a serious architect. He drew his plans right into reality.* He created mountains of achievements and made history."

"He sure did," Teddy became intrigued. "*That's phenomenal.*"

"*Notations of time rolled on,*" Jarvis kept talking. "Other achievers were: Joseph Winters who patented the fire escape ladder in 1878; Garrett Morgan patented the gas mask in 1914 and invented an inexpensive traffic signal that featured STOP and GO signs in 1923. And, what about Percy L. Julian, who was noted for synthesized medicines for treating rheumatoid arthritis and other inflammatory conditions. In addition, he used a soy protein to produce a fire extinguishing foam, which suffocates gasoline and oil fires."

"Umph," his mini lecture gave me something to think about, "that's interesting. You're on a roll. Keep it going… we're listening. No more interruptions. Scout's honor," I saluted.

They chuckled.

"In modern times, another figure inducted into the National Inventors Hall of Fame who crosses my mind is Dr. Mark Dean. He was one of those who invented the 'bus,' which permitted add-on devices to be connected to the motherboard. Dr. Dean has developed all types of computer systems and holds many patents and patents pending. His developments and success trails are endless. He is an outstanding scientist rolled into the 21st century who stands on the threshold of making historical achievements. Progress never ceased. As I have said before," he glanced at us, getting back to making his point, "many people are to be commended for whatever their purpose was. We even have a purpose, right now, that has to be fulfilled. That's what I meant by the torch of flames. We have to remember those who are flames, and the torch causes them to shine in our minds. And the ribbon of trophies, that we should treasure, are the flames. The ribbon is valuable because the people are connected to honor, which is the ribbon, as they are united as one."

"*Man,*" I edged in, "*I feel like Freddie; I like that.*"

"*Oooooooooo,*" is what dribbled from Freddie's mouth, "*that's heated.*"

"Sure is. What you just said, Jarvis, is memorable."

"What you have shared with us about Ms. PeggyAnn, Devin, just brought it on home," was his response. "We have to remember those before us. Many have gone through many things in life that brought us luxury in this day and time compared to back then. Quite honestly, some of the things they endured then would send some people, now, to the mental ward."

Freddie laughed. "Yeah, that's about right!"

My comment was, "I'm glad somebody had a dream in more ways than one."

Jarvis chuckled. "It had to be placed there and they had to enforce the vision."

Freddie batted next. "We should be thankful and never take things for granted as you have already said, Jarvis. I agree with you, whole-heartedly, brother."

"In my book of records," their eyes slid in my direction, "I've noted Ms. PeggyAnn as part of the flame."

Jarvis smiled. "I can certainly understand why. I'm sure there's much more to her history, in addition, to what we have already heard."

"If you *only* knew, man. You've only heard a fraction of her story."

Freddie picked up his cup of soda again. "I would love to hear more—"

We were distracted.

One of the pilots announced over the speakers about the nice weather conditions. Trying to hear and continue the discussion was difficult. Water had been thrown all over our ringside chat.

I glanced at Freddie and Jarvis and said, "Maybe we can get back to Ms. PeggyAnn later."

"That'll work," Freddie agreed and sat back to relax.

"That's fine," was Jarvis's response. He seemed to be on a mission, reaching for his laptop. "I'll just let that smolder in my thoughts until we can pick it back up. I need to do a little research here."

Freddie chuckled and turned toward us. "That's the kind of conversation that will be hard to burn out."

"I agree," said Jarvis. "That will be hard to forget."

The aircraft was gliding above one of the states that is known for its cowboys and Indians. Spurs and bows and arrows are how I saw it. It was a place where Indians always kept their ears to the track. They had keen ears for tracking down locomotives from very far away. Never did understand that one. Must have been from the dance of the earth. They were different in their own unique way. Apache blood ran deep. Like the snap of a whip, they flew on horses seizing choo-choo trains as if it was their last meal. Their raw hides had to have been smokin'. If the poor horses had it their way, they most likely would have gone into hiding. Their cousins have to be glad because that's just too much entertainment for a pony. *Who would have ever known that they were kin?*

Drawn from deep thought, from a little unexpected turbulence, I noticed that the pilot had finished his array of announcements. My eyes traveled toward the closest window, but I saw very little. Not having a window seat was a disadvantage, at times. From what I could see and remember, viewing the natural features of the earth was broad. Never could tell where one region separated from the other. It was designed artistically like a jigsaw puzzle neatly glued together.

By this time, Jarvis was clicking away on his computer and in a world of his own, and Freddie was slowly drifting into a dream world. I, on the other hand, was winding down and ready to relax, too.

As a stewardess was headed our way, I caught her attention. "Miss, I would like a cup of tea, please."

Immediately, Freddie and Jarvis slung their heads in my direction drawing attention to themselves. Their heads turned as quickly as a pop willy; their necks must have snapped, crackled, and popped.

Her eyes danced with approval. "Sure!" she replied, energetically. Her smile blossomed.

"*Smooth tea?*" Jarvis asked with quickness.

Freddie tuned back in, too. "Uh-oh!" his eyes widened, seeming to have forgotten how sleepy he was.

A surge of laughter was coming on. "*Gnaw*, man," I shook my head almost stumbling over my words. I was stunned by their reaction. "I don't think big bird has my kind of story-telling tea. I have to be intoxicated with the right stuff."

They laughed.

"Intoxicated, huh?" Jarvis joked.

"Yep, caffeine is about as good as it gets."

A couple in front of us snickered.

Jarvis shook his head and kept clicking on his keyboard.

A warm mild-flavored tea was what I needed. The aroma spiraled up to greet my sense of smell. The tea tranquilized me right into my own quiet world of seclusion— meditating. When I finished drinking it, I was in for a ride. It was more than what I had bargained for...

… how could anyone forget
the sound of this beat…

ROLL 'EM

Film production is an art,
clip after clip,
rolled through a projector,
scanned by the eye of light,
a motion picture,
black and white or,
colors of mixture,
a plot driven as the key.

Scenes create motion pictures,
captured into captivity,
a conglomerate of events,
the present,
the past,
facts or fabrications,
dreams and histories,
fantasies and mysteries,
the makings of art,
a cast destined for the part.

Plots unfolds over time,
raising the flat line,
an escalation,
rippled beats,
dancing in the heat,
rainbowed from the dark,
branded on the heart.

... *"ACTION!...ROLL IT."*

1920's

Chapter 5

PEGGYANN

"HELP! MAMIE, STOP!" I shouted at the top of my lungs. She flew across open land as fast as a missile.

A balloon of questions surfaced, *Why is she flying like that without warning? Where is she going? This is unlike her.* They popped at the sound of a voice.

"PeggyAnn! Wait! Where are you going?" Josephine shouted then stopped, as we shot past her. She dropped a handful of daisies, staring as her mouth opened. In our circle of friends, she was known for her gold-medal expressions. Her eyeballs bulged with intensity. Her oblong face that encased her large brown eyes danced to the rhythm of Mamie's feet. Her yellow and white cotton dress with smiley faces on it flowed in the same direction. They blended well with her own happy face—cocoa, hazelnut skin—until she became confused.

I looked behind and hollered, too, "I don't know! Mamie won't stop!"

Josephine was still standing in the same spot—frozen.

When I turned my head back around, I shouted, "Slow down, Mamie!" It felt as though she didn't hear a word I said.

Mamie kept right on going.   She couldn't be distracted.

Looking around for the last time, I saw Josephine run a few feet and stop with her hands in the air. She shouted something, but I couldn't hear her. Between the sound of Mamie's feet and the wind merging against my face and ears, everything else drowned out. When Josephine realized that Mamie had no plans of stopping anytime soon, she tried to catch up. Mamie's speed was no match for her own. I knew she would lag and disappear the farther we went.

The ride became horrifying as I slid a little toward Mamie's neck. I pulled on the rope but she still kept running at full speed. To keep from sliding even more, my knees pressed tighter and tighter against the sides of her body. Her silky brown coat made it that much harder, especially since there was no saddle on her back. I was not a pro at speed riding.

She sprinted past Mr. Jackson's wooden-framed-yellow-house surrounded by patches of thickets and up the dirt road.

Again, I turned to see if Josephine could be seen, but there was no sign of her. All I could hear now was her faint voice screaming my name, and collapsing in the swooping wind. Thoughts ran wild in my mind, *Where is she?*

The ride was bumpy, shaking me all over. It was enough to cause coins to spew right out of a piggybank. *Oooh…I don't know how much longer I can hold on.* I tried to concentrate and remain calm. Gripping the rope tighter was a psychological haven. I tried to brace myself. Trying to raise my body and bend forward while pressing against Mamie's stocky build with my knees was very difficult. Locked in position, with my head steady to regain control, was my last chance. Being nervous, that option worked temporarily but failed. Her coat was just too slick. There was nothing on this horse that could help make this situation easier. My height, 4'11", was a disadvantage. Someone always had to help me up on a horse's back.

For some reason, Mamie shifted her course and slightly turned to the left off the road. She surged across large expansions of land covered with fuzzy-green grass. Mamie had all the space she needed to jet stream to wherever she was going. In the direction we were headed, there wasn't another farmhouse close by to scream for help. If I had only seen Mr. Jackson when we flew past his place, he would have probably put an end to Mamie's stride, but no one appeared to be home. I didn't even see his dog, Smokey. It was strange, as if they had gone into hibernation. There was usually some activity going on at his place. He was always working on his land; farming was his hobby.

Exhaustion set in. We must have gone as far as two miles. Trying to find a way to stop this expedition was useless. Endlessly asking myself where she could be going was branded in my thoughts. The mystery lies only in Mamie's roadmap; her brain held all the road signs. The farther we went, the more I wondered. *Why this route? What could possibly justify all this?* There was nothing in this area that was significant enough to warrant this kind of attention. All I saw was Mamie's kind scattered very far away on inclines like miniature toys. We were isolated zooming across somebody's land. This is not quite what I had in mind. As quickly as Mamie was moving, nothing could stop us now.

"Mamie, what am I going to do?" were the only words that spilled from my trembling mouth, pleading for answers.

She slowed her pace significantly and finally stopped at a creek.

I slid to the ground with relief and slowly stood up. My chest was still pounding; my equilibrium was just as shaky as my legs. *"For heaven's sake, Mamie, why did you run off like that?"* While catching my breath, I looked down and brushed off my dress with my hands. There was a trickle of water droplets that had brewed on the sides of my temples. Sweat had accumulated from the fear.

Simultaneously, her head scribbled in the air as her long, black ponytail waved—horse-talking.

I stroked her silky coat when she suddenly did it again. "What is it, Mamie?" I looked at her now, confused.

She was beginning to move impatiently.

But why? I thought.

Slowly, she moved forward.

"You're acting really strange today. Where are you going now?" I asked, on the alert. Holding the rope, I walked alongside her. This was puzzling.

The sun was beaming, and sweat was just waiting to seep through the surface of my skin.

Mamie stopped. We were now standing under a shade tree.

"Oh," I thought out loud, "you want to rest under the tree. Too hot out here *for you, girl?*"

She snorted and moved her head wildly.

Watching her confused me more than ever; her behavior was a mystery. My senses were on the rise like steam from a teakettle. Paying close attention, I observed and made a complete circle. From what I could see, there was nothing to be concerned about. My eyes moved downward. There were no snakes in our vicinity or wild animals. It was very quiet. A perfect spot for anyone to lie down and take a nap under a tree. It was late spring. One of the best times of the year.

The only thing that stood out was a nearby wagon that was posing on a slight incline with four wheels. It was still in the same place where it had always been. It was painted bright red and the wheels were dark green. Bundles of straw were stacked neatly in it. Beside the two wheels were two large red baskets filled with artificial, shiny-red apples, coated with dust. It fit the country environment, and blended well with nature as the perfect view. It was a part of the property. Someone was creative.

Mamie intensified the mystery. You would think the way she was beginning to move her legs that she was trying to kick off a pair of shoes. She had my full attention.

I stared at her, searching for answers that she could not give.

Her eyes were round like owls, bouncing her head up and down.

Now, my eyes fell on her long nose thinking, *This is bazaar.* I don't know what else to do or what to look for. Knowing what I was about to say was a fantasy didn't stop me from speaking my mind into the quiet air, *"If only you could talk."*

The wagon shook.

"Huh?" My neck stretched.

Mamie started moving closer, but I restrained her by gripping the rope again.

She sure is bold, I thought. Almost tiptoeing, I followed her lead. Turning around to run all the way back home was a thought since I was too short to jump up on her back.

The wagon moved, again, breaking the silence. Something inside was heavy and the poor wagon was stressed from the weight of whatever was in it. Sudden movement caused the wheels to squeak.

We stood still.

I waited for something to jump out. *Maybe it's a dog or some other overgrown wildlife,* I reasoned. Whatever it was, it made no sound. That was the strangest thing. Seems like it would have barked, growled, or something. Not a paw or head could be seen. My curiosity finally ran out. A surge of bravery overcame me. "Let's see what this is, Mamie. This is getting ridiculous. Come on." I pulled the rope to guide her as I walked forward with caution. It seemed like it took forever to get to it.

With sudden movement, it rocked a third time, but that didn't stop me.

Surprisingly, when I finally reached the edge of the decorated wagon, there was nothing but loose straw piled in front of the bundles. I couldn't believe that there was nothing there. Analyzing, I walked slowly around the wagon while rearranging the straw. When I made it to the other side, I reached down, again, grabbing straw quickly.

Mamie pulled back. Her hesitation distracted me.

As I turned my head to glance at her while reaching down for the last time, I gripped hold of something heavy and familiar. I dropped it like a hot potato.

A mound of straw undraped a rising mass; a figure rose, staring me *right in the face*.

I dropped Mamie's rope. My mouth fell open...

Chapter 6

PEGGYANN

We both screamed in horror, as I slipped and fell to the ground from shock. I was almost crawling backward as my hands accommodated my feet. Whoever it was, their eyes looked like they had been blown up with helium. They shone brightly as two moons through strands of straw.

We breathed rapidly, as if we had run in a marathon. Words of intensity rang out, *"Wh-Who,"* we both stuttered and said at the same time, *"a-are you?!"* Our pronunciations were like locomotives blowing out steam. We were seriously shaken.

He looked at me.

I stared at him.

After realizing that one was just as spooked as the other and that we were not getting anywhere, the entire scene was turning into a comedy.

Silence was shattered as Mamie moved in closer. The sound of her presence had broken our trance.

Our eyes traveled in her direction. Then, our eyes met again.

A buildup of laughter was waiting to be exhaled. We could no longer hold our peace when, gradual inclines of laughter spilled into the air and turned into an explosion. At this point, we both needed a good laugh.

My eyes were watery from watching this kid's innocent reactions.

He blew a few strands of straw from his lips as he laughed hysterically. "What a fiasco," he said. It looked like he was holding his stomach with his head facing the sky.

Easing up off the ground, I replied, "I must say it is." My eyes fluttered trying to see clearly. I was a little off-balanced. Leaning on Mamie's build was my only support as I laughed really hard. The mixture of comedy and horror was an adrenaline rush. The back of my ears were starting to hurt. I wiped my eyes with the sleeve of my dress.

Something was odd. When he spoke the second time, the thought of introducing myself had vanished. A burning question raced to the tip of my lips. *"What's wrong with your voice?"*

Silence filled the air. It left as quickly as it came and was overshadowed by the continuous flow of laughter. We couldn't seem to control it.

Even Mamie heehawed in a language that horses understood.

That really took him a notch higher. *"Myyyyyyyyyyyy… voice?"* he managed to say.

There was no point in saying another word until we got it out of our systems. We just could not seem to get out of our heads how we met, face-to-face, some minutes ago.

As good as this was getting, ever since Mamie took off like a bolt of lightening, had me wondering what more could possibly happen. There was so much action that it felt like a fantasy turned into reality. It deserves a gold medal. The chain of events could have even been rollin' on film.

The laughter soon faded.

Meanwhile, I straightened my clothes. I had fallen twice within the past 20 minutes. Streams of tears stopped flowing. Finally, I said with a raspy voice, "Yes, your voice."

Getting over the initial drama, he tried to respond. "Hmmm," he cleared his throat, "there's nothing wrong with my *voice*."

Now, I was looking at him in disbelief. I thought, *Either he's a good actor or, he's...strange.* Never had I met anyone this complicated. Some puzzles were difficult, but this one took the cake. How could a kid his age have a voice as deep as a man's? *"Are you joshing?"* I asked seriously. I visualized multiple images of clowns circling his head because I thought he was the best comedian ever.

He shook his head. "No, I'm not joshing." It was obvious that he was struggling to suppress the urge to laugh again. My expression didn't make it any better.

Who would ever believe this? I wondered. *Maybe that runs in his family. Umph, an unusual trait.* He didn't seem concerned about it, so I moved on to my next question. "What's your name?" I asked him the same question that he probably wanted to ask me. Obviously, he wasn't from our neck of the woods.

He began brushing straw off his arms and head. "My name is Devin." The straw was plastered all over him.

"What's your name, Miss?" he asked when it was his turn.

"You can call me PeggyAnn."

The youngster began scratching and popping his neck.

I giggled.

He grinned. "What's so funny, Miss PeggyAnn?"

I spared him. "You're using your hands as a flyswatter."

When he visualized how comical that must've been, he saw the humor in it himself. "These straws feel like bugs sticking me."

If he remained in that wagon any longer, I probably would have started scratching, too. "Maybe, you should come down out of that wagon," I told him. Psychologically, I felt mild stings on my skin. An urge to scratch was tempting. I refocused and thought about something else.

Devin stood up.

My mind tried to tally up his measurements. "How tall are you?" I was curious observing his height.

He looked puzzled that I asked. "The last time I checked, I was 6'4" tall."

"You *can't be* 6'4" tall," I laughed slightly.

He was trying to figure out what humored me until he looked down. His expression showed confusion. *"How could that be?"*

"How could what be?"

"Where did the inches go?"

"You look tall, but not 6'4"."

He carefully leaped from the wagon. Mumbling seemed to come easy for him. He was stricken with confusion, studying himself. Since he was standing on the ground, it was better to determine how tall he might be. Trying to understand, he asked with a blank expression, "How tall do I appear to be?"

"Maybe 5'8" tall…give or take a little."

"Umph," he thought out loud and said nothing else further about his height. Soon after, he walked up, looked down at me, and reversed the question, "How tall are you?" His height well surpassed mine.

"I'm 4'11" tall. A little short for a 15-year-old," I replied a little self-conscious.

Devin picked up on it. "You sound dissatisfied. You shouldn't be." His response surprised me a little.

"I know. You're right."

"You still have time to grow."

"You're starting to sound like an old man. How old are you?" If I didn't know any better, he was shifting in and out of maturity. My eyes were fixed, waiting for an answer.

"How old do you think I am?"

"You must be arooooound," I paused, "I would say between 12 and 14-years-old." All I had to go on was his youthful appearance and what seemed logical, other than his voice stirring from his Adam's apple.

He really looked dumbfounded. "Between 12 and 14-years-old!"

Alarmed, I asked, "Did I miss something?"

He guffawed as he entertained the question. "You wouldn't believe that I'm—" he held his thought.

"Believe what?"

He rephrased his answer saying, "We best leave that one alone."

I surrendered. "Well, if you say so," I shrugged my shoulders. This conversation was getting stranger by the minute.

"By the way…where on earth is this place? Because *I know* I'm dreaming!" One thing led to another.

"Why do you say that?"

In awe, he spread his arms with his mouth opened and looked down at himself, again. "What are these clothes I'm wearing?" He appeared petrified.

"Come on, now," I stared at him. "You're in the 1920's. Remember that?" Now, I was confused again.

Not believing what I just said, he laughed out loud. "The 1920's?!" Understandably, since nothing added up. He was in denial. He may have thought the same about me as I did about him that I could be in my own world.

I reconfirmed, "Yep, the 1920's."

He looked at me as if I had spoken in another language. "You *must be* mistaken."

Shaking my head, I answered, "I don't *think* so."

His jaws collapsed. He turned in the opposite direction with his hands in the air and said, *"The 1920's?!"* His voice echoed so far that I felt as though we were the only humans that existed. He was overcome with questions that he could not understand.

"Yes, it is."

Slowly turning back around, his eyes scanned the view. *"This can't be,"* he whispered. He looked lost.

"Yes, it is," I reiterated.

"And when did that happen?"

I shook my head, giggling. "And when did that happen?" I repeated him, not taking him seriously. He had to be practicing his role for some play. My eyes were fixed on him.

"Yes," he replied starry-eyed.

"You would make a good actor, Devin."

"I've heard that many times before, but I'm not acting."

"Sure you are."

His next statement was, "Ms. PeggyAnn, *really, I'm not kidding."*

My expression changed. "You have me confused."

"You're confused...*I'm really confused!"*

My eyes wondered off, gazing this place too. From his reaction, he had me second-guessing myself for a minute. Seeing that he was not joking, I couldn't help but be concerned. "Do you not know where you are, Devin?" The thought of amnesia crossed my mind but, *how could that be? He remembers his name.*

"In the United States."

"Well, you got something right."

His eyes grew. "Whew!" was his reaction to knowing he hadn't completely lost his mind.

Testing his geography, I then asked, "Where in the United States?"

Upbeat, he answered, *"I live in California."*

"California?!" I blurted. Just about everything he said was striking. I was tickled by his humor.

"What's so funny, Miss PeggyAnn?"

"You're a long ways from there."

"I can see that." He stared at nothing but grass, trees, and a wagon. "This place is so country, even King Kong would sit down and cry."

From the sound of that remark, I had to laugh at that. "Who is *King Kong*?" I asked. My eyes batted from the mystery.

Devin grinned. "An oversized ape."

My eyes stretched. *"How big is that?"*

"Toooooo big to comprehend," he said. "He's used to the wild all right, but on a totally different level."

"Talking like that, you're most definitely *not from around here.*"

"Now do you believe me?"

"You have some kind of imagination."

To defend himself, he said, "PeggyAnn, that's not my imagination."

I froze. "I wouldn't tell anyone else that."

"Why?"

"They would probably lock you up."

He laughed so hard that he turned another shade. "Someone else thought of that," he shook his head, "*not me.*" Under the circumstance, it's a good thing he's laughing instead of crying.

"Umph, umph, umph," was all I said.

"Anyway," he moved back to the main topic of discussion, *"where is this place?"*

"You're standing in Seminole County."

"See me what?"

"Seminole County."

"Where is that?!"

"In *Oklahoma.*"

"Oh, Lord!" he laughed out and held his stomach. *"Home on the range, where deers and the antelopes play. This is too MUCH."*

Seeing how comical he was, I fell out laughing, too.

Wanting to make some sense out of what seemed impossible raised a lot of unanswered questions. He was caught between reality and what seemed like a fairytale. I couldn't help but wonder, *Why is he here? How did he get here? How long has he been here? Does he have family? And, how on earth is he going to get back to where he came from?* Since we both were overwhelmed by his mysterious visit, I didn't bother to ask, for now, anyway. I thought trying to figure out how cows could run on two feet was hard, but this was *too complicated.*

"The 1920's, huh?" he rehashed. It finally sunk in.

"What year did you think it was?"

"Not the 1920's. The thought of the early 1900s sounds historic."

I blinked, as my neck stretched. From his answer, I didn't know what to expect next from him; I had been entertained well since we'd met. One surprise seemed to lead to another. Under the circumstances, it would be inevitable. Baffled, I asked him, *"Why historic?"*

"You are many steps ahead of me."

"Of course I am. I'm older."

"I know this is going to sound strange, Miss PeggyAnn, but, I'm older and younger than you think."

"Huh?" I slightly drew back. "That makes no sense."

"But it does."

"How?" my head tilted as my eyes wondered beyond him. I waited to hear something that sounded logical.

"I'm older in age and younger in wisdom."

Thrown off, I looked up at Devin and said, "First time I've heard that saying."

"I'll explain later because you will not understand right now."

"I agree. That's probably a good idea."

"Trust me, it is."

"Well, back to my earlier question," I remembered eagerly. "What year did you think it was?"

"Do you really want to know what year I thought it was?" he asked a question with a question.

"Yes, that would help," I answered, realizing that we had not moved from this spot since we both screamed.

At some point, Mamie had already left our circle and was standing under the tree. I guess she needed a change of pace. When I glanced at her, my eyes were attracted to the scenery. Mamie was a stallion standing there surrounded by the background of open-wide territory. Momentarily, the beauty of it all captured me. Her brown coat blended well with nature as her ponytail swayed. The tree, which she stood under, was spread like an umbrella. The sunrays were vibrant, casting a beam of light between the separations of leaves. The grass was glazed by the bursting sun. Hands could not have crafted it any better. All I could do was retain it in my photographic memory.

Easing away from the wagon, Devin followed alongside of me.

The long conversation never let up as he laid another bombshell on me and slowly said, "The *21st century.*"

I stopped.

He stopped.

A crease formed in the center of my forehead. "You're right!" I told him. This topic grew from a hill of mysteries into a mountain.

He glanced at me and said, "Right about what?" He knew he had said many things and wondered what scored him to be right.

"*You are dreamin'.* I thought maybe you were off by a few years or so, but—" my sentence chipped away. "The 21st century is not even here yet!"

Dryly, he said, "Doesn't look that way."

I was more concerned now than ever, and I had a feeling that some things would never be the same.

Chapter 7

DEVIN

For sure, I was confused and trapped between two worlds. PeggyAnn didn't know what to think and neither did I. I suddenly realized that I was homeless and had no place to go. Being at her mercy was crippling since I didn't know anyone or have a map of this county. I was not certain what brought me here or why. Whatever adventure I was on was going to be interesting because I didn't know what to expect. Being caught between both worlds had me puzzled. I felt as though I was shifting in and out of maturity. If I'm really a young kid between ages 12 and 14, as Miss PeggyAnn guessed, this would not be easy to digest. Knowing that I was a young man and... *Gnaw, that can't be!* My mind kept flipping pages for an explanation to understand why. No matter how many reasons I came up with, it still wouldn't matter because, I didn't know what the solution was. It was too early to know and not long enough to show. "Oh, well..." I mumbled. Seeing that I wasn't going anywhere, anytime soon, I tried to accept things the way they were until a change came.

We talked part of the way to wherever we were headed, replaying what had already happened so far, and talked briefly about her family. I called her Miss PeggyAnn because, from what I saw, she seemed older than her age. She was caring and very friendly. Being the oldest child in her family, I

sensed she wore many hats and held the leading role. Even
though she was 4'11", she carried weight and style. She was
unusual for a teenager and what amazed me even more was
that she rode her horse in a *dress*. Maybe this was a onetime
incident, but I had a feeling that this was customary. I can't
recall ever watching a lady, or even a teenager, ride a horse
in anything other than pants. *Did all the girls dress that way?*
Her characteristics and style were an even match, blended
with her brown, even-toned skin and tender eyes. She had
black, shoulder-length hair, which was combed backed,
wrapped behind the ears, and curled under.

After walking about a mile, we spotted, what appeared
to be, two teenagers heading our way. One of them, a girl,
shouted from afar.

Miss PeggyAnn's arm shot up in the air. Her hand
waved like a flag. "That's Josephine and Joshua," her voice
raised, glad to see them. She smiled in between Mamie and
I, guiding her with a rope in one hand.

After all that had happened, Mamie looked as though
she had not been on the run all day. The sound of her feet
rhymed with our footsteps walking up the dirt road.

Looking down toward her, I asked, "Are those your
friends or relatives?"

"Friends. Josephine is Joshua's sister."

"Do they live close by?"

"Yes, they're our neighbors."

"Umph," I snickered.

PeggyAnn's eyes slid up at me. "What's so funny?"
Her eyes were filled with wonder. She had no idea how that
sounded to me.

Grinning, I answered, "From my observation, it looks
like neighbors around here are at least a block and a half or
more away from each other. And so far, I've only seen three
houses."

She grinned, too. "That's correct. How far apart do
you live from your neighbors where you're from?"

"Definitely, *not that far apart*. Much closer."

"How close?"

"Some houses are from here to where your friends are up ahead and some even closer."

"*You're kidding*?" she stared.

"No, I'm not kidding."

"That's *too close*."

"Just as I feel that these houses are too far apart. Miss PeggyAnn," I snickered again, "if a bear entered your house, no one would hear y'all scream."

"Devin, there are no bears around here," she laughed, amusingly.

"*Whew*," I comically wiped my hand across my forehead, "*that's good to know*. I wondered about that."

"There are—" she stopped talking when her attention was diverted. We did not realize that her friends were within talking distance. We were deep in conversation.

"PeggyAnn, *what happened?*" the girl asked breathing heavy with worry. "*We've been looking all around for you.*" Her face was shinin' with beads of sweat dryin' along the hairline of her face.

"It's a long story, Josephine. I'm too drained to explain."

Her brother was relieved. "We're glad that you're all right." He looked like he had been running from the dampness around the rim of his shirt. "Josephine came home and told me that you were riding on a runaway train. I followed her lead since she saw which direction Mamie was going in."

Josephine snickered.

PeggyAnn glanced at her. "*A runaway train?* That's a good one, Josephine."

Defending herself, Josephine said, "He knew what I meant."

Joshua nodded his head, "Yeah, I did. That's one of her codes."

"Well, I've learned something," PeggyAnn said.

I smiled, agreeing with her since I had never heard of a horse categorized as a runaway train.

Joshua looked at PeggyAnn again. "The main thing is that you're all right."

PeggyAnn smiled at him. "Thank you, Joshua, but I'm fine."

Then he and his sister looked at me and realized that we had not met.

"Joshua and Josephine, this is Devin," PeggyAnn immediately introduced us.

"Hi, Devin," they both said.

"Hello."

Their mouths opened wide. I had forgotten about my voice.

"*No way*," Joshua said as if amazed.

Their eyes rolled in PeggyAnn's direction like marbles.

Wondering what she would say, I glanced at her, too.

"*How did he do that?*" Josephine asked her. Her eyes grew to their limit.

"Do what?" she played it off.

"You know...*sound like a man.*"

"*How did you do that?*" Joshua chirped, zipping through his sentence without breathing, now facing me. He had a grin that would not release itself. "I need to learn how to do that." He stood straight rubbing his hand around the contour of his chin, as if he was acting.

Josephine then asked, "Are you an actor?"

"No, I'm not an actor," I replied, wanting to reverse the question because her expression was hilarious. I couldn't help noticing the smiley faces that covered her dress. They contrasted with her personality.

They were confused.

PeggyAnn seemed to be just as amused. She knew, as well, that it would be hard for them to understand.

Joshua asked stunned, "PeggyAnn, *is he your cousin?*"

My eyes met hers.

"No, he's not." Her eyes revealed that she would have rather concealed as much information as possible.

"*Who is he*?" was his next question. "*He's a star in my eyes*." He was determined to know.

Josephine joined him. "*He sure is. Wow, that's incredible*."

"He's a friend and we'll leave it at that."

"Devin, how long will you be around?" Joshua asked me, question after question.

This is going to be a long day, I thought, then answered him, "I'm not certain; I'll be around until time for me to go home."

"*Cool*," he smiled, "*you'll love it around here*."

It felt like time had stopped. At any moment, PeggyAnn looked like she could bust. She knew how I felt.

"You think so, huh?" *If he only knew,* I thought. That was a comment that made me feel like laughing in hysterics.

He grinned, and spread his arms as if to show me a palace with red carpet. "Sure, you would. You can't get any more country *than this*." His humor was apparent.

"Tell me about it," I agreed.

Joshua and Josephine were puzzled by my remark.

He asked, "Tell you about what?" What I said went right over their heads.

It dawned on me that we were from two different worlds. For clarity, I said, "What I meant is…you're so right." Lingo in this day and time was probably off the map. Some communication gaps were likely to happen.

"Oh," the confusion fizzled away, "that's what you meant. I've never heard that line before. Where are you from?"

With intensity, all eyes were on me.

"California is where I live."

"You're a long ways from home," Joshua responded, as a thought fumbled in his mind. "Now I understand."

"Understand what?"

"Your response to what I said about this country place. California, from what I have heard is, *much different from Seminole County.*"

I glanced past his shoulders and replied, "Yes, it is," hoping that, by the time I blinked again, this would all disappear.

With an interest, he then said, "Before you leave, you have to tell me what it's like there."

Grinning, I nodded, "One day, I will." The 21st century would be the fieldtrip of his life.

Josephine spoke with excitement, changing the subject, "Oh, by the way, PeggyAnn, what are you doing Sunday afternoon?"

"We're going to a program."

"*Really?*"

"Yes."

"*So are we at the high school.*"

"At Earlsmoth High School?" PeggyAnn asked, puttin' two and two together.

"*Girl,*" Josephine's voice escalated, "*we're going to the same program.*"

PeggyAnn's face beamed. "*That's great.*"

"The Give All You Have program is what we've been waiting for."

"Sure has," said Joshua, "and I'm looking forward to it. This will be my first time going."

"You'll enjoy it," PeggyAnn assured him. "It will be my second."

He looked at me, bright-eyed. "Devin, have you ever heard of the Give All You Have program?"

"No, I haven't. What kind of program is that? I'm already broke."

They looked at me from head-to-toe then suddenly laughed, uncontrollably. I wondered what humored them.

"*You're already broke?*" Josephine kept staring. "*You look straight to me.*"

I snickered. "Umph," I muttered, realizing what I said was comprehended the wrong way, "what I mean is…I have no money to give away." I couldn't tell them I came here without any change. Only PeggyAnn would know that.

"Ooooh," they chorused.

Joshua explained, "You don't need to give money, Devin. The program means to give all that you want to share with us."

With curiosity, I asked, *"Like what?"*

PeggyAnn stepped in. "When I went last year, some read their favorite poems, educational skits, another person talked about the greatest thing that ever happened, someone else talked about family. Those kinds of things are what I have witnessed."

"Oh," I got the picture now, "that sounds interesting."

Joshua gladly said, "You can go with me, if you want. How 'bout it?"

At that moment, I wasn't quite sure what to say. I looked at PeggyAnn. She was waiting for my response too. *"Welllllll,"* I paused with uncertainty, "I don't know…" That question was hard to answer because I didn't even know where I was going to stay overnight.

Seeing that I was struggling, PeggyAnn said softly, "I think it would be great if you went." The look in her eyes told me not to worry.

"Well," I felt myself about to give in, sounding like a kid again, *"all right.* I guess it wouldn't hurt." There were too many things on my mind right now that I couldn't answer or understand. Life felt very complicated. It was like a math problem that didn't even exist.

Joshua grinned. "No, it wouldn't hurt," he appeared entertained, so did his sister, but PeggyAnn's expression showed compassion. If Joshua and Josephine had only known my situation, they probably would have reacted differently. "Anyway, I don't think our parents would mind."

"We'll ask them tonight," Josephine said. That was one more thing added to the list of things to worry about. *Who were their parents?*

How much time had passed since we met up with them was a good question. We had walked and talked for some time now about other things up until we saw some man waving at us.

"Hello, Mr. Jackson," the three shouted. They waved back, including me, even though I didn't know who he was.

"Well, I have to be going," Joshua said. "Wish I could hang with you cubs longer, but you know, PeggyAnn, I have things to do."

Josephine joined him. "I have to run along, too."

PeggyAnn smiled and nodded that she understood. "I'll see you both later."

Joshua asked one, last question, "Where should I look for you tomorrow so I can let you know what our parents decide?"

That was one question *I wanted to know* because, I didn't have a clue. Keeping a straight face, the only thing I could think to say was, "I'll be around."

Quickly, PeggyAnn stepped in to cover me. "We'll stop by your place tomorrow, Joshua. That will give Devin a chance to see more of Seminole County."

He looked relieved since he didn't know where he could find me. "All right. That's even better."

They both waved and left.

I exhaled. "Thank you, Miss PeggyAnn, for saving me."

She smiled with sincerity. "You're welcome, Devin. You must have been nervous."

"Yes, I was. That was close. The less people know the better."

"I agree," she looked down toward her shoes. "Who would ever believe your story?" She shook her head while looking up at the sky as if she wished it would rain.

Looking at her, I asked, *"Do you?"* I wanted to know what she really thought.

She stopped. "Yes, Devin. I have to admit...*I had a hard time believing you, at first*." She slowly starts walking again.

"And what changed your mind?" I began walking, too.

She glanced at Mamie with the rope still in her hand and answered, "The way Mamie was carrying on was very strange and putting both scenarios together confirms my suspicion. Some things still don't add up but sometimes its best to leave the unknown alone."

Before I could get out another word, the man who waved was just a few feet away. Walking up the dusty road to his property, he pulled off his hat. "PeggyAnn, how yuh doin' dere, damsel?"

His salutation was definitely strange to my ears; his dialect had a southern spice, and "damsel" wasn't even in my vocabulary. Quite frankly, I had forgotten the term existed.

When we finally reached him, she smiled and said, *"Great, Mr. Jackson."*

He put his hat back on. "Dat's whut I like tuh hear, and who's dat young fella?"

"Mr. Jackson," she said, "meet Devin." PeggyAnn looked at me. She knew once I spoke that he would be swirling with suspense, just as shocked as the others.

He stepped closer. "Another lad," he said with a kind smile. "Nice meetin' yuh." His style was innocent.

After dusting off my hands on the surface of my pants, I reached out my hand and said, "Nice meeting you, too, sir." There was residue still left on them from the straw.

His eyebrows rose, as he reached to shake my hand. "Dat's some voice yuh 'ave dere, lad." Entirely thrown off, he gleamed, as if he had seen something spectacular.

"Well, sir, I don't know what to say." From all the attention I had been getting, I was fresh out of words.

PeggyAnn giggled. She had been observing, from the very beginning, scene after scene of what happened next.

Mr. Jackson was in a trance. "I'm *confuuuuuused*. If I didn't *kno' no better, I'd 'ave thought I is talkin' tuh uh grown man.*" He pulled off his straw hat, again, and scratched the corner of his head where a distinguished patch of gray hair grew. An imprint from his hat was neatly carved in his wavy hair. In stature, he appeared to be 5'5" tall and in his fifties. He was wearing overalls. No matter how old time gets, overalls will never be obsolete, especially in the country.

Mr. Jackson still had some youth bursting through the boulders of his shoulders. The strength in his handshake was powerful, and his grip revealed muscles bulging from his tanned forearm. It was apparent that he was kind in nature, and it showed from deep behind the walls of his eyes. Talking with him put the icing on the cake because his humor never ran dry. His expression kept the comedy going as he continued, "*How old are yuh, lad? Maybe, I'm mistaken and need tuh get some…glasses.*"

I knew that would be the next question since I couldn't seem to pass the initial inspection test. Speaking before thinking, my answer really had him baffled, "Twenty-first century—"

PeggyAnn kindly cut in. "Mr. Jackson," she said, breaking his trance, "I tried already and believe me, you don't want to know." She glanced at me.

Then, Mr. Jackson landed his eyes on me again. "Try me. I've heard many thangs and one mo' tellins' can't be dat bad."

The diversion PeggyAnn had in mind was not working, and we both were searching for a way out.

Wanting to be honest, I came out with it. "I'm not sure how old I am right now, but I'm a 21st century type of man."

He coolly laughed, shaking his head while looking down.

I shrugged my shoulders at PeggyAnn wondering if that was a good enough answer. Maybe he'll let it go…for now anyway.

"Oh, yo're a comedian. *Dat's uh good one.*"

"You think so?" Maybe my answer *was* good enough, but I didn't think he would see it as comedy.

"Yez, I do."

"I've heard that many times before."

"Oh, 'ave yuh?"

"Yes, I have."

"Yuh kno' what's funny?"

I grinned. "What, Mr. Jackson?" I felt PeggyAnn's eyes.

He then gazed past me. "I don't think uh *good actor* could act out his voice fer dat length of time."

PeggyAnn's eyes were waiting to get my attention when my eyes finally met hers. There was plenty eye movement going on. It was like a drag-race competition.

Since I took so long to answer, he continued. "And, whut's even funnier is dat, I believe yuh." Mr. Jackson kept his eyes straight ahead.

It was a relief to hear that someone else, who was an adult, actually believed me. I felt like a pound of worries had deflated.

PeggyAnn said in disbelief, "Mr. Jackson, did you say that you believe him?"

"Yez, part of it."

We were both swept right into a net.

He looked at me again. "I believe dat yuh don't kno' yer age, but dat stuff 'bout da 21st century don't sound right. Yuh probably 'ave amnesia. Yer voice sounds too natural tuh be *actin'.*"

"But, Mr. Jackson," PeggyAnn said, feeling that she needed to intervene, "*I don't think he has amnesia.*"

"Little damsel, anytime someone starts talkin' like dere experiencing blanks and 'ave twilights on dere *lips is needin' some checkin'.*"

Staring at him in disbelief, I repeated, *"NEEDIN'
SOME CHECKIN'?"* I hoped he wasn't thinking what I
thought.

"Yez," he verified, nodding his head. "Uh good *doctah
will do yuh some good. Do yuh 'ave any folks 'round here?"*

"No, I don't, sir. They're—" I coughed, trying to draw
attention away from the topic.

"Der where?" he remained focused. He didn't let up.

Shaking my head, I sighed. "It's a *loooooog story."* I
took another peep at my surroundings. Slim chance to think
nature could come to my rescue.

Mr. Jackson slightly grinned, with concern. "Lad, it
can't be much worse than whut I already *kno'."*

PeggyAnn's eye inflated when she tried to warn him,
*"Mr. Jackson, he's not kidding…it's a loooooong story, and he's
gonna need more than just an apple a day."*

"Let's hear it. It can't be dat bad!"

He has no idea, I thought. *What will he think when he
hears the rest of the hidden truth?*

Chapter 8

DEVIN

*P*o' *Mr. Jackson.* By the time PeggyAnn and I had told him everything, his eyes were *stuck in space.* He had us to repeat that story twice before he finally decided to turnaround and go sit in a wooden chair nearby. He took his hat off and swiped sweat from his face. He looked like someone had poured a bucket of water over his head. Until everything soaked in, only two words, jet streamed through the tunnel of his mouth, *"Oh, Lawd."*

Hours had passed, but how many, I didn't know. So many thoughts lingered in my mind. This has been one of the most eventful days of my life. So far, the intensity never seemed to let up. Today had been lit up like a fireball, and it was like going from, scene to scene, acting out a movie or play. And no matter how many times I flipped the pages back, I was stuck on previous scenes wondering, when and how this mystery would unfold. The way things were happening, we could roll right into another episode. The chain of events was still whispering. Moving forward was going to be quite interesting the ways things were going. For the time being, there were no pages to turn going forward without change. The day that happens…it's history—a fine art that's hard to find.

PeggyAnn and I were on our way back to Mr. Jackson's home after going back to where this chapter all started. The whole purpose was to backtrack to the mystery wagon where we met, and maybe, something would jog my memory. We were back to square one, replaying the rough-cut. What was very strange was that Mamie didn't even take off like a whirlwind, which was the beginning of the scene, *according to PeggyAnn's version*. Instead, she strolled along as her horseshoes echoed against the drum of the earth. It was as if she had jetlag. It would have been good if she had started her lines from the top of the script as history was noted since I'm a 21st century type of guy. Our intent was to roll this film from the very beginning, no matter *how many times*, before the final cut was developed and completed. *But why was I a part of the cast?* the thought occurred to me.

Mr. Jackson thought this exercise was a good idea. He wanted time to think so he could decide how he could help. He needed a break. Intermissions could never come too soon.

When we saw Mr. Jackson from a distance, he was unloading, what looked like, stacks of hay from a wagon that appeared as if it hadn't been moved in years.

Vaguely, I remember seeing that wagon earlier but, from all that was happening, it was as if that clip had been erased from my mind. At this point, I didn't want to see another wagon anytime soon.

Walking up to the front of his property, I noticed for the first time that he lived on a large piece of land. A big barn built out of natural wood was off to the far left. There was animal chatter going on inside. A big sign over the large wooden door read "JACKSON." It couldn't be missed from the extremely large letters painted in dark yellow with a white background. Next to the barn was a wooden dog house with "SMOKEY" written on it. Of course, it was scribbled the same color as the other sign. There was another wooden building painted in yellow on the right side of his property and a barrel near the road. Most of what was on his property coordinated with his pastel, yellow-wooden house.

Everything we passed were farms. *Hmmmmm, where's the city?* the thought radiated. Missing my world, one thought raced after the other. *Umph, I haven't seen a car yet. Straaaaaange.*

After hearing the sound of Mamie's feet, Mr. Jackson turned around and took off his gloves. He walked toward us with a smile. "Anything new?" He put his gloves in his pocket.

"No," I shook my head. "Nothing new."

Mr. Jackson's head twitched. The thickness of my voice reminded him that he was not dealing with an ordinary youngster. He looked at PeggyAnn.

"Maybe soon," she said, trying to be positive. "Look on the bright side, Devin. If Mamie had not led me to where the wagon was, we may not have ever met."

Mr. Jackson's smile grew. "Dat's right," he patted me on the shoulder, "and another day is uh comin'."

"Aaaaaamen to that!" I perked up, being optimistic.

They laughed.

"I see da comedian side of yuh has awakened again," Mr. Jackson noticed.

"I might as well make the *best* of it."

"Champ, yer uh star."

"You think so?"

"*I kno' so*," he said, with definition. "*I can jus' feel it in dese bones!*" His statement hit a funny bone.

A spark of laughter was ignited and burned until we couldn't laugh anymore. He was acting out his role extremely well to the point that PeggyAnn and I were half bent over. Apparently, he didn't realize the southern impact of his own, unique style. Standing straight as a sergeant, he swung his Popeye arms. The spears of his words soared dynamically, aiming for the rainbow of hope. What neither of us understood was not black or white, but in between, losing its neutral hue. Shades of gray lost their grade to colors of vitality that would help change anybody's world of uncertainty.

PeggyAnn's eyes were watery, and so were mine. When we refocused on him, again, our vision was blurry from tears splashing from the flap of our eyelids.

Forming my lips to get a word in was difficult because, even his laugh took it to another level. It came from way down in the belly. For the time being, I tabled the thought.

PeggyAnn was scuffling to speak, when she finally said, "Mr. Jackson, you're funny in your own way. All these years, I had no idea."

"Sometimes, situations can bring da best out of yuh."

"Out of curiosity," I chimed in, "where are you from?"

"Lad," he chuckled, remembering the days of his youth, "I'm from da *good ol' South*."

"Where in the South?"

"The southern states of Georgia and Mississippi. I'm uh southern boy."

"Look!" PeggyAnn shouted with horror.

Alarmed, Mr. Jackson and I zipped our heads toward his barn but saw nothing.

"Over there!" she pointed.

We turned our heads the other direction.

"It looks like smoke from a fire," I said.

Mr. Jackson stepped forward, looked as far as he could and wondered, "Where could dat smoke be uh comin' from?" His eyebrows joined when bells set off in his head. "Dat looks like dat smoke maybe comin' from yo' place, little damsel."

"*It sure does*," PeggyAnn's mouth gaped.

Mr. Jackson backed up and said quickly, "Let's help yuh up on dat horse and see whut's goin' on over dere." He locked both his hands together for PeggyAnn to place one foot in. Like jumping cables, he raised his hands to lift her up on Mamie's back.

PeggyAnn held on to the rope that was looped around Mamie's head and neck.

Facing me, Mr. Jackson then said, "Lad, yuh welcome tuh ride wit me."

I said swiftly, "I'm ready."

"*Stay here*," he told me, walking toward the barn. "*I'll be right back.*" He opened the door of the barn and hurried inside. It was dark in there from where I stood.

"Umph, is that where he keeps his car?" I mumbled.

PeggyAnn turned and glanced at me but didn't understand a word I said. "What was it that you said, Devin?"

Staring where he had disappeared, I replied, "I was wondering if Mr. Jackson's—"

PeggyAnn's eyes shifted toward the barn.

There was a sudden outburst of loud noise.

From her expression, she soon figured out what I was possibly trying to say.

A few chicken feathers were floating in the air, landing as parachutes.

"*Whaaaaaat*," I said flabbergasted. My eyes felt as though they would pop. It looked like *The Last Wagon* had jumped off a television screen, rollin' in high gear. For sure now, that movie would never get old. When I glanced at PeggyAnn again, she was waiting and anxious to let Mamie flow in the wind.

I gasped and said stunningly, "*Miss PeggyAnn, is that what I think it is?*" I was getting a little light-headed from the exhaustion of being overwhelmed from one countryside hit after another.

She kept a straight face and nodded several times.

Mr. Jackson was guiding two horses attached to a wagon. He pulled on the leather straps to slow them down to a complete stop as they reached the edge of the dirt road. "JUMP ON, LAD!"

Not wasting any time, I jumped up in the seat beside him, starry-eyed.

Mamie took off like lightening. We sped behind them down a winding road.

Between the urgency of getting jolted and watching Mamie glide in the wind, I recalled the conversation PeggyAnn and I had. She told me about her terror ride earlier and how she was not the best at running a horse at top speed. Anxious to get home, she learned to ride Mamie at whatever cost it took, and she rode her well.

"Oh," Mr. Jackson said, during what felt like a high-speed chase, "I've done uh lot of *thinkin'*."

"*About what?*" I glanced at him, bouncing around, as if I was a salt shaker.

"Until we can figure out whut's goin' on, yuh can stay wit me."

I felt as though I went from rags to riches, knowing that someone cared. "Thank you, Mr. Jackson."

"Sure, lad. Since it's gettin' late, yuh might as well stay at my place. Don't yuh worry, sooner or later, it will all make sense."

"Yeah, I know."

The smoke got thicker the closer we got. Not believing what I was seeing, I saw oil wells on a farm in an oil field. It looked like the closest one near a house may have been about 100 feet away. Amazed, I said counting, "Wow, there are at least ten of those rigs out there!"

"Little damsel lives dere," Mr. Jackson let me know.

Shocked, I exclaimed, "*It's a good thing those are not on fire.*" That concerned me, but yet, I was relieved. Those oversized grasshoppers had taken my attention completely away from the blaze ahead.

"I kno'," I heard relief in his voice. "Dere's not enough water *'round heah* for that kind of catastrophe."

From a distance, we watched PeggyAnn slide off her horse and run into the house. She probably stopped there to alert her family.

Looking ahead, Mr. Jackson then said, "*Dat fire is at John Bailey's place.*" The fire was small but large enough to draw a lot of attention.

Observing from the onset, more and more people were coming to help in any way they could.

Transportation was colorful. I had never seen so many horses, and, wagons, seem to be a delicacy around here.

As soon as we pulled up, Mr. Jackson jumped down off the wagon. His speed was quick.

Of course, it took me a little longer. Seemed odd not reaching for a car-door handle first. "I can help, Mr. Jackson," I offered.

The fire spread rapidly, burning the green pasture. A wagon was also on fire with what may have been lumber in it and many bales of straw around it. The fire was headed toward his barn.

"Lad, stand uhside. We may need yuh tuh do somethin' shortly."

There was so much going on; it looked like a circus. People were running, and dogs were barking. The dogs were making just as much noise as the horses and wagons that were approaching with intensity.

There were men quickly moving with buckets of water swinging from hand to hand.

"Hmmm," I thought out loud, "where are they getting the water from?"

There were two other wagons that pulled up with tubs of water in them. They jumped off and reached for buckets they brought to help; they scooped their own water into them.

I didn't know who was who. My head turned everytime I heard someone holler out another person's name.

"Smith," a man shouted, "needin' more water!"

"More comin' up!"

Looking up the way, there was Joshua with buckets in his hands, too. He handed them to the man called Smith.

"*Lad,*" Mr. Jackson shouted from a distance, "*we need yo' help now.*"

Running to where he stood, I asked, "What do you want me to do, Mr. Jackson?"

Brushes of heat swepted past us.

He pulled out his hankerchief. "Follow dat lad dere. We need mo' water." Then he wiped his forehead.

"All right." Spinning off past a crowd, I rushed to meet Joshua. He was walking fast and was empty-handed. "Joshua!"

"*Devin*," he stopped, surprised to see me again so soon, "*your visit was timely.*"

"Yes, it is," I caught up with him. "I'm here to help."

"We need all the help we can get."

"Where are we headed?" I followed him.

He moved his head upward indicating which direction. "Up the way." His eyes were trying to pinpoint the exact spot but he could hardly see for all the commotion.

Two men were standing idle trying to catch their breath. "*Joshua*," one shouted, "*over here!*"

We rushed to meet them.

They looked exhausted with sweat running down their faces, dripping on their shirts, soaking their clothes and more. "You can take these to the well." Two buckets were on the ground in front of them.

"All right," he said, charged.

The two men pulled out their handkerchiefs and wiped a flood of sweat from around their heads and necks.

Joshua bent over. "Here," he reached for one of the empty buckets for me to carry, "you'll need this." Then, he grabbed the other one for himself.

I followed his lead again. Looking around, I asked, "How far is the well?" The heat was starting to bake my skin. I mopped my hand across my forehead.

Our buckets wobbled with intensity as we got out of the way of others rushing by.

Feeling the heat, he wiped his forehead, too, with his other hand. "*From here*, about half a sweet potato pie away."

I stopped, and so did he.

"*To get some water?!*" my eyes inflated. A patch of dirt floated in the air from my feet puttin' on brakes. Trying to figure out what could be the equivalent to half a sweet potato pie was baffling. I couldn't come up with a calculated answer. Whatever the distance was, it sounded too far for comfort.

"Yes," he almost grinned. "Why you asked?" We picked up our pace again, joining in the marathon. Our mood was changing despite the setting.

"*That sounds like a loooooong way, man, to lug some water in buckets,*" I told him, forgetting their southern exchange of words.

He slightly laughed, seeming to forget that we were on a mission. "Wow, I like that."

"Like what?" the thought of walking far kept pounding.

"You called me a man," Joshua grinned. "I feel privileged, but you're the man. I still can't get over your voice."

Trying to throw him off, I said, "Well, I can't get over what I'm experiencing today." I did not want him to ask me about my age, but I knew sooner or later he would. For now, I was not ready to deal with it. The less he knew, the better, and it was best to keep it that way.

Keeping his mind occupied and off the fiery scene, he kept the conversation going by asking, "Why you say that?"

"Let's just say…it has been very interesting."

He sensed some disbelief in my response. "Give it some time…you won't regret it," he assured me.

"Maybe not," was all I could say.

"It's not that bad…*really*."

"Like anything else, I guess it takes some getting used to."

"You're right about that. California is far from the country way of living."

"It's different."

"How? This is a good time to fill me in until we make it back from the well."

"What do you want to know, *cub*?" I shot back at him from earlier today.

He slightly laughed. "You can call me 'man.' That's a nice exchange."

I joined in his spirit of laughter. "All right, man." He had no problems getting used to his new role, which was just between us.

Two men were standing at the well.

I noticed the rafter and a rope around the wheel for dropping buckets down into its mouth. *That's a neat setup*, I thought wondering how deep it was, but this was not the time to ask.

As we approached them, Joshua handed them his bucket and I handed them mine.

In exchange, they gave us a bucket each, already filled, to haul all the way back.

I figured out why Joshua wanted me to fill him in about California until we made it back. The distance was about half a block. We needed to stay mentally occupied while carrying the heavy loads.

After a while, gritting my teeth created a happy face without me even trying. "Man, how much water is in these buckets? Do you know? They're very heavy." I couldn't wait to get back. It wasn't long before the discussion about California vanished.

Joshua struggled himself, but he wasn't to the point of grinning—not yet, anyway. "These buckets hold up to three gallons." He was walking fast and so was I.

Before long, I had to stop for a minute. "Go ahead, I'm right behind you." Catching a second wind, I picked up the bucket and continued. I had to stop a couple more times to rest my arms.

By the time I finally did make it back, firefighters had arrived. Equipped to handle disasters much quicker, they put out the smokey blaze to a humbling hush.

Daylight was closing its eyes.

Joshua and I were standing at the wagon when Mr. Jackson finally walked up after chatting with neighbors who were observing the site of charcoal. All three of us gazed at the damages, for the last time, before leaving. No one seemed to notice I was even there.

Mr. Jackson was in no rush to return home. We crept along, talking about the disaster, until he said, changing the subject, "Lad, whut do yuh kno' 'bout wagons?"

"Not too much," I grinned, intrigued about why he had asked. "I know that they're designed to remain in the *good ol' days.*"

He laughed so hard that tears streamed down his cheeks. His eyes were nearly closed revealing slight features branching from the Indian side of his ancestors.

After momentarily watching the role he played, I exploded. I laughed right along with him after realizing the impact of my statement.

"*Whew!*" he blew out with force, "*dat wuz funny.*"

"I guess it was," I said, on the verge again.

He pulled out his handkerchief and wiped his glassy eyes. "Umph, umph, umph," he shook his head, "yo're one of da most funniest lads I've ever met."

"I wasn't trying to be funny, but that's how I feel. I'm used to either a 10-speed, an automobile, or a train. Wagons as transportation are like fairytales where I'm from."

Mr. Jackson chuckled. "Yeeeeeez, sir." He was thoroughly amused.

"*Gee,*" I said, wanting this scene to speed up to *The End,* "*this is unbelievable. What's next?*"

Still grinning, his words were, "I reckon ya'll find out soon enough."

"I don't know if I can take too much more," I glanced at him. "Are there any hospitals around here?" I don't know why I even asked; I felt like I was on a safari trip. Everything was *so* far apart.

He looked at me. *"Uh hospital?"* the words fumbled from his mouth.

"Yes, a hospital."

"Why yuh asked dat question? Hospitals are fer sick folks." I guess he was trying to understand why I would be needin' to go to a place where folks are dressed in white.

I paused. "I know."

"Are yuh all right?"

"For now. Somewhere down the line, I may have to check-in."

He chuckled, again. "I don't think yuh'll be needin' uh doctah. Yuh gonna be jus' fine, lad, jus' fine."

"Yeah...I know," looking straight ahead.

There was silence, then without warning, Mr. Jackson stopped on the side of the road, as if it was a two-lane highway and said, "How 'bout if yuh guide these horses da rest of da way?" He held the straps in front of me as a teaser, smiling.

For some reason, the sudden rush to try something different became enticing.

"Here, take it," he firmly said. "Tam and Sam won't mind."

"Tam and Sam?" I chuckled, glancing at his horses. I took the straps.

He smiled. *"Dat's dere names."* Mr. Jackson stepped down and patted the horses' noses as he walked to the other side. "Slide over, lad." He stepped up and sat in the seat. "Let me kno' if yuh need my help."

"I will," I assured him, nodding my head.

"Roll'em," he said, sounding like he had been in the entertainment business of ridin' 'em high. That was one of Major's famous words on *Wagon Train.*

I snickered at his humor. Taking control, I lightly popped the straps. "Let's roll." Although bumpy, I passed the driver's test.

It was interesting watching both horses pull our wagon. They were strolling along, side by side, as if they were enjoying a perfect evening.

When we made it back, nightfall had opened its eyes. It was dark and there were no streetlights. The moon was hidden behind dark clouds as if it had been swept under a rug.

Just before reaching the barn, which had to be pitch black inside, Mr. Jackson said, "Wait here." He hopped down and headed in that direction. His footsteps penetrated the silence. The outline of his stature faded with distance, blending in the dark.

I couldn't see much of anything on the side or across the road. The night was quiet and still. It felt like we were being secretly watched by nature.

In the meantime, I jumped off the wagon. Forgetting that I was no expert yet, and did not have eyes as scanners in the dark, my knees hit the ground. The landing was a little rough. I lost my balance. When I tried getting up, I felt a set of teeth against my ankle. I heard a grizzly sound. My world started shaking. Quick as a jackrabbit, my body stood up straight as a bowling pin. I felt a rush of fuel blaze to my brain. My eyes flipped on like headlights. They were on high beam. The scare tactic worked. My battery was charged, sending juice to my feet. I took off toward the barn and ran inside as the door suddenly swung open.

Mr. Jackson's eyes grew to the size of bowling balls while holding up a lamplight at eye level. The significance of his expression ran deep like the woods were to a city boy. "SMOKEY," he shouted, "*come here.*"

The dog started barking in his baritone voice.

Not realizing that flyin' past him would take me to another level, I ran *right into a zoo.* I put on brakes, and staggeringly, made a complete circle in a trance. I was now surrounded by screamin' chickens, walking geese, two oversized snorting pigs, a mule, two other horses heehawing in melody, a cow that mooed, ringing a bell around its neck, staring me in the face. I felt this was one of those scenes where I had been captured into captivity.

I twitched when Mr. Jackson tapped me on the shoulder. "Lad, it's Smokey. Yo're safe now."

Numbed, I asked out of breath, *"Are there any more surprises? I had no idea there was an army in here."*

He strapped his hand across his mouth, trying to remain intact, ignoring the question. "No need tuh be skeered. Yo're *protected* 'round here."

"What is it that you don't have? You have a flock of animals in here." The movie, *Noah's Ark*, flashed before my eyes.

His eyes were flooding. "I 'ave uh nice little collection, and Smokey helps keep 'em inbound. And now since Smokey kno' who yuh are, yuh won't be having any trouble out of him."

"Good," I said, beat, "I'm tired now."

I wondered how many times Mr. Jackson called on the Man Upstairs, because, I was sure gonna need it.

Several hours later, my eyes flipped open and oscillated at the sound of a rooster crowing at 4:00 a.m.

Chapter 9

PEGGYANN

S aturday morning was going to be a good day. The heavy clouds were gone from the previous night. There were scribbles of dusty clouds that looked as thin as paper, slowly gliding across the sky as the sun shined cheerfully. The weather was not as hot as the day before; it was just right.

It was early and I assumed that Devin stayed with Mr. Jackson overnight since he had no place to go. I did my chores very early and was off to see how my friend was doing since I knew he might need some help adjusting.

I tied Mamie around a tree in Mr. Jackson's yard then knocked on the wooden door. When it opened, drafts of good smelling food floated past me. "Good morning, Mr. Jackson."

"Well, good mornin' tuh yuh, little damsel," he acknowledged, smiling. "Yuh must be lookin' fer da lad?"

"Yes, I am."

"Would yuh like tuh come in and 'ave uh seat? He's jus' finishing up eatin' breakfast."

"I'll wait for him outside, Mr. Jackson, if that's all right?"

"Sure it tis. I'll let him kno' yo're here," he said, and closed the door.

I sat on a bench close to Mamie under a tree.

A few minutes later, he came out with baggy overalls on, and a dark blue tee shirt. *Hmmm, those must be a pair of Mr. Jackson's overalls*, I thought. They were some inches way above his ankle.

"Miss PeggyAnn," he said, gleefully.

"Hi, Devin," I smiled, seeing that Mr. Jackson was taking good care of him.

"*I'm sure glad to see you.*"

"Is everything all right?" I asked, wondering why his voice slightly escalated with emphasis.

He stood next to Mamie and patted her on the back. "A nice horse ride to the point-of-no-return sounds good about now." He looked seriously, gazing past Mamie, as if in deep thought.

Baffled, I asked, "Why you say that, Devin? Isn't Mr. Jackson a nice man?" I felt my eyebrows join, hoping the answer was what I wanted to hear.

He glanced at me. "Yes, Mr. Jackson is a kind-hearted man. I'm grateful and couldn't ask for a better person to help me."

I was mystified now. "Well, why would you want to ride off to the point-of-no-return? That's not an everyday statement."

"Let me explain," he said, walking to the other side of Mamie, as if that would help his thoughts flow easier. "I don't know where to start."

"Start with what happened first," I told him, hoping that would help.

"I couldn't believe it yesterday when people, including Joshua and I, were lugging buckets of water all the way from a well, which was, half a sweet potato pie away, as Joshua puts it."

"*What?*" I said, not expecting to hear what he had just said.

"*Helloooooo,*" he said strangely, dragging the word, but comically, "*what time is it?*"

I laughed so hard, I couldn't see well. My eyes were filled with tear water.

He was silent, watching me bubbling over, nonstop. His facial expression was blank.

"That is the funniest thing I've heard in a long time. Well...since yesterday that is." I shook that thought before I involuntarily went into suspension. *"What do you mean?"* I laughed, again.

From all the disruption, he lost his train of thought and had to laugh himself. He cleared his throat and continued, "When Joshua said the distance was half a sweet potato pie away, I had no idea he meant *that* far. He has an unusual way of calculating measurements. I must admit, that was a good one." He drew in a deep breath and exhaled. Then, he said, "I'm not telling it in the exact order but I'm telling you what happened as it comes to me."

"That's all right, Devin, I'm listening."

"Also, when Mr. Jackson rocketed out of his barn on a wagon like a missile, I thought I was dreaming. Then, when we made it back to his house last night, Smokey turned the evening into fright night. Honestly, I thought a grizzly bear was on my tail. And what tops it off is when I ran into the barn, not knowing he had a stash in there."

I said puzzled, *"A stash?"*

"Yeah, a stash, as in where he hides his animals. I thought he had a few chickens in there and a couple horses, but, *he has a fortress.*"

"Well, Devin," I said, humored by his reaction, "some families around here have, what you call a fortress on their property, with or without a barn. *Where have you been?* Oh," I remembered, "you're not from around here. *You must've thought you dead-ended into a corral.*"

"Umph," he shook his head in total disbelief, then added, "and, what puts the icing on the cake is, during the silence of night, *what do I hear?* I heard a rooster singing at 4:00 a.m. in the morning, nonstop, until it got tired."

This was funny. The seriousness in his voice and in his expression was a matching pair. *Who could have told it any better?* I thought his theatrics were dynamic.

"I don't know how many times I turned over in bed. Last night was draining, and even more exhausting by the time my eyes wobbled to sleep from listening to the same bugle play over and over." His story increased with intensity, "*I tried covering my ears; I tried tuning it out, but nothing worked. What do you do?*" He raised his arms like he was waiting to catch anything that fell from the sky to answer him.

"Devin, there is no easy way for me to answer your question. The best way to deal with it is to get used to it, and *you will.*"

"*How do you get used TO THAT?*" his voice increased in volume again. "*That bird got louder and louder.*"

I drew back. His description of a rooster threw me off. "*Bird? That's a rooster.*"

"They all look alike. It still has feathers."

"Well, that's something they have in common," I couldn't deny.

He took a deep breath, "I don't know, Miss PeggyAnn."

"You don't know what?"

"I don't know how long it will take to get used to all this, or if I can even adjust. I'm stuck on a merry-go-round and can't seem to get off."

My next comment was, "Life sounds extremely different where you're from."

"Convenience and the way of life have been easy. Luxurious, I might as well say, compared to this lifestyle of living."

"Look at it this way, Devin. You will get the best of both worlds."

"Isn't that the truth?"

"We should never take anything for granted. You will always have something else to treasure because it is treasure. Someday, it will all become a memory."

"It'll be *history*."

To help his situation, I thought maybe I should clear up some things for him. "I understand how you must feel, but wagons are not the only way of getting from place to place around here."

He wondered if he heard me right. "What? Not a pony or a mule?" he looked with tension.

I giggled. "Oh no, no. I don't want to traumatize you no more than you already are."

"Thank you," he smiled. "What else is there? I have only seen wagons and horses."

"We have cars, too."

Devin's mouth dropped. "*Really? Where?*"

"Everyone doesn't have one, but some do."

"Well," he glistened, "that's good to hear." I knew the next question that was coming, when he asked, "Do your parents own a car?"

"Yes. A Model-T Ford."

"*What a classic!*" he almost shouted.

"Mr. Jackson has one, too."

Curiously, he asked, "*Where?*" His voice dropped from baritone to bass.

"It's probably locked up in that little hut."

"Oh," he looked in that direction, "*you're probably right.*"

"Devin," I gazed at him, "you must think we live in the stone ages. Automobiles do exist, but sometimes, I still walk to school and ride horses and wagons, too. And, back to the water buckets…we get our water from the wells around here."

"Everybody?" his eyes grew extremely large.

I nodded my head, "Yes, most of us."

"Are you saying that every time you want a drink of water, you have to walk to a well to get it?"

"Yes," I saw his smile diminish.

Devin stared at me. "Aaaaaaand, are you saying that every time I want to take a bath or wash my clothes, I have to walk to the well and get the water?"

"Yes."

Then he asked, "And how many buckets is that on an average?" He did not blink.

I sure didn't want to be the one to tell him, but on the other hand, maybe it was best that I did before he decided to escape for good. "On an average, 3-4 buckets to bathe in. We usually use the #3 tubs, which are the largest size."

Devin said, "By the time I go to the well 3-4 times carrying buckets of water that heavy, I'll be too tired to even take a bath."

"We're used to it. Even I get my own water."

He looked shocked. "You have to be kidding?"

"No, we all do." Then a thought surfaced, "Didn't you go to the well this morning to get water to wash up?"

Quickly, he answered, "No. When I got up, Mr. Jackson had already put one of those decorative pans filled with water in my room with soap and a wash cloth. He told me to leave it there when I was done. I don't know where the water came from."

"Well, what about a washroom?"

"Oh, yeah." That question seemed to jolt him into a coughing spell. "I forgot about that. Now that you mention it, when I asked about the restroom last night, Mr. Jackson said he would show me where it was. When he headed for the door, I didn't put two and two together. I thought maybe the door inside was jammed. He opened the front door and said, 'The private room is outdoors in the back.' Of course, I had to see what he was talking about, so I followed him. When he raised the lamplight and pointed it in the direction we were going, I felt my back crack from stretching my neck like an ostrich. *My eyes were spinning like coins.*"

I snickered. He was captivating.

Devin rubbed the back of his neck. "My neck has never been jacked that high!" He went on to say, "AS DARK AS IT WAS OUT THERE...MY OWN WELL WENT DRY!"

Silence fell.

"*What do you mean by that? You don't own any wells out here, do you?*"

He could barely grin and shook his head. "That's not what I meant, Miss PeggyAnn." From the dry look on his face, I couldn't help but put the pieces together.

"Oh," I finally caught on. Tickled, I replied, "*I see your point.*"

"*Whew,*" he said, "*I don't know how much plainer I could get on that one.*"

"*That was a good one,*" I paused for a moment to recollect, and then said, "but I can understand because it gets very dark around here in the rural areas."

"*It was pitch black. Smokey's eyes were shining like two fluorescent lights.*"

My eyes were starting to flood. Devin was a good actor. I didn't know how much more I could take listening to him go on and on.

"*Talk about running track,*" he kept it going, adding more explosives to the fire, "*my brain commanded everything to head in reverse.*"

My eyes slid upward, thinking about what he just said. "Running track?" I mumbled.

Devin stared at me, seeing that, once again, I didn't quite make the connection.

Like flashcards, the answer appeared. A burst of laughter erupted. Finally, I stood up holding on to a tree branch. I felt like I would tip right over.

Mr. Jackson opened the door. "Are yuh two all right?"

"Yes," we both answered, and fell out when he shut the door.

"*OH, BOY,*" Devin realized something then he looked around as if he had never seen this place before, "*this is too much. I'm on a funny farm. I haaaaaave never seen anything like this before. Gee...*"

Mamie's head danced in the air, making her usual sound. I guess she wanted to be part of the script, too.

"One other question," I said, remembering now that I had wanted to ask him something else earlier, "Devin, what about your teeth?"

"My teeth? The last time I *looked*, they were all there." He touched his mouth to double-check.

Amused, I laughed under my breath. For clarity, I rephrased the question, "How were you able to clean your teeth?"

"I asked Mr. Jackson if he had a spare toothbrush and some toothpaste that I could use, and he said that's what the cup filled with water was for and to use the other cloth for scrubbing my teeth."

"What did you use on your teeth?"

"He gave me some baking soda."

Even though his teeth were bright, I tried to offset any other uncertainties from rising in his head, when I commented, "Your teeth are pearly white. The baking soda did the job." Devin already looked like he couldn't take too much more of what seemed to be outdated, as far as he was concerned.

"That's better than not having anything. I figure he was just out of toothpaste and hadn't made it to the store to replenish his toiletries yet."

So he wouldn't think that he was all alone in the toiletries-deficiency department, I added, "I don't know what Mr. Jackson normally uses, but we have always used baking soda. Don't feel bad...we make do."

"Well," he glanced at me, "sometimes you have to do what you have to do. I don't feel bad; I've used baking soda before as a whitener."

Relieved, I told him, "I'm glad that didn't traumatize you. That's one less thing on the list."

"Baking soda…I can deal with, *but the rest*," he snickered, "has me dumbfounded."

Even though I wanted to laugh, I suppressed it. "It's funny and it's not funny. I feel for you."

"I agree. It will be funny…*very* funny when things are back to normal again."

"I'm glad you can at least see the comical side of it all. Hopefully, this is the turning point."

"Maybe," he smiled and said no more, and neither did I, hoping that he was beginning to see the brighter side of the country way of living.

We heard a door open and close. Mr. Jackson was coming from the backside of his house walking fast. He appeared to be on a mission as he put on his straw hat.

Smokey ran to meet him.

He threw a ball in the air as he walked toward the barn.

We met Smokey after he ran to retrieve it.

Devin was somewhat reluctant to go near him. After last night, who wouldn't be skeptical? Smokey's shiny coat was black and he had brown honey eyes that softened his features. He was a plump, large German Shepherd. His mouth was clamped around the ball.

"Good dog, Smokey!" I praised him. He released it in my hand and started sniffing Devin.

"Hey, Smokey," he said, but kept his hands in his pockets. Devin watched the dog. "You tried to bite me last night, grizzly."

Smokey just stared at him and sat.

"Uh-oh," he said, "I know that look. He reminds me of Jordache."

"Jordache?" I repeated. "*You have a dog named Jordache?*"

"I sure do. *Thaaat's my dog,*" he joked.

"They're nice to have around; they make good guard dogs, too."

"Yes, like Smokey, but you don't have much to worry about around here."

"Why you say that?"

"*Because*, Miss PeggyAnn, no one in their *right mind* would come around but the postman."

"You may be right about that," I told him, because, I knew he had a point.

Finally, Devin patted Smokey on the head. "That's all right," he looked down at Smokey, again, letting his guard down, "you were just trying to hold down the fort. You thought you caught a midnight snack, didn't you?" He started teasing him by ruffling his coat.

Smokey shifted his head and jumped in the air, ready to play.

Devin began moving around, dodging him, and then said, "*Maaaaaan, you have a lot of territory to guard. You can handle it.*"

Surprised, I said, "You seem to get along with dogs quite well."

Grinning, he replied, "So far, so good."

We saw Mr. Jackson walk out the barn. He looked, and started laughing and shaking his head.

Curiously, I said, "I wonder what humored him."

"He probably can't get last night out of his head."

Laughing to myself, I told him, "That makes two of us because it will be years before I forget the expression on his face from yesterday when we dropped the bomb on him."

Rekindling the memory caused Devin to laugh out, unexpectedly. "That scene will never get old."

"That's the truth," was my response. We both looked at Mr. Jackson for keepsake.

A few minutes later, he stood in the doorway of the barn. "Lad," he called out to Devin, "will yuh come and give me uh hand?"

We rushed to where he stood. When we stepped inside, all the animals seemed to be looking in our direction, as if time had stopped. *Is this just my imagination?* a teakettle thought was percolating. *Or, maybe they remembered Devin from the previous night. Nah, that can't be. That was a funny thought*, I grinned.

"How can I help, Mr. Jackson?" Devin asked energetically.

"Shortly, I'd like yuh tuh fill dis bucket here wit some water at da well."

Devin glanced at me. Now, he knew for sure where Mr. Jackson got his water. *"Sure. Where is that…half a sweet potato pie away?"*

I looked the other way to keep from laughing. Devin's humor was somewhat unexpected, at times, and confusing.

Mr. Jackson grinned with curiosity in his eyes. "Are yuh hungry, lad? Dere's mo' left tuh eat."

Devin chuckled realizing that Mr. Jackson had no idea what he was talking about. "I'm fine," he steered away from what he really meant. "Just point me in the right direction." He reached for the bucket on the ground.

"Hmmm," Mr. Jackson stood there, scratching the side of his temple, distracted by what seemed to be an instant thought, "'ave yuh ever made butter befo'?"

Devin replied, "No, I haven't."

Mr. Jackson smiled and asked him, pushing his hat back further away from his forehead, "Would yuh like tuh learn da process and master da technique?"

"Definitely," Devin answered gung-ho, "when can we start?"

"We can git started right now," Mr. Jackson said, just as anxious to show him.

"I can help," I offered. Knowing Devin, my assistance may be needed.

"Do yuh 'ave time, little damsel?" Mr. Jackson asked concerned. He did not want to infringe on my time. "I do not want tuh complicate yer day."

"It's quite all right. I've done my chores for the morning and afternoon already."

"Yo're fast."

"I'll just say that I was determined."

"Yer help is appreciated. Thank yuh fer volunteering."

"You're welcome."

Mr. Jackson faced Devin. "Yuh 'ave uh great friend here, lad."

Geared, he replied, *"Miss PeggyAnn is great."*

"Yez, she is," Mr. Jackson smiled.

We followed Mr. Jackson out the barn.

"Little damsel, I 'ave cream already. I'll bring it out soon. If yuh could show him how tuh get da cream, den we'll be already set fer tomorrow."

"Sure, Mr. Jackson."

"Oh yez," he turned toward Devin, "befo' da day runs out, I'd like tuh take yuh into town. Yearly, der's uh program at uh school—"

Devin kindly cut in. "The Give All You Have program?" Then he glanced at me, as if he remembered something, and so did I. We probably thought of the same thing.

Mr. Jackson looked surprised. "Yez. How did yuh kno'?"

"Actually, Mr. Jackson," I stepped in, "we all were talking about it yesterday."

"That's right," Devin said, "Josephine brought it up."

"Oh," he smiled, remembering that we four had been together yesterday, "word spreads fast. Der isn't uh lot of time befo' then. Since da program is tomorrow, I'd like tuh get yuh somethin' da wear, that tis, if, *yuh wanna go.*"

Smiling, I thought that was a great idea and that it would be good for Devin to do a little sightseeing. To see more of the population would probably be a breath of fresh air. "You can't pass that up," I told him.

"I'd like tuh take yuh tuh da program."

He couldn't resist the invitation. "Sure," I'd like to go with you, Mr. Jackson."

Sometime today, we have to let Joshua know, the thought surfaced again. Going with Mr. Jackson seemed to be the right thing for Devin to do, for now. He probably preferred to avoid untimely questions anyway.

"We're not da same size nor da same height, so, yuh gonna need somethin' else tuh wear other than whutcha 'ave on."

Our eyes were now on Devin, observing him from head-to-toe.

He stretched out his arms, looking down at himself. "Well," he chuckled, "you have a point."

Mr. Jackson then asked, "Do yuh go da cherch on Sunday mornin'?"

"Yes, I do."

"Good! Yuh'll be all set tuh go. I'll let yuh two alone so yuh can get started. Take dese." He gave Devin a pair of gloves to protect his hands, then pointed in the direction we needed to go.

When we made it back to the barn, I noticed beads of sweat had formulated around Devin's forehead. "Give me a minute," he said, breathing rapidly. "I need a little water." He sat on a stool not far from a cow to rest.

I sat on the other stool near the door.

Mr. Jackson walked in with two cups and a dipper. "Thank yuh," he said, reaching for the bucket to put on the homemade wooden table, too. "Help yo'self. I'll be back shortly."

"Thanks, Mr. Jackson," we said in unison, as we walked over to where the bucket was. I poured water in the cups and gave one to Devin.

He raised his hat and said, "My pleasure. And, little damsel, Lillybell dere is da prize." He nodded his head toward the cow as Devin quickly drank his water. The water must have plugged his ears in the process because he never responded. Mr. Jackson had already put a bucket in place underneath the cow.

After a few minutes of rest, I stood and took my stool to where Lillybell was. "Mr. Jackson probably wants us to use a little of the water to rinse the butter clean."

"That's interesting but, sounds impossible since butter is slippery," Devin said, blindly.

I sat on the right side of Lillybell. "You'll see once we get closer to the final stage of the process."

Devin asked, "What are you doing? There's no butter over there."

I rested my head on Lillybell's flank to begin step one, as Mr. Jackson had asked earlier, before we began making butter from the cream he already had.

His mouth opened in horror. "Oh no, I know you're not going to do what I think!"

Mashing down on one of Lillybell's funnels, I responded with, "How else can butter be made? So you'll know, this is step one. You will first need cream from milk before doing anything else and it has to sit for several hours."

Silence fell.

"Miss PeggyAnn," Devin finally muttered, sounding very far away, "I feel a lullaby coming on…"

Chapter 10

PEGGYANN

Mr. Jackson walked in at the *right time*. *"Yuh all right, lad?"* he asked, very concerned. "Maybe we should continue with this later."

Devin slowly stood up. "Give me a few minutes; I'll be fine. I need some air," he deeply inhaled, and then exhaled a gush of rushing wind from the cavity of his chest.

As he walked toward Mamie for a breath of fresh air, his steps seemed to be weighed down by sadness and worry. He stood under the tree, gradually scoping the perimeter and beyond. Eventually, he laid his praying eyes on the colored-blue sky.

Mr. Jackson and I stood near the opening of the barn.

It was quiet and still.

I couldn't imagine his despair, but I knew at some point, that things would work out for him.

"Maybe we should give him some space right now," Mr. Jackson said, hoping that things will soon change. He stared far ahead, as if to find a quick fix to solve Devin's problem. "I'm goin' tuh wait uh couple mo' days, and if nothin' surfaces, then I 'ave no choice but tuh take action."

"I understand, sir," I stared, too.

"But yuh kno', little damsel," he gently smiled, "everything is gonna be all right. Yuh jus' wait and see."

My head slightly tilted. "Yes, everything will be all right."

"Yeeeeeez, sir," his words were dancing to the rhythm of hope. "Don't yuh worry...I can jus' feel it in dese bones." He took a few steps further and gazed across the painted pastures.

Nodding my head was verification. "I'm not worried; he'll bounce back."

I saw Smokey trotting in Devin's direction. He sat next to him. The onset looked like a framed picture of Devin, Mamie and Smokey posing under the fully bloomed tree.

"I guess I should run along now, Mr. Jackson," I turned, walking toward the table for water to rinse my hands.

"I want tuh thank yuh again, little damsel, fer sticking around tuh help."

"Really, Mr. Jackson, I didn't mind at all."

He reached for a cup. "Can't thank yuh enough. I can pick it up from—" he stopped, distracted, and put the cup down.

Smokey was barking.

We rushed, out of curiosity, back toward the door.

A Ford rolled up into the yard. It was sparkling black with shiny silver wheels.

One car door opened, then the other. Two men got out dressed in casual attire wearing baseball caps.

I said while in shock, "Mr. Jaaaaaackson."

He grinned very wide. "Well... I don't believe it," his words trailed, slowly.

When I saw Devin, his whole countenance had changed. He appeared to be just as shocked as I was, looking back and forth.

"Excuse me, little damsel." He walked up the way.

Devin and I met up not far behind.

"*Moses...David...*" we heard Mr. Jackson say.

"Paul!" they replied, smiling. From their reactions, I could tell they had not seen each other in a while. All three of them shook hands, hugged and patted backs. It was perfect timing because silence was rewarded with laughter.

Dazed, I said, "Paul is his name. All this time, I never knew Mr. Jackson's first name."

Devin blurted, "*They're triplets.*" He snickered.

I wondered what humored him then said, "They look so much alike."

"The same height, and practically, the same size and complexion, too."

I stared. "This is my first time ever seeing something like this."

"Join the club."

When I was about to question Devin, Mr. Jackson glanced at us and said, "Little damsel, lad, I want yuh tuh meet some of my folks."

We walked to where they stood, and he introduced us.

When Devin spoke, his brothers looked at each other and grinned. The one, named Moses, raised his cap and scratched the side of his forehead.

Devin smiled. "I know…my voice, right?"

"Well, yes. You sound like a grown man, but you look extremely youthful."

David joined him. "That is some voice you have there."

"I have it honestly," Devin told them. He seemed to be getting used to the attention. From all the responses he has gotten since yesterday, everyone's comments were probably beginning to sound like a broken record.

We heard something fall. "We'll check it out for you, Mr. Jackson," the sudden racket caused words to hurdle from my mouth. The noise came from inside the barn. Once again, *perfect timing.*

Gazing toward the barn, wondering what the noise could have been, he muttered, "Thank yuh. It's probably nothin'."

"It was nice meeting you both," Devin nodded.

"Yes, it was," I smiled.

They acknowledged us by raising their caps.

Walking away, Devin sighed. "Saved by the bell." When we stepped inside the barn, nothing appeared to be out of place. "I wonder what that noise was."

"I don't know," my eyes roamed, staring at animals, straw, tools and a tractor. Everything was neat and orderly. Nothing else stood out other than daylight filtering through cracks.

"Well, I guess we should continue where we left off."

"Left off?"

"Yes, I'm ready now," Devin said.

"You don't mean—" my voice echoed.

"*Yez*," he laughed, and so did I. His humor was timely. "*That's what I mean, Miss PeggyAnn.*"

I was taken by surprise. "You actually want me to show you the process?" After his lullaby episode, I didn't think he would ever want to get near that topic or see another cow, for that matter.

"Why not?"

"When you left out for some air, I thought you just had enough and couldn't take it anymore."

"I had no idea that I would have to get *that close* to a cow."

Smiling, I said, "You're learning. In no time, you're going to be a pro."

"You're right! I'll get the best of both worlds by the time my lessons have ended. I'll probably teach you something."

A combustion of laughter rang out because we both knew that was very unlikely.

"Well, Miss PeggyAnn," Devin looked at me wanting to know of my lesson plan, "I don't have a clue *what to do*."

"Well, let's get started," I told him, walking toward Lillybell to sit down.

"Better yet, let me sit there, Miss PeggyAnn. I want to learn hands on."

My mouth dropped. "Whatever you say." As his tutor, I showed him what to do.

When he was done, he jumped up. "*Whew*," he comically said, wiping sweat from his forehead, "I'm glad Lillybell didn't *kick* me."

As funny as that sounded, I laughed out. "You must know what you're doing."

"*No*," he shot back, reminding me that he had no prior training. "*You're a good teacher.*"

"Thank you. I'll try to go easy on you."

He shook his head. "Interesting. Do you do this often?"

"Yes, twice a day. Can you hand me that bucket, please?"

"Sure," he reached for it and then commented, "you're the pro."

"After years of experience, you get used to it. It's just another daily chore."

Devin gulped. He probably said a quick silent prayer and was glad he didn't have to worry about being subjected to tending animals, routinely. "When do you have time for milking cows other than the weekends? You go to school, cook, wash dishes and do your homework, don't you?" The look on his face revealed that he couldn't imagine when I found the extra time.

I grasped the bucket and answered, "I keep busy. On my schedule of things to do, I milk cows early in the mornings before school and when I return home."

Question marks were dangling in his mind. "Everyday?! Why so much? Oh," something occurred to him, "your family drinks a lot of milk, *is that it*?"

All I could do, for the moment, was grin. Controlling my emotions, I stayed on track to further educate him and continued, "The milk is fresh for drinking and we also use it for other things, like butter."

"Back to making the butter, what is the process?" he now asked, wanting to move on.

I covered the bucket and placed it on top of the table for Mr. Jackson. Reaching for the container that he already brought for me, I raised the top and glanced at Devin, "Look inside here."

"What kind of contraption is that?"

"It's called a churn, which has a dasher on the inside. After you milk a cow, you wait several hours for the cream to rise to the surface. Then, you separate the cream from the milk by pouring it through a strainer. The cream collects on top and the milk runs through. You'll know the difference because the cream is another form of substance."

He asked puzzled, "What do you do with the milk on the bottom?"

"You can use that and drink it."

"Then, what?"

"Let the cream turn to clabber and then you can put it in a churn similar to this one."

"That resembles a tall slow cooker, and the top looks like a broom stick attached to it. What are those slats at the bottom of the dasher for?"

"That is what beats the cream to help thicken it. Watch me," I instructed him, closing the churn by putting the top back on. I moved the dasher up and down, repeatedly. "This process takes a while. You'll know when to stop because the substance will thicken."

"*Whew*," Devin said, as we took turns, "this is work. You should have muscles like *Bruto* by now because this is brutal. I need spinach like Popeye."

"You're funny," I laughed, lowly.

"Yeah, so they say," he kept a steady pace the best he could, eager to know what to do next.

"Once done with this step, we're ready to put the butter into another container resembling that wooden bowl there. We separate the butter from the buttermilk using a butter paddle, or another object similar that will do the job."

"What about what's left in the churn?"

"Oh yes, the buttermilk that's left can be used as a drink." My last statement seemed to have deadened his hearing because he had no comment.

Hoping that was the end of the process, he asked, "Is that it?" He picked up his speed with the dasher.

"At that point, you wash the butter with small amounts of cold water. Use the butter paddle compressing the butter on the sides of the bowl. After you have gotten out the excess liquid, you would add one teaspoon of salt per pound of butter."

"Hmmm, and what's the purpose of that?" Devin asked.

"To keep it fresh." Adding another tip, I said, "You can put the butter in a mold and then wrap it in butter paper. That's about it."

"So, *that's how it's made.*"

"That's all there is to it."

"Miss PeggyAnn, that's enough," he stared. "You have said a lot."

Thinking of something else, I said, "One other thing. Once you have wrapped the butter in paper, you can take them into town and sell them to businesses."

"Now you're talking my kind of language," he chuckled.

"Oh, how so?"

"Maybe not by making butter, and I don't know how, but I need to make some money." He stopped motioning the dasher and gazed out the door, "Someway, somehow, I'll figure it out."

After Mr. Jackson's brothers left, he set up for plowing using a Georgia Stock that had two handles for pushing. He hooked a harness to the horse and pushed his straw hat down on his head for shade.

Devin was observing. "It looks like Mr. Jackson is ready to do some serious work," he commented. He had been watching, mysteriously.

"He's about to plow," I said. "You're not familiar with farm work, are you?"

"No. Only what I have seen on television," he stood up off the bench. "Maybe I should give him a hand."

I stood, also. "Let's go and see."

We walked to where he was standing.

"Mr. Jackson, I see you're about to carve the earth," Devin said.

"Yez, I am," he chuckled. "Some of da comments yuh make, lad, is comical."

Devin grinned. "I know."

"And whut do yuh kno' 'bout plowing?"

"Not a thing, but there's no better time than now for me to learn the trade."

"Yuh hang 'round long enough, yuh'll be an expert. Let me sho' yuh what tuh do."

"I can show him, Mr. Jackson," I offered, giving him the opportunity to do something else.

He looked at me. "Little damsel, I can't ask yuh tuh do dat. Yuh already 'ave done enough."

Devin was in disbelief. *"Miss PeggyAnn, you know how to plow, too?"*

I coolly laughed. "Of course, I do."

He was amazed. "Is there anything that you don't know how to do?"

"I don't know everything, but I have learned to do most things as a country girl."

Impressed, his comment was, "I knew you wore many hats, but I had no idea…" Devin's mouth slightly opened.

I put my hands on the handles. "Let me show you."

Mr. Jackson said in a hurry, "I don't kno' 'bout dis."

"It's all right, Mr. Jackson. I'm used to it."

He nodded. "Well…if yuh insist."

I pointed, "See this, Devin?"

"Yes."

"That's called a Georgia Stock, which farmers often use to bust the ground between two rows of plants."

Now, he was intrigued. "What is the purpose of that?" He scanned how long the rows were.

"Its purpose is to throw new dirt on each side. Fresh dirt will prevent weeds from taking over."

Devin's eyebrows rose. "Oh," he caught on, "that makes sense."

"Little Damsel," Mr. Jackson eased in to say something, "I see yuh *do kno' somethin' 'bout plowing*. Yuh doin' good."

"Thanks, sir."

"She's a good teacher," Devin told him.

Mr. Jackson smiled. "She sho' is, lad. Yo're in good hands."

Devin asked out of curiosity, "By the way, what kind of plants are those?" He was staring at them, intensely.

"*Cotton*."

His eyes darted in my direction. "*What year is this?*" He scratched his head.

Mr. Jackson and I laughed out.

"*Never mind*," he let it rest, shaking his head. "I forgot."

"Over there, you probably recognize those," I pointed.

"Yep, I know what those are. Corn!" he nodded, verifying that something looked familiar to him.

Mr. Jackson said quickly, "I'm goin' tuh check on somethin' else. Let me kno' if yuh need me."

"We will," Devin and I said, simultaneously, as he walked away toward the house.

"Ready?" I asked, picking up where we left off.

"Yes, let's begin."

Keeping my hands on both handles, I steered the way walking down the row as dirt was thrown on both sides. The plants were awakened and sprouting more as each day rejuvenated its existence. Looking across the field, I saw that stalks of corn appeared to be as tall as my shoulders. Mr. Jackson had an army of them and many rows of cotton that were newborns. I guess Smokey was used to the routine because he was waiting on the other end. "HAW!" I shouted.

Devin laughed. "Do you mean HEEHAW?!"

I stopped, and laughed. "No. You supposed to say 'HAW,' commanding a horse what to do."

"*They're that smart?*"

"Yes, they are some intelligent animals."

"What does that mean?"

"It means to go left."

"How do you tell them to go right?"

"You would say 'GEE' and that's all to it."

Devin grinned. "*Oh, I can handle that.*"

"I can do another row," I told him.

With excitement, he said, "I'm ready to take it over, Miss PeggyAnn."

He put his hands to the plow and walked down the next row. "This is some work, but good exercise—for a man, that is, not a woman. I admire you, Miss PeggyAnn. You are a hard worker. I don't think *too* many females would like this type of work."

"Like you have said, Devin, you do what you have to do."

"I understand. This definitely is not something I would want to do for pleasure either, but I can handle it."

Walking behind him, I said "You're doing very well." By the time we made it to the end of the row, he shouted, picking up speed, "HAW!"

The horse turned left.

"*Oh, no,*" my voice raised.

Devin's eyes enlarged to twice their normal size. "OH!" he stumbled, losing his balance. "OH! WAIT, HORSE-EEEEEEEEE." He skipped and stumbled being pulled the whole time, running into bundles of straw and was headed straight for the barn, which would have been a disaster. "*UH, UH,*" he stuttered, clearly seeing that they were in trouble, "GEE!"

The horse then turned right, but by that time, they were a distance away from where he was supposed to be plowing.

"DEVIN," I shouted, "IT'S WHOA!"

The horse heard the magic word and slowed down, probably just as confused, itself.

"WHOA, WHOA, HORSE-EEE!"

The horse stopped.

Devin bent over trying to catch his breath. He had turned another shade. His mouth shook with frustration, "I don't know what's worse—*plowing or milking a cow.*"

For some reason, Mr. Jackson had missed all the commotion. I don't know what he would have done if he had seen a comedy in live action.

Without thinking, I gave in. "Whoops. I didn't mean to laugh."

"*Go ahead,*" he encouraged me, resting his hands on his knees, "*I know it's funny.*"

"I'm sorry, Devin, I forgot to tell you the most important command."

He must have replayed that scene in his mind because he suddenly laughed in hysterics and couldn't stop. "Like I said, this is a funny farm."

There was something approaching from behind him. When I realized what it was, my eyes felt like they were going to bust. "Devin, whatever you do, *don't move,*" I whispered.

"*What is it?*" he asked, terrified. His face was strained with tension.

Very slowly, I whispered again, "You don't want to know. Just trust me."

He was still bent over in the same position as his head slowly moved downward, facing the ground. We both were locked in an awkward, but similar position.

A skunk wobbled between his feet and stopped.

Devin's eyes bulged.

We both stared at the black and white creature that could potentially spray an odorous shot of cologne on us if we dared to move. Its tail was fluffy, curled up. I never could understand why such a nice looking animal was made to be a health hazard.

I shut my eyes with intensity.

"*Hey, little damsel, lad!*" we heard Mr. Jackson shout from a distance.

We didn't move or say a word.

I kept my eyes shut.

"*Is somethin' wrong over dere? Why yuh two bent over like yo're ready tuh begin uh boxing match?*" We heard him walking in our direction.

My eyes were squeezed so tight, they felt drawn together by a rope. I didn't know how much longer I could remain in that position. Mr. Jackson walking toward the ringside circus made matters worse. The intrusion made me shake. My feet sweated and water accumulated around my head. Running and screaming left without me. We were frozen, soon to be dripping icicles. My dress was getting soaked. *Oh no*, I heard my inner self say. *No, Mr. Jackson, no.* My eyes reopened, fluttering. I tried to think of other things before I made a mistake. Josephine crossed my mind. The thought of her being here, at this very moment, would have been a catastrophe. This is just the type of situation that would make the headlines. She probably would have accidentally stomped the skunk out of fear. Josephine and Devin were two of a kind and a handful when it came down to life. I had no idea what he was thinking at this very moment, and I didn't want to know, as comical as he was.

Finally, the skunk turned.

One of Devin's pant legs shook like a leaf. His hands shook like spasms and his lips quivered. He probably wasn't far from needing respiratory therapy...

Chapter 11

DEVIN

After the last two disasters, Mr. Jackson laughed until he decided he would resume farm work on Monday. He had a difficult time erasing our version of my experience plowing and the skunk from his blackboard. A horse gone astray and a popular black-and-white-North-American mammal were branded in his memory. He tried to get his mind on something else by talking about other things, but winded back to the same story. The script was just *too much* for him to bear. He laughed most of the way into town. Instead of one handkerchief, he had to use two. I couldn't blame him seeing how PeggyAnn and I had been trapped, on display, as live mannequins. That was the best play I'd ever been in—it took our breath away. When Mr. Jackson realized a skunk was between my feet, he stayed far away and told us not to move. He wasn't taking any chances of getting intoxicated by its fumes. The skunk took its time leaving.

This is some kind of day, I thought over and over. I was plagued for hours with constant flashbacks. Visioning everything that had happened since I came on the scene caused me to stare, without blinking, for long periods of time.

Mr. Jackson's Model-T Ford was just where PeggyAnn had said; it was parked in the other building where it could not be seen. It was identical to the one that his brothers drove, and surprisingly, as we rode into town, there were more. I saw a showcase of automobiles just about every which way I turned, similar to his and other makes. There were some horses and wagons, but for the most part, cabbies on wheels with an engine had the majority in this town, parading classics. It was a busy town that day.

Stores were built out of brick or wood, and were unevenly stacked like ABC blocks. The scenery was neither elaborate nor up-to-date like modern times as I knew it, but it was worth seeing the melodies of change that had rung out over the course of time. It would become a reflection of history, a story shared for generations to come.

Following Mr. Jackson, we walked toward the front entrance of a clothing store. "Whatever yuh do, lad, it probably would be best dat yuh said nothin' unless yuh can disguise yer voice. If I had uh hard time believing it, yuh can jus' imagine whut others would think 'bout uh young person with uh voice like yers. Yuh don't want tuh raise any suspicions."

"All right, Mr. Jackson," I said in another tone of voice that was so high that I almost squeaked.

He chuckled.

I cleared my throat. "Very well, sir." This time I got it right. My vocal cord needed no training at this point.

Mr. Jackson smiled, slowly motioning his head vertically. "Not bad, lad, not bad."

We walked inside.

I was looking forward to owning an outfit in my size. Wearing Mr. Jackson's clothes were odd since his size was out of my range.

After looking at one outfit after the other, I couldn't make up my mind. I shook my head, disapproving apparels that just weren't appealing. All I could think about was how outdated the clothes were. If the shoe was on the other foot, they probably would laugh at how people dressed in the 21st century. It was a battle trying to make a decision since my taste was apparently off the Richter scale. The apparel just wasn't spicy enough. Nothing in the store, resembled a Ralph Lauren, Perry Ellis, Savane, or a Sean John label, or reminded me of *home sweet home*. Not even a *Glad* sandwich bag. Finally, when I walked to the far corner, there was a 2-piece set. A coordinated pair of pants and a matching shirt caught my eye. I held it up to observe as Mr. Jackson walked up.

"Dat's uh winner, and I say dat yuh should take dat one. Whut do yuh think, lad?"

I slowly nodded, "This may work." It was time to end the search, besides, I wasn't the one buying. Suddenly, remembering that I was in an unpeculiar place and had no right to be choosy about brand, it didn't matter, as long as it fit. There were more important things to think about. As confused as I was right now, I was ready to take whatever I could get.

Next, we walked into a music store.

My eyes lit up as I stood in one spot gazing at instruments from left to right. "You play," I began to ask then switched scales, "*music, Mr. Jackson?*" I almost forgot to elevate my tone of voice from the excitement.

All eyes were on me, gazing with wonder.

"I sure do, lad," he answered, grinning, walking toward the counter. He probably was impressed at how quickly I had exchanged roles.

"Here you go, Mr. Jackson," the man said, smiling at the beauty.

Mr. Jackson held it in position facing a mirror, admiring the shiny piece of art. "Yuh haven't changed, Goldie."

My head tilted slightly. *You haven't changed, Goldie? What does he mean by that?* I wondered. The horn glazed in gold was so shiny that I saw my reflection as I walked up to get a closer look.

He chuckled, looking it over.

"That's a nice sax," I stared.

"Yuh like it?"

"Yes, I do."

"Do yuh kno' how tuh play one?"

"I try."

"Well," Mr. Jackson paid the man, "she's been repaired and ready tuh go. I want yuh tuh be da first tuh put her tuh da test."

Shocked, I said, "You want me—"

"Yez," he quickly said, before I could say another word.

"Here's your change, Mr. Jackson. Let me get the case for you," the clerk told him.

I held the saxophone in place and played a few swift notes.

Heads turned.

The man slightly laughed, standing between two red curtains behind the counter. "Not bad," his eyes sparkled.

Mr. Jackson walked toward me. "Dat was good, lad."

"You think so?"

"I sure do. Yuh may need tuh teach me uh thing or two."

"*Nah*," I shook my head, "*not me.*"

Mr. Jackson turned toward the man to say, "We're goin' tuh move along. Much obliged for your help."

"You betcha," he smiled, ready to help the next customer walking through the door.

On our way back, Mr. Jackson pulled into the parking lot of a restaurant. Before he turned off the motor, I asked, "Where are we?" With as many cars and wagons that were there, I assumed this was the spot for dynamite meals.

"We're in Earlsboro. Whut can yuh tell me 'bout Earlsboro?" he grinned.

Looking at a nearby sign, I answered, "All I recognize is an ear."

Mr. Jackson looked baffled. *"Ah whut?"* He opened his door and got out.

"An ear," I repeated, and began spelling it out as I closed the other door. "This place has only one ear."

He looked at the sign that I was staring at before he caught on. "Oh," he laughed, amused, "dat's uh good one. Never heard dat befo'."

I chuckled. "Neither have I." Noticing the large sign above the building, which read *Name It and Eat It*, got my attention. I was astounded and it showed.

"Lad, whut's wrong?"

"No disrespect, but, *maaaaaan,*" I said in baritone, shaking my head with great concern, "you probably want to think twice about eating here."

Mr. Jackson laughed, holding his forehead, as if that would release the pressure of rain that was beginning to flood in his eyes forming tear droplets. "Whut ever made yuh say dat, Devin?" He pulled out his handkerchief and wiped a river of tears running down his face.

"Mr. Jackson," I hesitated, "I've heard that many times in my younger days, and I'm not interested in any cow's tongue, or anything else other than chicken, seafood, or turkey meat." I was holding on to the doorknob.

"Whut ever gave yuh dat impression?" he stared, blankly, wanting to know.

A big truck, loaded with cows, was headed our way. I pointed at the animals passing by, mooing, and said distinctively, *"Like cow's tongue—fried, baked, or stewed. Name It and Eat It* means only one thing."

"Whut's dat?" his eyes froze.

"You wouldn't know what you're eating. It's deceiving because it looks like neatly sliced roast beef. Surprise! Surprise! Surprise!"

He laughed again, running out of breath. "Dat's not how it goes at dis restaurant," he smoothly gagged, trying to assure me. He gestured his hand for me to release the doorknob so we could go inside before I talked him out of it.

I was ready to hear this one. "There has to be a trick to this." I walked around the car to where he stood.

He put his keys in his pocket and explained, "Yuh tell 'em whut yuh want and they'll bring it. It's dat simple, lad. Name whut yuh want, and eat whut yuh want." He opened the door of the restaurant and we walked inside.

"*Whew*," I blew out, relieved, "I can deal with that."

"I kno' how yuh feel; I would have tuh pass on dat one myself. Many people love dat part of da cow."

"*Not me*," I quickly said.

"Dat makes two of us," he grinned. "Yuh'll like it here—very popular place."

"I thought so." Turning toward the door, I remembered something. "Mr. Jackson, you forgot Goldie. You can't leave her alone, all by herself," I joked. "We have to watch out for her; we don't want her to get kidnapped."

"Dat's unlikely 'round here."

"It's better to be safe than sorry later."

"All right, lad, if yuh insist."

"I'll get her."

"Yuh go ahead. I'll wait fer yuh here."

As I walked back inside, a waitress approached us wearing a white apron and a pair of shoes that nurses wear in hospitals. She wore a net on her head with a white sailor cap shaped like a canoe turned upside down. "Hello, gentlemen," she kindly smiled, acknowledging our presence.

"Hello," we both greeted her, ready to be seated and eat.

"This way." She took us to a table draped with a large red and white checkerboard tablecloth with long wooden benches.

We sat, glad to finally get a chance to relax and enjoy the upbeat atmosphere.

The place was packed with people. The sunrays shining through the windows were spotlights on the wavy white smoke that floated in the air. The aroma of meats and vegetables brewing wafted through the entire place.

"Jackson," she said, and then glanced at me, "I see you brought a newcomer with you."

"Yez, I did, Ruby."

"What's your name, young man?"

"Devin, ma'am."

She smiled. "You can call me Ruby. That would be fine."

"Ruby, what's cookin'?" I asked her. "It smells appetizing."

"Well, Devin, we cook a variety of food. Right now, you're probably smelling pork chops, chicken and maybe the scent of cow's tongue."

I glanced at Mr. Jackson.

He courteously intervened. "Ruby, can yuh give us uh few minutes?" He knew it was intermission time.

"Sure, Jackson. Just let me know when you're ready to name it." Then she handed me a menu to look over.

"Thank you," I said appreciatively.

Refusing a menu, Mr. Jackson said, "No thank yuh, Ruby, I don't need one. I kno' whut I would like tuh order."

"I'll be back." She walked away in a rush.

Customers were piling in.

Playing it off, he suggested, "Take uh look at da menu. I'm sure dere's somethin' yuh 'ave uh taste fer."

It took a few minutes to scan through everything that was listed. "I think there is," I grinned, and laid the menu down. Just in case we came back another day, I wanted to make sure I already knew what to ask for.

Ruby was about to walk by when Mr. Jackson got her attention. "Are you ready?" she asked.

"Yes," we both answered.

Before walking away, she noticed the black case. "Is that an instrument?" she glistened, asking me the question since it lay next to me.

"Yes. It belongs to Mr. Jackson."

"Maybe he'll be able tuh teach me somethin'," Mr. Jackson smiled. "He plays good from da little dat I've heard."

"Oh, *does he*?" she seemed interested.

"I believe we have uh musician here."

"Devin, there's a chair over there if you want to play something for us."

From the gesture, I was startled. "Ma'am," my voice started weakening, "I've never played music in public. Thank you, but I'm not a professional."

There was music playing in the background. It sounded like country music. A few heads were rocking like pendulums, ticking to the beat of a banjo and harmonica. Can't say it was harmonious, but the tempo definitely reminded me of, good old-fashioned knee slappin' and clappin'—a beat I can grin to.

Mr. Jackson chuckled. "Lad, yuh sound uh lot better than yuh kno'. Take da offer."

"We do not often have instrumentalists play here," the waitress let me know, "but we've decided to try something a little different around here, especially for teenagers."

Umph, if she only knew, I thought. My youthful appearance really had everyone fooled.

Heads turned when a bolt of light shined through the door. A man walked in and sat down dressed in a suit and tie. From the expressions, no one seemed to know who he was.

"Hmmm," Mr. Jackson wondered himself, and then shifted his train of thought. "Goldie is uh callin'. Can't keep her waitin'."

Opening the case, I pulled her out and attached the strap. We were already close to where the chair was. I stood to follow Ruby.

No one paid any attention. The chatter filled the air throughout the place.

Two other waitresses took notice, but kept serving as if nothing was happening.

Mr. Jackson sat up straight, waiting.

"You can start anytime you're ready," Ruby said, before walking away. "Let me know if you need anything."

Clearing my throat, I whispered, "Water would be fine. My throat is getting a little dry."

"Sure. I'll get that for you right away."

The music stopped.

The clock inside my head fast-forwarded, searching for tunes that I was familiar with. I did not wait for Ruby to return. Getting right to it, the first note rang out loud and clear, bouncing off the walls into deaf ears.

The entire place stopped.

My mind was ticking for a beat. Reaching down under my music cap, I thought of a melody that I had composed during my spare time as a hobby. That's all it's ever been, just a hobby, passing the time away. Never had I taken it serious enough to want to go public. In my mind, I found a quiet place and blocked everyone out, playing Goldie, note after note, at a snail's pace. It was just music, only music that I knew. My eyes were closed imagining my own private viewing.

Nearing the end, I couldn't help but pick up the beat, spinning into the melody of a nursery rhyme that I had learned as a beginner. Keynotes were floating in my head, vividly letting my imagination carry me gliding across sparkling, waves of clear aqua-blue water, somewhere tranquil. Silky miniature waves slid down the path of my nerves giving me a tingle of satisfaction until I finally stopped. I opened my eyes. Surprised by the generosity of giving, my mouth dropped, as the drawing of my facial expression could not be hid. Mumbling, I thought, *How long was I up here?* I don't know how many times the clock ticked before I stopped.

There were coins and dollar bills covering the soft, rich-black-velvet-lining inside Goldie's case.

Ruby's customers laughed, including Mr. Jackson. He must've laid the case beside me.

As I glanced around the cozy, country restaurant, there were more friendly, smiley faces than before. "Thank you," I said, gratefully to the crowd, hearing my voice dance across the eatery. I immediately went from having nothing to gaining something. I was so broke that if something hadn't happened soon, counterparts in my brain would start limpin' the blues. My eyes looked upward, and I quietly mumbled again, "Thank you." As eventful as the day had been, I couldn't imagine what more could happen.

Ruby's eyes met mine. She broke out with a big smile, and so did Mr. Jackson, as she handed me a glass of water.

Thirsty, I drank the water then joined him.

While leaving, I noticed an advertisement on the wall about the Give All You Have program featuring the Electric Keynotes. I stared at the poster. *"Interesting,"* I mumbled. *"I wonder who they are."*

Not even five minutes had passed after returning home when there was a knock at the door. When I opened it, there stood Moses and David, Mr. Jackson's doubles. They looked like they had stolen his identity. I couldn't tell one from the other. "Hello, again, Mr. Moses and Mr. David," I said, as my eyes bounced between them both, hoping that I labeled them correctly by name. I saw the same confused look on their faces as before.

"That's all right, Devin, I'm Moses."

"And, I'm David," the other one said, chuckling.

Slightly laughing, I invited them in.

Mr. Jackson walked in. "Brothers, yo're back. Good timing. Devin and I jus' got back."

"*This is* perfect timing," Moses agreed. Seeing that I was still confused, he looked at me and said, "Just remember that David has a mole above his right eyebrow. That's the clue."

Mr. Jackson then added to the unraveling mystery, "And I sound like da southern boy. Dat's not hard tuh remember, is it, musician?"

"Not at all," I grinned, shaking my head and wondering why I hadn't thought of that before.

All three of them stood there together as if they were posing for a snapshot so I could get a good look at them to find more clues. It got more interesting as I witnessed the humor in them blossom.

"Hmmmmmmmmmmmmmmmm," Moses slowly hummed a thought until he ran out of breath, "did you say musician, *Paul*?"

I thought soon he would start singing from the deep. I laughed.

Mr. Jackson answered, "Yez."

"I think you've started something, Devin," David chimed in.

"Yeah, I think so, too." Immediately, the thought occurred, *In more ways than one.* There was no way I could disguise my voice now since I had already spoken to them, freely, earlier.

Moses observed inquisitively. "Paul, I thought maybe he was acting when we stopped by earlier, but, now," he shook his head, "I'm not so sure."

As they sat down, someone knocked at the door.

Saved by the bell again. I felt relieved.

Mr. Jackson opened the door. "Ahhhhh, here's Joe... Joe Johnston, and he brought along uh friend. Come in."

"Joe!" the guys greeted him. "How have you been?" Oddly, the other two spoke in unison.

"Great, my friends."

Joshua walked in behind him. He surprised me.

There were so many voices ranging out with glee, I could hardly hear myself speak when I approached him. After all the salutations and being introduced to Mr. Johnston, I nodded to acknowledge him as we were leaving. We went outdoors to talk privately. On the other hand, the timing was perfect.

"Man," Joshua said with so much excitement, "we heard!"

My eyes bucked. "Heard? Heard what?"

"We heard that you played a saxophone at *Ruby's restaurant*."

"*You got to be kidding. News around here travels fast.*"

"*It doesn't take long.*"

"*I see.*"

"*I knew it!*"

"*Knew what?*"

"*You're a star, man.*"

At this point, I was scrambling for words, and then said, "*A star?*" The next thing that fumbled out my mouth was, "WHOA!" I put my hands up as if to protect myself from anything else he had to say.

"*Whoa?*" Joshua looked around baffled. "Where's the horse?"

I was startled by his comment. "What horse?" I looked around confused, too. Maybe he was trying to humor me.

He gazed at me like I had lost my mind. "Oh," it occurred to him, "were you trying to say 'stop talking?' "

Seeing how innocent he was, I chuckled. "You can say that. That word is glued to my scull." I was having a flashback.

"Why you say that?"

"Because I've had an interesting day and 'whoa' was the only word that saved the day."

"That bad, huh?"

"Yeah," I answered and told him the story.

He was shaking his head and gagging the entire time. "Oh, boy," he tried to shake it off, "that's one of the most hilarious things I've ever heard. I bet you have some *stories* to tell."

"If you only knew. That was just the tip of the iceberg."

Joshua's eyes swelled. "So, *there is more?*"

"*Yep.*"

The front door opened. Mr. Jackson was walking fast with a lamplight in his hand. "Where on earth could he be going with a lamplight? It's not dark yet," my eyes followed him, puzzled.

"Hmmm," Joshua wondered, too, "he may be headed for the cellar."

"*The cellar requires a lamplight during the day?*"

"Usually, it does since it's in the ground."

"He may need our help."

"It doesn't hurt to ask."

We met up with him as he bent over and opened two wooden doors that looked like an opening to some sort of pit.

"Mr. Jackson, let me help you," I offered. Looking down, I couldn't see too much of anything but dirt beyond several steps.

"Maybe I should go down in da cellar dis time, lad," he looked at me gratefully, but chose to go in himself.

"I can handle it. What do you need *down in that pit?*"

Barely chuckling, Mr. Jackson shook his head. "I need uh jar of milk down dere on da bottom shelf tuh make some dessert. Yuh think yuh can handle dat?"

"*No problem,*" I said, taking the lamplight from him.

Joshua said, offering his assistance, "I'll follow him just in case he can't seem to find it."

Mr. Jackson smiled, "Thank yuh." He watched as we went below.

The glow from the lamplight illuminated our path the more we hit the darkness. All I could hear was Joshua and I breathing without the hawk of cold weather. When we reached the bottom, I held it up and saw shelves above and below the built-in wooden countertop.

"It should be on da bottom shelf," Mr. Jackson reminded us, trying to guide us.

"There it is," Joshua pointed. Containers were neatly labeled, written in pencil and dated.

I reached for it and handed it to him.

Joshua went up the steps and handed the jar to Mr. Jackson.

Impressed by the neatly arranged dungeon, I scurried to the other side before I headed back up the steps out of curiosity. "This is unbelievable," I said, and held the light high above my head. When I looked up in front of me, my eyes exploded, dropping the lamp, squawking. Scared stiff, I tripped and staggered up the steps, hand and foot, feeling frail. My knees collapsed like bowling pins. *I PASSED OUT.*

Chapter 12

DEVIN

"*Aaaaaaaaaaaaaaaaaaaah*," Mr. Jackson echoed, as tears rolled down his face the more he looked at me, "*oooooooooooooooooooh*." His eyes and face turned red. He couldn't get out of his mind what happened in the cellar yesterday.

At first, the whole ordeal wasn't as funny to me as it was to him, but his reactions alone were enough to cause a gush of tears to flow into a river around the entire Seminole County borders. As weak as I was, I had been bombarded by a sudden laugh attack, sending me into hysterics. I was leaning on the door, crunched in chorus, right along with him—one scaling in alto and one in baritone. The more I thought about it, the funnier it got. The scene was so vivid; the film in my mind rolled and rolled and kept on rolling. It was hard to turn it off or put on pause to take a break; it stayed on replay.

"Lad, I don't kno' who wuz mo' shook up, Joshua or yo'self. From da expression on yer face, I started tuh run *myself*." He shook his head and broke down laughing, again. His script hit every funny bone in my body. "Ooooooooooooo," he went on.

After the comic book in his head stopped flippin' pages, I asked, "You eat *hogs' heads, man*? I have *never seen* a hog's head hooked, dangling from a rooftop." I put the picture on pause.

That question made him howl, again.

People in passing cars stared in bewilderment.

The way things were going, it didn't look like this conversation was going to get very far. He had been thinking about that most of the morning.

I released pause and couldn't help replaying that moment. I held up that lamplight and saw a large head facing me at almost eye-level, 2-inches away with large vacant eyes. Its snout was aimed in my direction like a machine gun.

For a Sunday morning, I hadn't been this teary-eyed in a long time. Reliving this role had me stuttering inside my head.

As we rode in his Model-T Ford to church, we shook, side-to-side and up-and-down, at times, from the bumpy roads. The sky was dusty blue as the sun poured its sunlight. The mild heat did its job, drying my face, while the wind blasted through the window like a blow dryer.

The scenery was the norm for a country town. There were large gaps between buildings, if any at all. It was not very much for me to pay too much attention to, *unless*, I was headed for another rude awakening. We were back in Earlsboro with one ear.

We sat on the third row inside a small church.

I felt a draft of eyes shift toward us like a sudden wind. *Have they heard, too?* I wondered.

Soon after, PeggyAnn, Josephine and Joshua walked in with members of their family. In no time, they spotted us and smiled.

The pews filled up. Footsteps echoed against the wooden floor announcing their arrival. It wasn't long before Moses and David strolled in and joined us.

The inside was plain, but nice and clean, with a small number of dark, wooden benches. The windows were stained in multiple colors, glowing from the beam of the sun. A ripple of hymns made it that much brighter, which was their custom.

There was one person facing the members, who was in charge, sitting behind the podium. He stood and spoke humbly, dressed in a black suit, white shirt and coordinated tie, which added a touch of polish to his formal message. The gleam radiating around his countenance, as a tall, chestnut colored man, shined brightly, that couldn't be hidden. Even though it was a sunny day, I wasn't so sure if a storm could come through and hide the brass of his teachings and charisma with a gloomy overcast. He was armed with a unique gift.

After service, I stood outdoors in front of the building. Looking around, there were more people on the streets than in the rural areas. Most citizens were friendly and respectable. Men bowing their heads or gripping the brim of their hats caught my attention. Oftentimes, it appeared as if they were briefly lifting their hats to give their crowns some air. Sunday wear was impressive. That was the one day of the week that people stepped out in their best array of apparels. Hats are just as popular and probably would always be in demand.

Without delay, the clan approached me.

"How are you, Devin?" PeggyAnn smiled, along with the others.

"I'm fine, Miss PeggyAnn."

Joshua chimed in with relief. "That's good to hear." I knew exactly what his comment meant. We both wanted to laugh and get more into what happened yesterday, but it was just between us.

"Devin, I wish I could have heard you play yesterday," Josephine stepped in. "That is the talk of the town."

"Yes, I wish I could've heard, too," said PeggyAnn.

"I'm amazed how fast news travel around here," I told them, looking around wondering, what the total population could be.

"Something like that is major around here. That's like hearing that a play on Broadway is coming to town."

I chuckled. "I guess so; I can see that."

"I sure would *love to play* like that, Devin. To get this much attention...*you're good*," Joshua raved.

"Do you play music at all?" I asked him.

"Some."

"He actually fiddles with the saxophone," Josephine let the cat out the bag, revealing how much he really knew. "I guess he just needs a booster shot or something."

"Ooooooo," I squinted, "a *booster shot. That hurts.*" I saw what side of the fence her humor came from. She was naturally funny in her own way.

They laughed.

Joshua came back on a rebound, "Josephine, I don't think anybody would be able to play an instrument following the jab of a needle but you, sis."

"Not that kind of shot," she clarified.

"Oooooh," the clan harmonized.

"Devin," PeggyAnn jumped in to sum it up, "Joshua has all the bells and whistles that he needs. All that he's been lacking is someone like you to inspire him."

"I'm ready," Joshua said, gung-ho. "Although, I haven't heard him yet, Devin has given me all the inspiration I need."

Surprisingly, I was taken by this conversation. "Do you own a sax, Joshua?"

"Yes, I do."

"Good," I said. "Next week, we're on."

He looked puzzled. "*We're on? We're on what?*"

Remembering that we were on two different plateaus, I rephrased the statement, "How about getting together next week?"

"*That* would be great. I would love for you to be my trainer."

"I'm not a teacher, but I'll do what I can to help."

"That sounds good to me."

Ruby and her husband walked up. "Hello," she looked at us, smiling.

"Hello," the group greeted her in chorus.

My voice switched gears. "Great food, Ruby." I almost left my hat on the shelf.

Mouths dropped. The clan was confused, except PeggyAnn. She knew exactly what I was doing and she understood why. Changing roles, part-time, was just as heavy a load as a full-time job. Remembering when to open and close the curtain of my mouth was work. This was one role that kept me on my toes.

"Thank you, Devin. I'm glad you liked it." Then she introduced me to her husband, James. I saw him just as we were leaving the restaurant.

"Ruby has told me about you," he reached to shake my hand. "I'm glad that I finally have the chance to meet you."

"It's a pleasure to meet you, too, sir."

"Unfortunately, I missed it. If you're as good as she says, then you better watch out. You never know where your pennies lay." Then he looked around, smiling, "How is everyone else doing?"

"Fine," they responded at the same time.

"Good. We must be moving along," they waved, walking away. "Maybe we'll see you all at the event later today."

"We'll be there," we waved back.

"Very important man," PeggyAnn made me aware.

Looking back at Ruby's husband from a distance, I was about to ask a question when Mr. Jackson and his brothers walked up and spoke to the gang. After they chatted for a minute or two, they were ready to sail on wheels. "Lad, we're ready tuh head out." His keys jingled, as he took them out of his suit pocket.

Whew, chimes rang out in my mind, *saved by the bell again*. I actually lost count just how many times the bell had rung.

PeggyAnn glanced at me in smiles. She didn't have to step in to be protective. After two days, I was getting used to it.

"I'll see y'all later," I waved, changing roles again.

Josephine and Joshua were still trying to figure it out. My escape was timely.

The one lane to Earlsmoth High School was congested. When we drove up to the school, people, cars, wagons and horses were spread out everywhere. It was colorful. Through my eyes, the view was a classic and reminded me of a combination of *Bonanza* and *Bound for Glory*. Everyone parked on the grass like an assembly line. Each mode of transportation was sectioned off in a class by themselves on the school's property, across and down the street.

I wondered just how many people the building could hold. Without a doubt, there were more people than space. When everyone was seated, it was filled to capacity. Latecomers brought chairs, and others stood to watch. The brick building was larger than it appeared from the outside with a row of windows staggered open for airflow. The humming noise from conversations traveled right out the window and so did the shrieking sound piercing through a microphone. Three stands were placed at the back of the stage and one in the middle. Observing, I didn't see anything else other than an old piano hidden to the far side behind the black curtains, which was no surprise. Most schools had one.

Someone blew into the mic. "Testing, testing." Another shriek pierced through the building, and then a tapping noise as the volume was turned down.

I asked, turning my head to the left without thinking first, "Mr. Jackson, how long does this program last?" I was surrounded by the same person on both sides. They were dressed alike.

He grinned. "I'm Moses," he responded, in a deep voice. His name was striking.

Inside my memory bank, a bell went off, loud and clear. "*Moses,*" I said, thinking back on a little history, "parted the Red Sea."

Heads turned.

Slightly leaning forward, I noticed the mole above David's right eye. He was sitting next to him. *A mighty warrior.* How could I forget a name like that.

Mr. Jackson chuckled, quietly, shaking his head.

Moses was humored. Shifting the topic, he said, "With a voice like that, for a young man, it must mean something."

"I'm afraid not, sir."

"Have you ever been in plays?"

"No," I shook my head.

"Skits?"

"No, sir, I haven't done that either."

Mr. Jackson glanced at his brother. "Yuh might as well drop it, Moses. It's uh mystery."

David got a word in to say, "I think he's an old man. You know…some people are gifted in different ways."

"That is true," Moses emphasized. "Maybe he'll capture his niche." He looked ahead as someone was approaching the microphone.

It was quiet. A man stood in front of the audience and said, "*Ladies and gentlemen*, it is my pleasure to welcome you to the fifth *Give All You Have* program and we have invited you to enjoy what will be a *spectacular* evening…"

Hmmm, a thought scrolled across my mind, *this is going to be interesting. I'm looking forward to this.*

Mr. Jackson leaned over, "Lad, I think yo're goin' tuh like dis."

Excited, I replied, "I think so, too, Paul." His name had a ring as well, just like Moses and David. *I'm glad he eventually saw the light.*

"Enjoy da program, Devin," he grinned, staring ahead.

I was intrigued, listening to children and teenagers participate with poems and stories they had written. Some were short and some were lengthy, but all were interesting. At times, the audience laughed. Laughter echoed during the plays and skits. Even a few adults rose to talk about legends and pioneers. They kept us rollin' during the course of their speech. There wasn't a dull moment. Dry spells didn't have a chance. This event had spice, spiked with a no-dose serum. Like professionals, each participant had a tight grip on our attention span.

Even PeggyAnn and Josephine played a part. They sang with a group of teenagers—all females.

My head had been swaying to the beat the entire time. They sounded like grown women.

PeggyAnn probably wondered where in the crowd we were sitting. They didn't see me, but I saw them. I had a good seat, in the middle, close to the aisle.

Surprisingly, Joshua walked on stage. *Hmmm, I wonder what he's going to do.* He stood in front of the mic to read a paper and said:

INSPIRATION

I was inspired,
by someone I admire,
who shook the gravity of my life,
to look into the depth of my being,
finding a chest of jewels,
hidden sparkles,
opened by inspiration,
for my flowers to grow.

There's a purpose,
why we live here,
since the day we came,
to live our story,
where's our next step?
to advance with time,
that's why nothing remains the same,
not making a change,
injects pain.

I came,
with a code called "Inspire,"
through sunshine or rain,
through pain,
my arrival will not be in vain,
to give back to a life,
a paradise to frame.

Now that I know of my strength,
I will aim with spears,
to reach a higher plain,
to excel,
what I have claimed,
to sore,
from beneath the crust of my fears.

Even my schoolmates,
your inspirations are diamonds,
when they can't find the chest of jewels,
show them their hidden treasures,
inspire them to achieve their goals,
to find their desires,
sparkling in a cove,
to spread like fire,
an inspiration,
that moves your souls.

Joshua bowed, and walked off the stage.

The audience clapped.

Before I knew it, I was standing, thinking, *When did he have time to write that? PeggyAnn just brought that topic up earlier. That was neat!*

"Someone really impressed him," said Moses, whispering to his brothers.

They nodded their heads in agreement.

Being that I was the only one standing, PeggyAnn and Josephine saw me and stood up where they were and clapped, too. It became a rapid chain reaction. Youngsters were standing up in every direction as the curtains closed.

Soon, the ovation ceased.

Footsteps drowned the moment of silence, drumming up suspense, leading to the sound of objects that were being shifted around, hurriedly.

This time, a distinguished lady, who was dressed in eveningwear, walked across the stage then eloquently said, "Now, ladies and gentlemen, we welcome the *ELECTRIC KEYNOTES.*"

Mr. Jackson, Moses, and David stood up.

My mouth ripped open.

Their names rang out in my head like fireworks, *Moses, David, and Paul! You got to be kiddin' me!*

They chuckled when they saw the expression on my face.

The audience clapped. Heads snapped and turned.

"We'll be back, lad," Mr. Jackson said and walked up the aisle.

"Excuse us," Moses said, grinning, so that I could let him and David pass by. All three of them walked in single file.

Gazing ahead, I wondered what their role was.

The curtains reopened.

Surprisingly, three men handed them a saxophone each. Their horns sparkled like diamonds.

Mr. Joe Johnston sat at the piano, and there stood an upright bass, guitar, and drummer. I couldn't believe that Joshua's pop was connected.

An electrifying shockwave commanded everyone's attention with a thumping beat. Thundering keynotes rippled to the core of our eardrums. The three musicians playing the bass, drums, and guitar began playing a striking intro. Then, they suddenly stopped. The snare drums rolled continuously, as the pianist trailed in softly. The bass player mastered his rhythm, slap style, leading them into their own world of musical seduction.

Looking around, it seemed like all heads rocked on time, from the left, then, to the right. The way the music swayed, reminded me of a ballerina, whose partner forgot to catch her on her way back from spinning.

When they had ended their rendition, one of them stood at the mic and said after the audience continuously clapped, "I would like for someone special and unique in his own way to come up and join us, if he would."

Everyone looked around, and so did I, after I had raised my head back up.

"Who is he talking about?" I mumbled, just as inquisitive. My eyes roamed to where PeggyAnn was sitting.

She was trying to get my attention. Her eyes were gleaming with surprise.

I hunched my shoulders, still wondering when the mystery person would stand up at his request. When I looked ahead, the *Three Musketeers* were staring at me.

I gulped. My feet felt like lead and refused to move. I felt lightheaded. *This can't possibly be happening.* My mind was running track.

They were smiling, holding their hands out, as if their extremities would extend all the way into the crowd and lead me. The other two on stage joined him, "Yes, you, young man."

Eyes were looking past me and around me. No one could seem to pinpoint exactly who they were talking about.

I thought, *Had they practiced this? Was this part of their script, too?*

As I looked to the other side of the building, I spotted Joshua. His mouth was moving until I finally caught on to what he was saying, "I'm inspired." He grinned.

Instantly, I chuckled. "Umph," tumbled out my mouth, as I stood.

There was a humming sound sweeping across the audience.

I heard someone whisper, "He's the one that played the saxophone at Ruby's yesterday."

As I walked on stage, it became so quiet that I could hear a pin drop. As quiet as it was, I felt as though I was standing before a grand jury.

"Devin," one the identical images whispered, "we thought you would like to join in and play some music with us."

"*Me?*" my voice escalated.

"Yes," all three of them smiled, "we would be honored."

I changed hats, again. "Mr. Jackson, what on earth would you like for me to do?"

Confusion covered his face, and not only his, but I felt a beam of eyes. I had to keep my voice secluded. Instantly, he wanted to laugh, but reserved his initial response for later, for more reasons than one. Keeping the record straight, he said, "I'm Moses."

"*I'm David.*"

"And I'm Paul!" he harmonized.

The audience laughed, wildly.

Their humor came so naturally that even I found it to be amusing. Everyone else probably thought it was part of an act. I was impressed. They were good actors. From what seemed to be turning into a stage play, was beginning to give me an adrenaline rush that I was familiar with.

"Mr. Jackson," I kept it going, since they started an opening act so everyone could hear, "what's next?"

Now all the musicians were looking at each other. I couldn't believe what I was seeing; they were good.

"We 'ave another saxophone yuh can play, if yuh like."

"Whatever you say, Devin," David spoke up, leaving it up to me.

"Young man, capture your niche," Moses's voice rang out in baritone, remembering our conversation while sitting in the audience.

Chapter 13

PEGGYANN

Josephine and I were sitting on the edge of our seats. Watching Mr. Jackson and his brothers go back and forth with Devin was very funny. *They are a match for comedy*, the thought flashed across my mind.

"*What's wrong with his voice?*" Josephine gazed at me, baffled. Her expression and response was so dynamic that her whisper sounded like laryngitis. As quickly as she moved her head, her curls should have moved.

Not wanting to entertain the thought any longer before I fell to pieces, I replied, "They're good, and so is Devin."

"I must say he is," her eyes zoomed on him.

At this point, I didn't know where this was going. Devin disguising his voice came natural. How much longer he was going to play musical chairs was a good question.

They had everyone's undivided attention.

Devin stepped forward and bowed.

"*Why is he bowing? He hasn't done anything yet,*" Josephine whispered again.

"Maybe that's it…maybe he's done."

Chatter filled the building, sounding like a hive of bees.

Devin glanced across the audience. "I have something else in mind," he smiled.

Surprised, there was a sudden hush.

"Oh," Josephine thought of what he may do, "maybe he's going to tap dance or something."

Devin clapped. He put his hand to his ear, waiting.

No one caught on.

He clapped, again.

The audience clapped.

He clapped, again.

We clapped, including the musicians.

By the time we clapped on the sixth round, we were spellbound by an instant flow of vocal music imitating a horn. Devin was vocalizing his own tunes. His fingers were rapidly moving, as if he was actually playing a saxophone. Enthralled by his performance, he then spread his arms and started singing, forcefully, like he'd been *singing for years*. He must have done this many times before; he was so good at it.

Josephine's eyes trampolined.

I giggled with amazement. *"This is unbelievable,"* I thought out loud. Now, I was just as baffled as Josephine.

The Jackson brothers looked at Mr. Johnston and the other musicians.

Devin's style was far from ragtime, hymns, or country music. He glanced at the saxophone players and nodded.

The audience was still clapping, keeping beat.

The bass player began to play, as the drummer joined in and intensified it all. They had it down pat, including the guitar player, when he merged in.

Devin kept singing.

All three brothers came in strong, taking turns, blowing their horns with vitality. They were juggling notes between one another until they began spiraling up and down the scale harmoniously, accommodating him.

"Woooooooow, they're good," I mumbled.

Josephine was just as mesmerized, "Yeah, this is better than the circus." Leave it to Josephine; she would say something like that.

Mr. Johnston's head was swaying, keeping time. At any moment, from the way his fingers were bouncing in midair above a range of keys, he would soon master what was electrifying in his head. Finally, at the perfect opportunity, his fingers touched down, blending in. At first, he was playing notes in spurts, but it wasn't long before he was all over the keyboard.

"*What song is that?*" Josephine asked. "*I've never heard that before.*"

"*I don't know. I'm not familiar with that one either.*"

"Thaaaaaat's nice."

"I like it, too," my head bounced, approvingly.

Before long, all the musicians were playing the song like they had played it many times before.

The audience was moved.

I had never seen Joshua clap so hard. It wasn't hard to see, being his first time that he was really enjoying himself, too.

Trying to get to Devin, after the program, wasn't easy. He was an instant celebrity. "How are we going to get past all these people?" Josephine wondered.

After seeing that we were heading straight for a roadblock, I had second thoughts, "Maybe we should stand here and wait. Right now, we can't get to him. Let's be patient. Besides, we know where he lives." *For the moment, anyway*, a sad thought occurred to me. I smiled at the thought of just meeting him. If Mamie hadn't sped off the other day, we probably wouldn't have met.

"You're right. What's the hurry?"

Even though we couldn't get to them, we inched our way closer, within hearing distance.

There was a big crowd around him, including youngsters, who were impressed.

Joshua was already standing close by, getting a taste of publicity himself. There was plenty excitement going on.

When I turned my head, I saw the Electric Keynotes talking to Ruby's husband, James, and some other man. *Who is he?* They were quite busy themselves.

"Maybe we should piggyback off them and get some autographs," Josephine joshed, drawing my attention back toward where all the excitement was coming from.

Humored, I said, *"As imposters?"*

"Sure, why not. We could call ourselves…uh…" She ran out of, what sounded like, nonsense. She always knew how to entertain, even when she thought of something that was too far-fetched to comprehend.

"That's what I thought," I shook my head, but I was enjoying the small talk anyway, and so was she.

"Can we take a picture with you and Joshua!?" we heard someone say, but could barely see them.

"Sure, you can," Devin answered the little girl, who was shorter than most of them.

Then we heard a gleeful response from the rest of the youngsters.

"Same question I wanted to ask," a gentleman said, holding a black case. "I'm a photographer, and would like to get a few snapshots, if you don't mind."

"No, we don't mind," Devin replied above the noise.

The grown folks stood aside and watched.

The cameraman aligned them by height. It looked as though they were preparing to take school pictures for a yearbook.

Devin looked around, puzzled. "Wait. I want, Miss PeggyAnn and Josephine, over there to join us."

The crowd looked in the opposite direction wondering whom he was referring to.

Joshua motioned his hand for us to come to where they stood.

"We may get mobbed over there," Josephine snickered, but was thrilled that he noticed our absence.

"Come on, Josephine," I led the way. Reflecting on her earlier comment, I refreshed her memory, "Did you not say you wanted to get some autographs?"

Her eyes grew. "Of course, but—"

Wondering if she would try to wiggle her way out of this, I then stated, "Well," I politely cut in, "here's your chance, and you can call yourself…uh…" I tapped my finger on the side of my temple as if trying to think of something appropriate that would suit her stardom.

She looked at me and smiled. "All right, PeggyAnn," she totally gave in, "we can just pretend. How about that?"

"Very well."

After we had taken a few pictures, a boy approached Joshua and said, "I liked your poem."

"Thank you," he looked a little surprised.

"You moved my—" the young boy's eyes wandered, trying to remember a particular word.

"Soul," a girl said, to help him out.

"Yes. That's what I wanted to say. You moved my soul."

"How?"

"You are my inspiration."

"Am I, little cub?" Joshua grinned.

"*You sure are*," he answered, comically.

"And mine, too," more of them admitted.

Another girl joined in, "I feel that I can overcome my fears now, knowing that I'm not alone. There are things I would like to do, but have been too scared to try."

Drawn into what was taking place, we had a clear view of who was talking.

"Umph," Josephine gazed at the girl with compassion, "I remember those days."

"Sometimes, growing up is not easy," I understood, looking back, too. "At that stage, we're just beginning and still have a long ways to go."

Josephine gave a hard nod. "It's not over," she commented, as her eyes shifted back toward Joshua, interested in the growing topic.

"Why were you scared?" He looked concerned.

The girl's facial expression suddenly drooped.

"Because," she looked down.

The rest of the kids were staring at her. Some of them looked like they, too, could relate to what was troubling her.

"You don't have to be scared of anything. For anyone to further help you, it would help us in knowing why you were scared," Joshua tried, again, hoping she would open up.

Another girl, who had been standing next to her, saw that she was struggling and spoke up, "She's scared of failure; she's not doing too well in school."

"Are you her friend?"

"Yes, I am."

"Are you afraid of failure, too?"

"No."

"Can you help her get over her fears?"

She glanced at her friend, and then looked at Joshua again. "Yes, I'll try."

"What's your code?"

All the other kids and teenagers joined in to answer and shouted, "INSPIRE!"

"Help her to make a change and you will not regret it."

"I will," she glanced at her friend, who was now barely smiling.

"We're here for a purpose. *For purpose* to breathe healthy and survive, change has to occur, *somewhere*."

Josephine and I looked at each other.

"*Is that Joshua talking?*" Josephine looked spooked.

"Yes, that's your brother," I smiled, impressed.

"What's gotten into him?"

"Looks like he's making a change himself."

Then Joshua turned and glanced at Devin. "See my friend here?" he put his hand on Devin's shoulders to show that they were pals.

"Yes," the crowd said, grinning at Devin.

Devin's eyes batted a number of times with wonder.

"I was inspired by him. He probably didn't know it before today, and probably doesn't even know how, but he did. Sometimes, we affect people and we don't even know it. And sometimes, we affect another person by choice. If you care, reach out to give back to a life to help them. You have a strength that you may not be aware of, but it's there. Use it," Joshua looked at the girl's friend, again, and continued, "to help her achieve her goals. I'm not sure what all of her goals are. And maybe, most of you need help in school. What can you do to help your friends excel in what they want to claim?"

Eyebrows were shifting with wonder in the crowd.

Joshua glanced at Devin. He opened the floor for him to say something.

Devin cleared his throat. "How many of you like diamonds?" Although, he was caught off guard, I sensed he was not afraid to talk before a crowd of people.

"I do," most of them said, but one.

"*Not me*," the little fella shook his head. "*They cost too much.*"

Everyone started laughing, including me.

"What does this kid know about the cost of diamonds?" I said to Josephine, tickled.

"Sounds like plenty and he probably will never get married."

I saw that Devin was trying hard to keep his composure and not laugh out. He cleared his throat, again, and asked the kid, "Let me put it this way. How precious is something that is very important to you?"

"A lot!" he answered, boldly.

"What do you have at home that means so much to you?" Devin grinned. Seemingly, he was intrigued to hear what he would sputter next.

The boy pondered then replied, "My mother!"

The crowd sounded like humming bees. His answer was unexpected but a good one that most kids probably wouldn't have even thought of.

Devin smiled. "Good answer! How much does your mother mean to you?" he asked next, enjoying the quiz. He wasn't the only one because the kid had everyone staring at him. He had our undivided attention.

The boy blurted, without hesitation, *"She means the world to me; she's precious."*

"If your mother is precious, then she has to be just as significant as a diamond, wouldn't you say?"

The boy thought. "What does *significant* mean?"

"Having meaning…special meaning."

"Oh," the light came on. "Well, *my mother is significant to me.*"

"If your mother is special and precious to you, then she's as significant as a diamond because she sparkles and radiates in the cove of your heart."

"Ooooh," a humming of approval rushed through the crowd. They understood better how all the questions and answers were connected.

Devin continued, "A diamond sparkles and stands out, which causes it to be noticed. It's a shine that cannot be hidden from either of us. So, I say to you, let your diamonds, as Joshua shared with you in his poem, be an inspiration to someone else."

"Did someone inspire you?" a teenager asked.

"Yes. Miss PeggyAnn inspired me," he gripped my wrist, pulling me beside him. "If your code is 'Inspire,' then all of you will definitely help to make a change."

"Hi," I waved at them.

"Hi," they said back.

"I would like to add that if we, meaning, you and you and you and you," I pointed at each of them as an example, including myself, "spread our inspiration like fire, *we all* can make a difference in this world."

Josephine stepped in to say, "Now, I'm inspired from listening. I have opened my treasure box and I am ready to start reaching in for my jewels. It's up to me to change without being afraid."

"*Can you do it?*" Joshua firmly asked them all, taking the floor again.

"*Let's do it*," a little girl said, who was so short, the crowd opened to see who was talking.

"Yeah!" they cheered. All the kids were excited, even the boy who thought he didn't like diamonds because of how much they cost. He now realized the value of its worth.

Joshua looked at the young girl who was too shy to speak about her failure earlier and told her friend, again, but differently, "Be her inspiration so she can grow."

"I will," she reassured him, smiling.

Those who were at a distance, turned around, wondering, what all the excitement was about.

The adults, who had been listening, were clapping.

"You just may get your autographs after all, Josephine," I teased.

"Yes, I may," she said spiel, as fantasy, with gleam in her eyes.

"Thank you for talking to my daughter about her fears." The girl's pop smiled and shook Joshua's hand.

"You're welcome, sir."

"Talking to her may be the boost she needs. And even with all the other children who may be in the same situation, this is good for them and has an impact. They know they're not all alone."

"No, they're not alone, and *that's* what makes it even more special. It lets them see that they can help each other," his wife commented. "I liked the poem."

"Thank you, ma'am. Maybe this will be a good spark for them."

"From their response, it looks that way. Did you write it yourself?"

Curious, we glanced at Joshua, too, since we just had this conversation a few hours ago on the church property.

"Yes, I did," he replied.

"You did a good job," she smiled.

"You sure did, Joshua," Dr. Andrews, the principal overheard, agreeing, as she walked up, "and I would like to feature your poem in the lobby at the high school."

Joshua was speechless. *"Sure, Dr. Andrews."*

"Stop by my office sometime tomorrow morning and we'll talk about it further."

"I'll be there."

"And, what is your name, young man?"

"Devin, ma'am."

She reached to shake his hand, "You entertained us well. You were dynamic."

"Thank you."

"I've never heard anything quite like that before but I like gospel. You should be making records as good as you are. If you haven't, you will be. *I'm certain of that.*"

"PeggyAnn," she turned toward me now, "it's good seeing you. You are a hard worker who is determined to learn. Anyone who loves school *so much* is to be admired. You're a very good student and an example for our students."

"Thank you, Dr. Andrews."

"Josephine, it's good to see you, too," she waved and left.

Everyone had dispersed. We had been bursting inside for the longest, waiting to speak to Devin, alone, ourselves.

"You were *great*," I said, being the first one to congratulate him in our circle.

"Thank you, Miss PeggyAnn," he grinned.

"We didn't know you could sing. You're full of surprises."

Joshua smiled, still amazed. "Devin, I enjoyed that. You really have inspired me in more ways than one."

"And I enjoyed your poem, Joshua."

"I did, too," said Josephine and I.

"I remember our earlier conversation, but I had no idea," Devin shook his head in disbelief. "Right now, I don't know what to say, which is unusual for me."

"You have said a lot, and have done more than you know," Joshua told him. "Everyone has their own set of eyes and ears. Things have been quite interesting since you've been in Seminole County."

Devin quickly glanced at me. "It's been *quite* interesting," he chuckled. Joshua reminded him of incidents that he'd rather forget, right now. He was just enjoying the moment.

Joshua belly-laughed. After moments of savoring that thought, he seriously said, "But, I'm glad that you came."

"*Oh yeah, cub?*"

Joshua's head was bobbing.

Devin added, "You know I had to shoot back one of your famous words, even though we're past that stage."

Past that stage, my thoughts got tangled.

Josephine leaned over and whispered, "*Past that stage? Past what stage?*"

"Your guess is as good as mine."

"We both know it's a man's thing now," Joshua kept the mystery going.

Josephine shrugged when I glanced in her direction.

Looking beyond her, the Electric Keynotes approached us, smiling, with James, Ruby's husband. They were just as electrifying as they sounded. Dressed alike in royal blue and mellow-yellow attire was enough to electrify the entire county, not to mention that three of them were identical. And honestly, I still had a hard time figuring out who was who.

"We have a *star here*," James immediately said, softly chuckling, as if he couldn't believe it. Neither could we.

"We sure do," one of the three said.

Our circle gazed at them.

They chuckled, noticing that we all were confused. Like 1-2-3, they said, amusingly, "I'm Moses."

"*I'm David.*"

"And, I'm Paul!" They were actually harmonizing their names up and down the scale.

We sprang into laughter.

"I think they got it now," James laughed to himself. He shook Devin's hand. "Now I see what Ruby was talking about. *Amazing.* You can sing and play music. You had us all in suspense while up there on stage."

"Did I?" Devin asked.

James laughed out.

Everyone looked at him and wondered what warranted his sudden attack.

"You're good, young man."

"I'm sorry, sir, I don't understand."

He tried to regain his composure. "As young as you are, you can't *possibly* have a voice like that. Your voice sounds like a grown man's. I have to give it to you," he couldn't seem to stop shaking his head, "you are also a *gooooood actor.*"

"*You think so?*" Devin replied with a straight face. No one really knew what role he was playing, except a few of us. And, no one really knew why he had been shifting his voice throughout the day except Mr. Jackson and I. I was surprised to hear him talking normal with all these people standing around. I guess it really didn't matter because they probably would have thought he was acting anyway, just as Mr. James did. It's good things turned out as they did. If it was the other way around, he would've had a hard time explaining.

"He's good at whatever he does," Mr. Jackson chimed in, to change the subject before anyone blew the whistle. "Lad, yuh reached da *regions of joy in my soul. I'm impressed.*"

"We all are," Moses added.

Mr. James saw Ruby at a distance. "Well, guys, I must be going. We'll talk soon."

"All right," the band said, and we waved good-bye.

"Goldie and I 'ave seen many days," Mr. Jackson looked at Devin, picking the conversation back up, "but not like dis one."

Devin flinched. *"You and Goldie?"*

"Yez, Goldie and I. She has helped me tuh win many gold medals in da past."

"Oh," Devin sounded shocked, *"that's why you called her Goldie at the music store yesterday. That explains it.* That name is different and for good reason."

"Yez," he nodded, "dat's why. Tuh me, she's uh special instrument. All she needed wuz jus' uh minor repair, dat's all, and I wanted yuh tuh be da first tuh play her at da store so I could jus' listen tuh her sing."

"Believe me, Mr. Jackson, *I was honored.*"

David chimed in, "We used to play on the road."

Devin stared at them in disbelief.

"Now, we're back," Moses proudly announced, surprising the rest of us.

"What!" we almost screamed.

"Yes, we are," the rest of the band said, gleefully, and then chuckled from the response.

We heard a voice. Everyone immediately turned around at the abrupt interruption.

Mr. Bailey swiftly walked up after calling Mr. Jackson. "Before I leave, Jackson, I want to say thank you, again, for your help putting out the fire on my property."

"My pleasure, Bailey."

They shook hands.

Mr. Bailey acknowledged everyone else. "All of you were great today."

A chorus of replies thanked him.

The more he looked at Devin, the more puzzled he became. *"Were you the one with Jackson when the fire broke out?"*

Devin nodded.

"Thank you, you and Joshua."

Devin and Joshua smiled, accepting his gratitude.

"Oh," he said quickly, as if in a hurry. "I would like to ask a favor." He faced Devin, specifically.

Everyone was waiting to hear his request. We didn't hear too many of those around here.

"Would you be willing to stop by my house sometime tomorrow and maybe sing something for my daughter? As dynamic as you are, you may make all the difference in the world to her." Then Mr. Bailey glanced at Mr. Jackson for approval. I guess he thought he was his guardian in some way or another.

"Well, lad, dat's yer decision."

"Sure, I will."

Mr. Bailey chuckled. *"Yep,"* he appeared entertained, "you'll *definitely* draw her attention." He thought Devin was acting with the deep voice.

The group chortled at his humor.

He began to walk away then suddenly turned back around. "Hmmm," on second thought, "I don't think it would be a bad idea if the three of you joined him. What do you say?"

We beamed with approval.

Chapter 14

DEVIN

With all the excitement from the previous day, Monday came fast. David and Moses left yesterday after the program. They continued on their way to their hometown to visit other relatives and friends. I no longer tripped over my speech when it came to analyzing each of them. Finally, I could figure out who was who. David was an easy give away. The mole over his eye was one good clue. Next, Mr. Jackson's speech was different from the others, but he decided to do something about it, especially after hearing Joshua's poem. PeggyAnn and I volunteered to help him accomplish his goal.

Now, it was only Mr. Jackson and I. We were back to routine, but things were a little different for me. The weekend had been a boost, like an injection of some sort that made things a lot better. I guess I can consider it a booster shot, as Josephine calls it, with a lot of serum. As much as I've been through, I needed the highest dosage I could get.

Looking back, it's amazing how we can get used to things that we have no control over—some things, that is. It was my fourth day there now, and it never ceased to amaze me how far behind things were, by design and structurally, compared to what I knew. Although, seeing the early 1900's as it was had been educational and interesting. At the same time, it was far more appalling. Puttin' it in a nutshell—

LAWD, HELP! Then I thought, *On the other hand, how would a person know the difference, if they don't know anything else better?*

After Mr. Jackson had been plowing for about 30-minutes, I took over. This time, I had my horse commands down pat. From the way things had turned out the first time, I started out slow. All I needed was for Mr. Jackson's horse to flee like sheep gone astray.

Absorbed with a new challenge, I lost track of time. My pace was beefing up some steam; sweat was forming around my face. Plowing became a piece of cake, but if I was not careful, watching dirt fly in both directions could send a person into a trance. But I considered it more as a broken record, something I would never forget. Sometimes, repeats can be a good thing—it was therapy.

After what felt like hours had gone by, I noticed Mr. Jackson heading my way. When he met up with me, he asked, "How's it going, lad?"

I stopped. "Doing fine, Mr. Jackson. *I think I got it now.*" However, Smokey probably didn't think so. He sat waaaaaaaay over yonder, looking. I snickered. Maybe he wanted to play it safe.

"It looks dat way," Mr. Jackson's voice popped the bubble of that comical thought. He remembered his vow and corrected himself, "I mean…it looks that way."

Surprised, I said, "Mr. Jackson, you're coming along well with your speech. You're not wasting any time, are you?" He had given it some deep thought at the program.

"I wuz practicing last night before going tuh sleep." He noticed that he made another mistake but kept right on talking, "I have," he said slowly, careful of how he formed his words next, "a long ways to go, *but I'll get dere.* Pay me no mind if my English is incorrect." He shook his head.

"You'll get there," I told him, being careful not to let him hear me mess-up, myself. Sometimes, I chopped off my words, usually leaving off the last alphabet. "You're going to make mistakes until you get use to it."

"Practice makes perfect, and thanks to yuh and da little damsel for volunteering to help. Those homemade flashcards you both made up really work."

"I don't mind at all. *That's what I'm here for.*"

Mr. Jackson had the strangest look on his face. "*How old did yuh say you were, or did you?*" He scratched the side of his head and thought about his question for a moment then quickly changed his mind, "You don't have to answer dat question. We'll come back to dat another time."

From the corner of my eye, I saw a horse galloping.

"Devin," a voice yelled out, waving. It was PeggyAnn. She was riding Mamie.

"You're doing good," Mr. Jackson turned, about to walk away, "Devin, you're doing good." I noticed he was gradually calling me by name.

"I'll be a pro before long."

He turned back around. "It looks like you're already dere." He smiled, and then said, "I'll leave you to your company."

"Hi, Mr. Jackson. How are you doing?" PeggyAnn greeted him, as he was leaving.

He raised his straw hat out of respect, as usual. "Fine, little damsel. How are you?"

"Swell," she gazed at him, as her response weakened.

Mr. Jackson smiled and kept walking.

She smiled with hope. "Did I hear him correctly?"

"Yes, you did," I verified, so she wouldn't think that she was imagining things. "He's been practicing."

"That's good!"

"Yesterday did him a lot of good."

"I can *see that.*"

"And he's not the only one," I told her.

Quickly, she asked, "What do you mean?" Her eyes were smiling with anticipation to hear some more good news.

"I actually was looking forward to helping Mr. Jackson do some farm work today, despite everything that has happened. *Can you believe that?*"

"Actually, Devin," she grinned, "no, I can't believe it." Her eyes became glassy from the thought.

I snickered, reliving that moment. "Neither can I. It seemed like each incident continued to escalate. I didn't tell you this, but when I came face-to-face with a hog's head that was just dangling from the roof of Mr. Jackson's cellar, my world was spinning, *out-of-control*, from the sudden rush, trying to get out of that dark hole."

"WHAT?!" her eyes expanded as she covered her mouth. In no time, her eyes were filled with liquid. A faucet of tears ran down her cheeks. She turned around holding the side of her stomach.

I stared at her examining the curls shaking on the back of her head. I made matters even worse when I continued and said, "I felt like," a chill ran down my spine, "running a *looooooong ways from here WITH GREAT SPEED.*" I could feel the horror rise, again, dancing in my veins. My legs were getting weak; I had to lean on the horse. I eventually joined in her spirit of laughter.

It took a minute or two before we both were able to see straight, or even think about saying another word.

PeggyAnn finally turned back around, wiping her face with the back of her hand and asked, *"Why didn't you? I would have."* Her eyes were large.

"When my world started spinning, *I was soon out like a light.*"

That was it. She couldn't take anymore. *"Excuse me."* She left.

"Miss PeggyAnn, *where are you going?*"

She walked so fast, I thought she was going to stumble and fall.

My mouth gaped from her sudden dismissal. *Where is she off to?* My eyes followed her. I was a breathing mannequin, just standing there, mystified.

"I'll be right back," she said, but never turned around.

What's gotten into her? was all that came to mind. *Umph, how strange.* I gripped the handles and continued to plow, remembering that I had a full day ahead of me. Mr. Bailey would be expecting me soon.

Before long, PeggyAnn came back.

I stopped. "Are you all right?"

She was smiling, "Here. I thought you may need this." She handed me a glass of water.

"Thank you, I needed that." I drank the water until the glass was empty. "You didn't walk away just to get me a glass of water, did you?"

"No, but I had heard enough. Before long, I would have been on my knees, laughing, begging you to stop talking."

"*Oh.* I thought I had insulted you or something."

"No, Devin, that's not you. I had to take a break. I didn't *quite expect* to hear some of the things that you said."

"*It happened.*"

"Well, I'm glad to see that you're holding up well. And, it looks like you have really been working out here," she observed.

Looking at how much work I had already done, my response was, nodding, "I have, I would say."

Then she asked, out of curiosity, "Have you milked the cow, yet?"

"No, I haven't."

"From the other day, I didn't think so, but I thought I would ask. Once you get used to it, it's a piece of cake."

I was not anxious.

PeggyAnn and I stood with Joshua and Josephine on Mr. Bailey's miniature concrete-slab porch. We stood one behind the other. It was very quiet and still.

I knocked on the front door. The knock sounded deep and alarming. It looked like a fresh coat of paint had been stroked horizontally across its plain, flat surface. The house was a wood frame, painted light blue with two square windows. The concrete slab that we were standing on was garnished with two high-backed wooden chairs on both sides of the door.

Looking around definitely was not a rainbow. Apparently, we all had the same thought because we gazed where the spread of fire had been engulfed with flames. The fire colored his property leaving behind a massive sweep of black memories. A large portion of his land was destroyed, including a wagon and other possessions. His house and barn were still standing, but welcoming, as if the colors of day were watching the dark destruction of night. The fire had carved out all the beauty of its purpose for country living. The grass was burned and bared no light against the surrounding it once offset. Its shadow was dark and deafening, yielding silence.

Mr. Bailey had a lot of open land. It bared only one tree. It had many leaves with a homemade swing hanging from it by two thick ropes. *Maybe that's Genesis's get-a-way spot*, I thought. *But...who is Genesis?*

As the door opened, the hinges slightly squeaked. "Hello," Mr. Bailey smiled, glad that we stopped by at his request, "Devin, PeggyAnn, Joshua, and Josephine."

"Hello, Mr. Bailey," we said in unison.

He stepped aside. "Come in." He held the door open.

A woman walked in. Her smile glowed, but was weak with great concern. She looked matronly but distinguished. "Hi, I'm Ms. Bailey," she glanced at me, "Joe's wife. I don't believe we've met." Her voice was soft. She smelled like pastries.

"No ma'am, we haven't. My name is Devin."

Her smile grew stronger. "I've heard much about you already. You have an interesting voice."

"He plays two roles," Mr. Bailey cut in to comment while closing the door. *"He's good."*

"I see," she agreed with him.

Joshua and Josephine kept grinning, but I could tell that they were just as lost as yesterday. On the other hand, I felt like, what's the point even explaining. They probably would find it hard to believe anyway.

Ms. Bailey quickly shook my hand then greeted the others she knew. After everyone exchanged greetings, she asked, "Would anyone care for some cookies?" From the smell, they were tempting.

"No ma'am," was our response, simultaneously. Instead, we savored the heavenly scent.

To speed things up, I said, "Thank you, but we're actually here to see Genesis." I had no idea who their daughter was, but it had to be important for Mr. Bailey to ask us over. I wondered how he thought I may be able to help; I had never seen or even met his daughter before.

"Come this way," Mr. Bailey said.

Their house had more space on the inside than it appeared to have from the outside, but it was still small. We walked into a short hall that had just enough room for all of us to stand. A person could only turn to the left or right to get to two rooms. The entrance into the kitchen was only accessible through the sitting room. If there was such a floor plan, it was one that I've never seen. I thought it to be suitable for only one person.

Mr. Bailey knocked then opened the door.

We piled into the room that had only a small bed, chest, and a wooden chair, enclosed by four cedar walls. There was no color except the spread that was on their daughter's bed, which was cream, and a couple of dolls that were propped on top of the chest for added flavor. It was cozy and silent. Light was bursting through the small window, which Genesis sat in front of. It was as if she had never heard us come in.

"We don't know what's bothering Genesis. She's locked up and can't seem to open up, and she cries a lot. Maybe you can help," he said, lowly. His personality never seems to change; he gave me the impression that he was always optimistic.

PeggyAnn looked at Mr. Bailey. "I've never seen Genesis like this, Mr. Bailey. She's always been so happy."

"PeggyAnn is right. Maybe it was the fire. That can be devastating," Josephine said, trying to think of an explanation to help unravel what was troubling her.

"Honestly, I don't know," Mr. Bailey shook his head cluelessly.

Joshua and I were observing Genesis who appeared to be between 10 and 12 years old. She never moved or showed any emotion. The only thing that seemed to visibly function were her eyelids. She blinked occasionally.

Momentarily, an untimely thought hit, reminding me of the day we both were lugging buckets of water to help put out the fire. Joshua had carried that heavy case around with him all the way here so we could practice later today but, on the other hand, he was used to the heavy load. It looks like we may be putting it to use sooner than we thought.

Joshua broke my train of thought and whispered, "What do you want to do?"

I was just as puzzled. "I'm not sure," I told him, quietly.

He put the case down on the floor. "Would you like to use my saxophone?"

"Maybe, you should take it out, just in case."

In the meantime, PeggyAnn approached Genesis. She bent down to ask her, "What's wrong, Gen?"

The girl still did not move. Sitting at the window seemed to be her only get-a-way. As if ready to begin turning the reels of a motion picture, she was naturally beautiful in the setting. Her stature was straight, and the strands of her long black hair trailed down to the middle of her back. She was casually dressed in a dusty pink dress. It was the perfect blend against the softness of her youth that blossomed from beneath the layers of her skin. Whatever was wrong stole her sunshine.

Mr. Bailey nodded, and then closed the door to leave.

When Joshua opened his case, his poem was inside.

PeggyAnn noticed it, too. "Joshua," she smiled, "your poem is still fresh off the press."

He slightly grinned as if surprised to see it laying there himself.

Josephine stood near Genesis gazing out the window. They both looked like statues.

PeggyAnn and I were thinking the same thing. "I have a plan," I whispered to both of them. We huddled and I explained the scene to take place.

PeggyAnn then joined Genesis and Josephine.

Joshua and I began practicing on his saxophone. In intervals, we talked amongst ourselves. I showed him a few things I wanted him to know. That was our first practice session, right there in the Bailey's home. We took turns shuffling the instrument, replacing the reed each time, drawn in our own world, and so were the young ladies. Every now and then, we glanced at them to see if there was any change in Genesis's isolated behavior. I wondered if the patchwork was working. Trying to interact with her had proven to be a hard wall to knock down. She had closed every door of communication, but, that did not stop us.

PeggyAnn and Josephine conversed whether she responded or not. At some point, Josephine was brushing Genesis's hair and enjoying it. PeggyAnn was drawing, but I had no idea what. They were busy utilizing their time.

Time passed rapidly. About 45-minutes had gone by, and still, there was no change. Mr. Bailey and his wife were probably wondering what was going on inside their daughter's room.

PeggyAnn signaled Joshua and I.

We stopped what we were doing.

She stood to exchange roles and said, "Genesis, I would like for you to meet...Devin."

I walked to where she sat. "Hello, Genesis," my voice raised some octaves higher, "it's my pleasure to meet you."

Still, she did not move. Everything was going just as I thought it would.

Dropping the act, I told her, "You're very beautiful."

She looked up. I knew that should snap her out of her trance. She knew she had not heard my voice before.

PeggyAnn and Josephine watched intensely, wondering if she would speak next. Their eyes were pleading for hope.

Joshua was still standing behind me, waiting.

Suddenly, Genesis laughed out.

Mr. Bailey and his wife heard her. They rushed in.

Soon, the room was filled with laughter. I almost forgot what the plan was.

"Your voice," she thought to be incredibly amusing. *"You sound like a man. How did you do that?"*

"It comes naturally," I answered her, and stepped back toward Joshua. We were on a mission that had to be accomplished.

PeggyAnn stole everyone's attention. She was an excellent, mature, and special young lady that I admired. Motioning her hands, gracefully, she spoke eloquently, "My friends and neighbors, please welcome..."

CUT

Stories and plays are creations,
from the mind of decorations,
imagination and animation,
discoveries or educational,
entertainment,
fiction or nonfiction,
making the cut.

Cameras steady,
cast ready,
action!—to roll the film,
from scripts to plots,
even behind drapes of a dream,
spotlights shining through rainbow eyes,
as private screens,
until the end,
what the message sends,
CUT!

Life plays on and on,
the "real" song,
not an act,
it's true to the facts,
scene after scene,
what life brings,
edited only by the Editor,
the Monitor,
controlling the dial of time.

… what's next?

Chapter 15

JARVIS

"*D*evin, Devin," I tapped his shoulder, "*we're on the ground, bruh.*" The plane was headed for the terminal.

"*Huh,*" his eyes popped opened. "*Cut!*" he stared.

A few passengers looked around then gazed in our direction.

Caught off guard, I glanced around. For a second, I wondered if we were on camera. His reaction came as a surprise. I was glad he didn't shout as if on a football field but, it was enough to draw some attention. Flagging my hand, I smoothly smiled at passengers, including a flight attendant, as a sign that there was no need to be alarmed.

They casually turned back around.

Concerned, I turned and said, "You all right, Devin?"

He glanced around as if lost.

"It's me, bruh…Jarvis. You were seriously dreaming."

He took a deep breath. Realization was sinking in. "*Whew!*" he finally spoke and shook his head, trying to get it together, "that was *soooooome dream.*"

I chuckled, relieved. "I see. A few times, you were shaking like a leaf."

He looked zapped. "Was I?" he glanced at Freddie, who slept through the commotion.

"Yes, you were. You probably should slow down on the tea," I reminded him, kidding about his magical potion.

"This time," he cleared his throat, "the tea was a good thing. I floated to the other side of the hemisphere."

Puzzled, I asked, "What hemisphere?" Making that statement, I knew he was back to normal.

"The hemisphere of my cerebrum."

I chuckled, again. "And what has your brain done for you lately?" As entertaining as he was, I *had to know* what flipped his switch.

"Its electrical wires brought a little history to life."

"*Oh*," I looked at him intrigued, "I'm anxious to hear what was curled inside your knapsack."

"Some history from waaaaaay back," he added with a smile, almost whispering. "It was so real." He looked like he was slowly rejuvenating, but needed a jumpstart. "You woke me up right at the time…" he paused.

"What time was that? It must've been interesting."

He exhaled, "It was, and the interruption occurred during an important scene. I wonder what happened next."

"Dreams are strange and you may not be able to recapture whatever it was."

"Brother, if you only knew."

"Since I've known you, Devin, your mind has always been decorated."

His curiosity rose. "Decorated?"

"Absolutely. You have some imagination, at times."

"That's a nice way of putting it," he chuckled.

"With all the bells and whistles, bruh. You don't miss a thing."

We laughed, quietly.

"I don't know if that's a good thing or not."

"That means you're able to bring some creativity to life."

He sat up straight. "Umph," he paused, "you kicked my mind right into overdrive with that one."

"It's the truth. Do you realize what you said waking up?"

"Vaguely." He thought back for a few seconds. Unsure, he asked, "Did I say 'cut?' " His eyebrows crinkled.

"Bravo," I clapped, without making a sound.

Releasing the strain in his eyebrows, he chuckled. "That's interesting. I guess it was fulfilled."

"I guess it was and hopefully on a good note."

"One day when we have some free time, I'll tell you all about it."

"Some dreams are short-lived."

He jolted in his seat. *"NOT THIS ONE!"* he came alive.

"Whaaaaat," I wanted to laugh badly. His animation was hilarious.

"Jarvis, my brother, *that dream was serious.*" His eyes were extremely large.

My eyes batted, feeling as though we were having a contest. "From the way that sounds, there must be something in that dream that stands out."

"For sure. There's a blaze between the early 1900s and the 21st Century."

Now, he had me curious. "What do you mean by blaze?"

"Things have really changed."

"Oh," I was starting to get the picture. "Is the connection, by chance, Ms. PeggyAnn?"

"Bingo!" Devin said.

I grinned. "I know that was deep."

"You have *no idea*, man."

"From our conversation earlier, I can just imagine and that's just the surface."

"Again, it was interesting but at the same time, moving. I admire her, and have a lot of respect for Ms. PeggyAnn. She's quite a lady."

"I've never even met her but I feel as though I have. From what I've learned, it's just something about her…she's special."

"In the dream," Devin said, staring into space, "*she was soooooo real.* I felt as though I had the opportunity to know her even better. She was smart, caring, intelligent, and knew so much for her age. She was advanced."

"I see you were viewing something deep through rainbow eyes from behind drapes of a dream."

He did a double take. "Run that by me again." His neck stretched.

I backtracked and repeated the statement.

"*Rainbow eyes,*" Devin mumbled, bewildered.

"Yes. Like I said, you have a decorated mind. From behind drapes of a dream, your creativity was viewed from your own private screen—your mind—for your eyes only. There was a lot of activity going on through your spotlights, which are the eyes of your mind since your eyes were closed."

"Oh," he caught on, "that makes sense."

I added, "Apparently, the viewing was colorful, meaning action packed and creative."

He confirms, "It was both entertaining and educational." Instantly, Devin laughs and couldn't seem to stop. He leaned forward to try and catch his breath. "Excuse me, Jarvis, I had a flashback."

"You most definitely have to share that thought someday."

"I can't wait! It's so funny that I can't even discuss it on the plane. G*et ready,*" he warned, "you're going to find out just how decorated my own viewing was."

"You must have a lot to tell."

"I do. *But, man,*" something else occurred to him, "*that was a lengthy dream.*"

"It probably just seemed long."

"No, I'm talking about four days worth of data."

"No one dreams that much at one time. Maybe you picked up where you left off from another time."

"I don't know. It must've been on fast-forward."

"Knowing you, *brutha*," I snickered, "*anything is possible*."

Devin chuckled because he knew that statement had some validity.

"Did you learn anything from this dream?"

"*Yes*," he stressed, "I could *NEVER* be a farmer."

"*YOU, A FARMER!*" That hit a funny bone.

"*Can you imagine that?*"

"Not really," my brain shifted gears to entertain the strange thought since he has always been a city boy, "but, on second thought, you would be the perfect one."

"You have to be kiddin', Jarvis?"

"You could adjust."

"Somehow, I don't think so."

Grinning, I added, "It may be a funny scene, but you have what it takes once you get used to it."

Devin's expression said a thousand words. "Jarvis," he shook his head, "I'm not feelin' that."

My eyes were flooding from the humor. I looked straight ahead to keep my composure then said, "It's all about what we've discussed before."

"Which is?"

"Change, bruh, change."

"That's a little much."

"Why would you say that?"

"*In this day and time, milking a cow is not at the top of my list.*"

I *fell out laughing*. "Oh," I could barely speak, "*now* I see what you mean. You don't need to say no more. *Milking a cow! I can't compute.*"

Because of the expression on my face, Devin began to laugh.

Once he got himself together, he said, "I can't begin to tell you what it was like for them back then in the dream. If you could have seen that, you would *beg* to be on the MIA list. Your feet would go into automatic-pilot mode."

"Missing in action...*I believe it.   I'd run far, far away.*"

"I know that's right."

"That's going in reverse. Things are so advanced now that there's no need, unless there was no other option. On the other hand, there's nothing wrong with being a farmer if a person wants to be one. Adjustments can be made, however, we have choices. Although, everyone is not cut out for the fixture."

Devin looked relieved. "That dream reinforced how thankful I should be."

"Always," I thought the same. "The Man Upstairs knows just how much we can take."

The pilot made an announcement after being delayed on the landing strip.   Once we made it to the gate, the engine stopped. Instantly, ripple effects of seatbelts were clicking. We were on Atlanta, Georgia's soil.

At that moment, our eyes fell on Freddie.

I told Devin, "It's a good thing that Freddie the Teddy is still asleep."

"Why you say that?" he glanced at me inquisitively.

"Because, bruh, you were *dynamic*. Not only can you sing, but—" I had to chuckle at his wake-up performance.

"But what?"

"You would make a good actor if you were given the opportunity. It comes naturally for you."

"Why am I not surprised," he responded, as if he had heard that many times before. "I'm glad you think so."

"I know so," I said, without a doubt. "Like I've said, it's a good thing Freddie is asleep because he probably would have awaken in a panic and tried to jump off the plane, especially after that gorilla story."

We chuckled then moved on to more important matters.

Atlanta's airport was not Kiddyland; it was a large facility. The walkway was crowded with people coming and going. Eateries and bookstores were goodie stops. Glancing through the glass was a sure invitation, a temptation to buy what was neatly displayed. The aroma of food floated across the pathway, tapping on the pockets of hungry passengers. And there were so many gates until it was difficult to see to the other end. It was an adventure that reminded me of a forest, trying to get around others to see our way. When we figured out where we were going, we headed down the escalators.

Catching the tram was like running to catch the subway. We stepped into what seemed like cyberspace. We were welcomed aboard by the summons of a robotic voice. It was a nice break cutting down a wide scale of steps to get from point A to point B. The final stop was baggage claim.

As we grabbed the last travel bag, we heard familiar voices heading our way.

"*Carlton*," I called out to get his attention. We were shocked to see the clan but glad.

They stopped and, with an explosion of joy, rushed to meet us.

"*This is a nice surprise*," he said. His eyes bounced between the three of us.

"*Yes, it is*," Carla chimed in, and so did the others. Her smile was bright as always.

There was so much sunshine, we drew attention. Eventually, we formed a conversation pit as his children waited at the carousel for their luggage.

"How long are you here in Atlanta, Jarvis?" Carlton asked, inquisitively.

"Our flight leaves out Tuesday evening."

"Wonderful," he grinned. "We're leaving Wednesday. Maybe we'll get a chance to get together."

"That sounds good."

"This is our last stop before going back to California."

"Oh, yeah," I had forgotten, "you did say that you would be spending a few days in Atlanta. Perfect timing."

"It sure is," Carlton said.

"This *is* a good surprise."

"I agree. I haven't talked to you in a few days, nephew. What brings you to Atlanta?"

Swiftly shaking my head, I said with excitement, "You *wouldn't believe it.*"

"No, you wouldn't," Devin and Teddy joined in.

Carlton's eyes sparkled. "*That good*, huh?"

"Yes, it is," I confirmed.

"Well, I can't wait to hear this. I'll believe just about anything these days."

I put my baggage down to release the pressure of weight off my shoulder. "On short notice, Devin has been nominated to sing."

"Nominated?" Carlton stared.

"Yes. It gets even better."

"Nominated where?"

"At a hospital. Rather, I should say requested."

Carlton and Carla glanced at each other, amazed.

"*That is interesting*," Carlton said, impressed.

My cell phone rang. "Excuse me." I took it off the clip of my belt.

"Take your time."

I turned, and walked away and stood next to an entryway for more privacy. "Jarvis speaking."

"Mr. Brooks, I'm calling from…" This trip was getting more intriguing as time went on.

After the business call, I joined the gang again. "Whelp, Devin and Teddy, you'll be appearing at a nursing home and rehabilitation center in Tucker instead." I made sure my phone was clipped securely.

"Did you say a nursing home and rehab center, Jarvis?" Devin's eyes danced with anticipation, wondering if he had heard me correctly.

"Yes. The location has been changed."

"That'll work, too."

Teddy grinned, "Wherever it is, I'm ready."

Carla smiled. "Looks like you're both greatly admired."

Carlton grinned and said, "They're in for a treat."

Based on my experience working with these two gentlemen, I said, "I believe it will be worth their while." I couldn't see it any other way.

"I definitely agree with you, nephew."

Humbly, Devin edged in, "We just hope that whoever it is, they will enjoy what we have to give."

"Uh hmmmmm," Teddy hummed.

We chuckled.

"They will," I told them. "From the sun to the stars to the moon."

"I like that," Carlton pointed toward me.

Devin nodded. "Mysterious, but I like that, too."

Carlton turned. "Well, I guess we're ready." He noticed his offsprings approaching with their luggage. "By the way, I almost forgot to ask," he remembered. "Which hotel are you staying at, Jarvis?"

"We're staying at The Georgian Terrace on Peachtree Street," I replied, searching for the itinerary to double-check the location.

"*O-o-o-o-ooooh*," he sounded happy, "this couldn't be better. We have reservations at the same hotel."

"*Now, that's what I'm talking about.*"

"Well, our ride should be waiting, Carla."

She smiled, glancing at the rest of the clan, making sure they were all accounted for.

"And how about you three?" was Carlton's next question. "Is your ride already here?"

My eyes raced toward the entrance. "We will soon find out." The crowds of people walking in and out the terminal made it even more difficult to see who was who since the sun had already gone down. The entire place reminded me of a crowded mall.

Everyone grabbed their travel bags and headed out the electronic sliding glass doors into the nice weather.

Atlanta's airport was just as congested as LAX. It almost appeared that we had never left, seeing that bumper-to-bumper cars were trying to escape the hustle and bustle just as others on the other end of the continent. *Some things never change*, was my immediate thought.

I could hear airplanes taking off. Their engines blasted one behind the other. The sound of thunder roared with urgency that people had places to go and people to see. Time schedules had to be met.

There were two, long black Lincolns that awaited us shining like pearls. The chauffeurs took our bags. Without wasting anymore time, doors opened and closed.

Distracted, Devin stopped, before getting in.

I became alarmed by the sudden, frozen look on his face. "Bruh, *what is it*?"

"Yeah, man, you all right?" Freddie turned his head and looked, too.

We were all staring in the same direction. Swarms of people were in our view.

His mouth dropped.

… hmmm, *why did the beat stop?*…

WHAT TIME IS IT?

Life meets destiny,
unraveling change,
rolling its red carpet,
when it's time to take control.

Time has a curfew,
as the knob turns,
to display its course,
of another wink at history,
to the signs of change,
dropped from the hang.

The companion of time is its lyrics,
together they grow old,
marked by the gray of its hair,
fully clothed,
the armour of time,
laced by the stories they unfold.

… time has some beautiful songs.

Chapter 16

FAITH

*I*t's a beautiful morning. I smiled, standing in front of the window. The open curtains brought cheer to the room. Several flights below, I stared at automobiles passing by on Peachtree Street. At 8:30 a.m., traffic was heavy as people drove with urgency. There's nothing like rush-hour traffic on a Monday morning, and where I'm from, is no different.

My eyes roamed toward the Fox Theatre, which was facing the hotel directly across the street. At night, the bright lights gave it personality. It was lively. Now that it was another day, it appeared to be asleep and looked like a ghost town.

Atlanta is an interesting city. This place was decorated with clusters of enormous trees. Being many floors up above ground level was necessary to look over the city. High-rise buildings were not a deficit. There were plenty and they soared.

After welcoming nature's gifts, I walked to the side of the bed and picked up the cell phone to return Devin's call. As his phone was ringing, I reflected back on his bubbly message. The replay came to a halt when he answered his phone.

"Devin speaking." He sounded wide-awake.

That's right, the thought filtered down, *Atlanta is hours ahead of California.* I wanted to just hang up and call back later, but it was too late, so, I took my chances anyway. "Good morning, Devin."

"Good morning, Faith."

"I forgot about the time difference," I was quick to say, feeling foolish. "I'll call back later." It must've been around 4:30 in the morning.

"It's all right, I'm awake."

"I thought so, but wasn't sure. You're up extremely early."

He slightly chuckled. "That's because we're in the same time zone."

"How can that be? You're in California."

"Right now, I'm in Atlanta."

"You're in Atlanta, Georgia?"

Amused, he answered, "As we speak, my friend."

I was sparked by his reply. "I'm impressed. You move around fast."

"This time, Faith, I have to admit that my trip here is much unexpected."

"What brings you to Atlanta?"

"My vocals," he softly sang the words.

His spontaneous humor caused me to laugh. "That's great!" I sat down on the edge of the bed to get comfortable. "Where are you singing?" Our conversation was starting to brew.

"We were scheduled at a hospital."

There was static, "Did you say a hospital?" I wasn't quite sure if I heard him correctly.

"Yes—"

From the excitement, I interjected. "Oooh, Devin—"

"But, that has changed."

Apparently, I had spoken too soon. I refrained from saying another word for the moment.

"The location is at a nursing home and rehabilitation center."

"That's just as good."

"What's even more shocking is that we were requested."

I smiled. "I find that to be a very special honor."

"It is," he almost whispered. His tone of voice sounded as if he had drifted into deep thought. Obviously, this new twist was more precious than silver or gold. He expressed gratitude about the opportunity and was looking forward to it. He was excited, and so was I.

After he filled me in on the details, I asked, "What hotel are you at?"

"I'm staying at The Georgian Terrace on Peachtree Street."

Surprised again, I had to catch my breath, "I can't believe it."

"You can't believe what?" his voice sounded far away.

"What a coincidence."

"*Not you*," he joked. His voice came through loud and clear again. "You're lodging at The Georgian Terrace, *too*?"

I replied, "I am."

He laughed. "We could have ridden *up-and-down the elevator to have this conversation*."

From his remark, I couldn't help but laugh out. I tried to picture how many times the elevator would have buzzed. *That would have been a long journey*, I thought. Usually, our conversations were lengthy.

Once we both calmed down, he said, "This trip, I must say, is timely."

"It appears that way, Mr. Fairchild."

"The others will be just as surprised as I am."

"I'm sure they will be."

"Have you had breakfast yet?"

"No, but, that sure sounds good right now. I am starving."

"Would you like to join us?" Devin asked.

"Sure," I accepted, sliding my fingers through my hair. I stood up and slipped my feet into my slippers.

"It is…about 9:15. Is 10 o'clock a good time?"

"Yes, 10 o'clock would be fine."

The hotel was spotless and inviting. The shiny ceramic floor sparkled, leading to gold-trimmed elevators. Valet parking was the final stamp. Their hospitality was the trimming of the South.

As I entered the restaurant, my eyes searched for Devin, Jarvis, and Teddy but did not see them. Watching my step, I walked down into the cozy dining area. I was fascinated by the eye of the interior decorator. This place was turned into a goldmine, especially for those who sought seclusion. With Southern style, this was the place to get lost in. The dark, subdued color coordination was catchy, and far more relaxing than most I had been to. The carpet and furnishings were exquisite and classy. This hidden-cove setting impressed me. Seeing that there was more to this island to be treasured, my eyes roamed straight ahead through the glass. For those who desired moments of outdoor dining for pleasure, that was another feature for dining as an option. My eyes then traveled to the left toward the back section spotting a spiral staircase. The off-white ceramic beauty spiraled to the upper level that is yet to be desired as a tucked-away haven.

Refocusing my attention on why I was there, I waited near the entrance since there was no sign of the others.

No more than three minutes later, Devin walked up with open arms. "Faith," he smiled, "am I *ever grateful* to see you?" He was casually dressed in black slacks, dress shoes and a polo shirt. He was clean from head-to-toe.

Welcoming his approach, I smiled, too. "We meet again."

"Yes," he raised a finger to make a point, "but *not* on the elevator." As usual, he was in a joking mood.

I smiled and said, "You're just as entertaining as your performances, in case you didn't know."

He grinned. "Ooooo," he looked surprised, acting, as if he didn't already know, "then I must be *good*." He was enjoying the chitchat. "Would you like for me to sing for you while I'm at it?"

I was speechless.

"Oh," he glanced at me, chuckling, "are you getting shy on me now?"

If he sang anything in front of all these people, I would pass out.

"Of course not," I tried not to let on. "However, I've never been put on the spot by a professional artist."

"Faith, I would never embarrass you. I know how personable you are. *At least I think I do*," he stared, as if he was searching for signs that he just might have been wrong.

I didn't move.

"Oh," he stood beside me, seeming to be as tall as a giant, almost whispering. "This is getting more and more interesting by the minute."

I peeked at him and said, "You think so?"

"What's really tucked away in your basket, Faith?"

There was comedy all in his voice.

Placing my finger against my temple, I replied, "I have a basket of fruit." My reply caught him by surprise.

"I like that response," he nodded. "Am I worthy of an example?"

"Sure, I'll share one," I answered, as my mind moved rapidly. At the moment, I had no idea what example that would be. Then, for some reason, I couldn't seem to control what I did next. Before I knew it, I began to spray some heavenly notes on him, singing lowly, not to draw attention to myself:

> "Your heart sings,
> Your voice rings,
> Bringing sunshine a heart full of gold,
> To touch the world,
> And reach boy and girl,
> Leaping from the mind of your soul,
> As an open flower,
> Hope for tomorrow,
> Showering joy and love."

"Bravo, bravo," Devin clapped softly. "I didn't know that you could sing, Faith." He chuckled as he turned his head.

"Neither did we," a crowd of familiar voices said from behind.

Hearing a multitude of footsteps, my mouth slipped opened. Devin had not mentioned who the others were. I grinned from the joy of just seeing them all. "Really, I was just sharing a note or two with—"

Carlton flagged his hand to intervene. "There's no need to explain," he spoke up first to my rescue. "We missed the performance."

"Aaaaaaaw," the group said in unison. One snicker after the other turned into a rupture of laughter.

"*Umph, what a shame*," Carlton shook his head. "We walked up as you were opening your eyes. When Devin said he didn't know you could sing, that was news to us."

Carla stepped forward and smiled. "*Is that really you, Faith?*" she said excitedly. "*You look great.*"

"It's me," I giggled with her, with an arm full of hugs. We were like sisters.

"I am so happy to see you, girl." She shook my upper arm.

"Hey, Faith," Jarvis shook my hand, "it's good seeing you again."

"Thank you. How have you been?"

"Doing well. Thanks to Him, the *Key* to all my situations."

"Amen to that," Devin agreed.

Then Jarvis said, realizing something, "You know that Camille is going to wish she had been here once she finds out that you and everyone else, coincidentally, met up in Atlanta, Georgia."

Finding truth to his statement, I couldn't agree with him more, "I think I would feel the same way if it were the reverse." There appeared to be so many of them standing in front of me until I didn't know whom to greet next. Instead, I said to the others, smiling, "Hello, everyone else."

They saw humor in my salutation. "Hello," they responded, including Devin jumping on the bandwagon. He always seems to find the humor in life.

Joy stepped forward. "Hi, Faith," she smiled and hugged me, too.

"*Little Angel,*" I remembered, from my conversations with Devin, a name that was fitting for a special girl who was so gifted. How could I forget? She had gotten a little taller since I had last seen her.

She said, "I would like to hear your song."

I looked down and gripped her chin, "If we have time, I'll share it with you."

"Great!"

Carla's offsprings: Jada, David, and Correy were just as elated.

Teddy's voice always stood above the crowd. His deep voice could not be missed, and I was glad to see him, too.

"We apologize for the wait," Jarvis glanced at his watch. "Shall we?"

"*I'm ready,*" the menfolk emphasized.

"Ladies," Carlton gestured with his hand.

Carla, Jada, Joy and I stepped down into the cozy dining area.

A waitress met us at the path. "Good morning, everyone."

"Good morning," we greeted her.

"Let's see if I can get you all seated together." We followed her toward the back.

After we sat and looked over the menu, she took our orders.

Carla and I chitchatted. We had a lot of catching up to do.

Later, during our meal, Jarvis stood, making sure he could see us all. "As you are all aware, Devin and Teddy have a performance this evening and you are invited to attend. The facility where it will be held has extended their invitation to you. We are welcome to bring visitors."

Carlton was hyped. "*This is the South…southern hospitality. What time does it start?*"

"At 5 o'clock sharp."

Carlton glanced at his watch.

Joy leaned forward. "Pops, I would love to be there with Cousin Ja, Mr. Devin, and Barry White."

Everyone came unglued, laughing, because Teddy's voice was just that deep. She looked at him, amazed, each time he spoke.

Carlton's head fell back to release what was tickling him. "*You're too much, Joy.*"

"*Does that mean we will be there?*" she asked for confirmation.

"Let's seeeeee," he paused. "That should be enough time but that doesn't leave us much room. After breakfast, we'll be on our way to the aquarium, and then come back to get ready. How does that sound?"

"*Sounds good,*" she smiled, bottled up with joy.

They glanced at me.

"Unfortunately, I will not be able to make it," I told them. "I have a busy day and a meeting to attend in the late afternoon."

"There will be another time, Faith," Devin said and smiled. That song was befitting because his heart seemed to always sing, reaching to touch someone. He patched the day. He could tell that I wanted to attend but knew, under the circumstances, that I had to take care of business first.

"That's all right, Faith, I'm taking you with me, anyway." Joy's comment turned heads.

Her sister and brothers stared, and so did everyone else at the table.

"*Uh-oh*," Jada buzzed.

"Joy, what do you mean?" Carlton asked confusingly. Obviously, he wasn't the only one.

"*You shall see.*"

Jarvis and Devin looked at each other.

Teddy looked like he was lost.

"Well," Jarvis said not surprised, "we *shall see*."

Wondering what she would say next, my eyes met hers.

"I'm taking you with me to the powder room, Faith." She entertained us very well with greater confusion.

This time, Jarvis and Devin chuckled, but no one understood why. She was an interesting little young lady.

"Oh, that's it," said Jada. "She has to be excused."

Smiling at the flower, I stood, "I would be happy to escort you, Joy."

"*Thank you, madam*," she said politely.

Eyes followed her until we were out of sight, and I certainly understood why.

Once we returned and sat back down at the table, I saw Devin reach in his pocket and pull out a piece of paper. "...I was dreaming on the plane and, surprisingly, remembered every word."

Apparently, we had missed some of what his topic of discussion was about. *Every word of what*, I wondered.

Everyone else was quiet and listened intensely. Jada, David, and Correy seemed to be on the edge of their seats.

"The name of this poem is 'Inspiration,' " he read.

He had my undivided attention and I was enthused to hear about such a vital and precious topic. Whatever he was about to read was worth listening to. I felt the listening ears of other customers within close range halt their own conversations. They were very still, straining to hear above the noise of eating utensils clanging against plates. When he finished, he folded the piece of paper and put it back in his pocket.

"You *dreamed that*?" asked Jada.

Devin tried to get a word in when David chimed in, "You *dreamed...that*?"

The fact that they repeated each other tickled everyone.

Joy gave her compliments, "That was a good dream. I like that."

Devin smiled as she beamed. "Do you, Joy?"

"Yes, that sticks to the ribs," she nodded her head.

Devin smoothly got Jarvis's attention by eye contact. I got the feeling they didn't know what to expect from her next.

"Joy, I understand," I told her, impressed by her intellectual ability, "that is something to remember, isn't it?" I knew what she meant in her own way.

"It sure is."

"You know, Mr. Devin," Correy stepped in, "that's a good motto, especially for my generation."

"For all generations," Carlton voiced strongly. "One never gets too old to inspire someone else or even to be reminded that they have a purpose, too."

"Although, I'm not—" Devin stopped talking.

All eyes were on him.

"What were you about to say, bruh?" Jarvis asked baffled.

Devin looked like he was either reliving something or he had forgotten what he was about to say. He finally said, "It wouldn't make sense, but I thought I would share that with everyone. Each of us care about life and we care about others. A day should never go by without wearing it as a stole. Reach out and touch someone."

Smiles could not be erased. We were moved by those few words.

My second thought was, *Change. Hmmm, life sure has a way with destiny, soloing change, unfamiliar tunes, strolling up the red carpet to take control.*

"Is that you talking, bruh?" Jarvis seemed impressed.

"The one and only."

Hmmm, I took notice, too, thinking, *is this Devin? I guess the knob is turning because time has a curfew. What time is it? I love the lyrics.*

"Mr. Devin," Joy tilted her head, "your brain sure has a lot of fat on it."

Carlton closed his eyes somehow drawn into meditation. Her comment sent a clash of ripple effects throughout the group.

Once again, Devin and Jarvis chuckled. I wondered why before, but now I knew.

Not too many phrases went past me. I was usually good about catching balls, but her statement froze in midair in my mind.

"Joy, are you hungry, dear?" Carla asked next, showing no emotion. It was a give-a-way that she was used to her unexpected crossword puzzles.

This time, Teddy joined them, amused. "This is almost as good as the *gorilla story.*"

"*WHAT!*" the course changed, as the word fumbled from our mouths, staring. Just the thought was appalling.

"Happy Thanksgiving," Jarvis joined Teddy, "because I'm glad I wasn't there to see it." Then they both laughed with teary eyes.

This conversation was on the loose. In fact, it was getting very intriguing, trying to make some sense between gorilla and Thanksgiving. From the expressions on our faces, we were strung-out on confusion and wasn't quite sure what to think.

Jarvis managed to say, "You know, Devin, Teddy has mentioned this on more than one occasion. Maybe you should relive it and tell everyone the story because *it's no secret now.*"

"Maybe I should," he agreed, "so he can hear it in its entirety. Well," he began drawing us into the mystery, "it happened in the state of Arizona..."

Listening from the beginning to end kept us rolling in tears. It was hard to catch a breath of air from all the peaks in his story. I grabbed a napkin from my purse and wiped my eyes, and so did Carla. Little Angel even had a difficult time getting a grip.

The timing was perfect when the waitresses walked up with plates in their hands.

By 2 o'clock, I left Publix with a vase full of cheerful flowers—pink, yellow, and lavender. Unlocking the car door, I smelled them, again. The fragrance reminded me of tranquility.

Up the street, off Lavista Road, I turned onto a driveway leading to Bentley Square. The sign couldn't be missed off the road. The driveway was long, curving to the parking lot. The senior living community set way back off the highway. It looked like it had been placed in a forest surrounded by a fortress of gigantic trees. Hardly, anything else surrounding it could be seen.

A breeze of cool air swooped around me as I opened the door to walk inside the off-white brick building trimmed in black. Candle scents greeted my entrance. The lobby was inviting and well designed. The high-backed Victorian chairs had curved wooden legs that matched perfectly with dusty-toned pictures, shadowing a homely imagination, framed in gold. The dark brown hardwood floor blended with the old-time setting that somehow reminded me of an actor, Victoria Bartley, on *Big Valley*. In my mind, I photographed what I saw as rich and royal.

As I strolled up the hall and turned to walk to the other end of the building, I passed by patients watching television, or just relaxing, passing the time away. Nurses were walking in and out of rooms working and tending to others. The inside was open and huge—clean and very well maintained. When I reached the last room, no one was there. It looked like a homely hospital room. Two beds had been neatly made-up, which were horizontal in front of a big window. I walked to the second one and thought, *Maybe she's in therapy*. I placed the vase on top of the bedside table.

A nurse stood in the doorway and confirmed, "She just went for therapy; she'll be back in about an hour."

"Thank you. I'll leave these flowers. They're for someone very special."

"Those are beautiful. I'll let her know you dropped them by," she smiled and walked away.

When I turned to leave, I couldn't help but notice a big beautiful plant on top of the chest next to the window. It had a tall stalk with a large pink flower at the tip. The flower had needle-end tips. The color was very soft with thin pencil marks, lined in light blue. It had wings of healthy-green foliage in an evergreen pot. As my eyes traveled to the long windowsill, I saw a few clowns softly painted blue and gray. They were lovely little eye-catching trinkets. Cards were lined on the sill adding more cheer to the little cove. I smiled at the colorful setting then slowly turned to leave for my meeting.

… this beat is steady rising…

CAST

Casts are chosen,
for selected roles,
operas and ballets,
movies and plays,
forms of theatrical presentations,
portraying as characters,
who are the actors?

Casts are like portraits,
developed or painted pictures,
each scene as a snapshot,
acting out their roles,
to be framed in gold.

Casts are colorful,
the roles they played,
a portrait,
masterpiece,
to be hanged,
remembering their debut,
cherished to salute.

… life is as roles, dancing to many colors.

Chapter 17

DEVIN

It was 2:30 p.m., and time was flying. While brushing my hair, I sang a few notes to brush-up on my skills. At the same time, my imagination kicked in with the sounds of drums, bass, lead guitar, saxophone, and piano. The rhythm that was pouring in was unstoppable.

As soon as I picked up my door-key from off the dresser and inserted it inside my pocket, the doorbell rang. When I opened it, Jarvis was standing there.

"Just wanted to let you know, bruh, we should be pulling out at 3 o'clock. We want to get on the road before the traffic gets thick."

"I'll be ready. You'll find me downstairs in the dining area."

"All right. I'll meet you there."

I shut the door and turned to make sure I had everything and left.

Walking through the bright lobby into the restaurant was as significant as blowing out a candle. It was similar to a revolving door, from sunlight to sundown. I sat at a table drawn into mystery. The spiral staircase toward the back of the restaurant caught my eye. *Why didn't I notice it before?* A warm smile surfaced. The obvious answer was *easy. That song Faith was singing surprised me.* Since I was her only audience, from my point-of-view, she was graceful and polished. Her style struck a match of creativity to my ears. A harmonious combination of elements rang in my head. A symphony orchestra would have been a perfect match. She had poise and sang with a swaying rhythm. *Hmmm, I would have never imagined that.* She laid her burdens all the way down, if she had any because, she was floating like a dove. Even though she caught me off guard, my heart pumped with the beat and jumped on the two-lane highway, going the same direction. I was feelin' that.

Snapping out of it, I refocused my attention and stared at the staircase again. Out of curiosity, I walked toward the back, looked upward and tried to see as much as I could. What I saw forced me to make a visit. "*Beautiful,*" I mumbled until I finally reached the top. I looked over the railing to see below. The upper level could not have been designed and laid out any better. It was paradise. The setting was for relaxation. There were extensions of the same furniture as downstairs but more plush. Islands of conversation pits circled around the entire floor with an attendant waiting to serve from behind a bar. The big screen television was the icing on the cake. Trapped in awe, I walked to the server at the bar and said, "I would like to get a cup of tea, if you have any."

"I can get that for you, sir," the waiter said. "Welcome to The Savoy Bar and Grill."

"Thank you." On second thought, I recanted my request and said grinning, "Not smooth tea, but the regular."

He chuckled, "I haven't heard of smooth tea, but we do have English Breakfast tea, and other flavors."

Although the English Breakfast tea sounded interesting, I was curious to know what else they had to offer. "What are some of the other flavors?"

"We have apple, cinnamon, lemon, mint, and peach flavor. You have a variety to choose from. Which would you like?"

After taking a few seconds to decide, I told him, "Lemon is good." Even though I wanted to try the English

Breakfast tea, I stuck with something I was more familiar with. "Right now, I don't need a dreamer. I have to perform this evening."

He softly laughed. "I can understand that." Puzzled, he asked, *"Aren't you, Devin Fairchild, the singer?"* I guess the word "perform" rang a bell.

"Yes," I nodded, "I am."

"I thought so. My eyes usually don't play tricks on me. You were on that series—" he snapped his finger trying to remember.

"Unforgettable," I helped him out.

"Yeah, that's it. I would say a year or more ago. That was some performance. You have some serious pipes."

"Thanks."

"You have to teach me a thing or two."

"If I was ordering smooth tea, I would have no problems," I joked. "But, I have to *at least* keep my mind from going into overdrive for the next couple of hours."

"What time is your performance?"

"At 5 o'clock."

"I see your point. What city?"

"Tucker."

His speed beefed up. "Let me get your tea so you can be on your way. You'll want to dodge the traffic."

"We certainly want to do that. Also, I'll take a few ice cubes on the side."

"Sure," he turned and vanished behind the doors. Not long after, he returned with my tea.

As I turned to go and sit in front of the television, I flipped my cell phone and called Jarvis. Since he didn't answer on the fourth ring, I ended the call. Before I could put it back in the holster, he called back. "This is Devin."

"You rang?"

"Sure did, man. Just wanted you to know that I'll be waiting in the restaurant on the second level."

"I didn't realize they had a restaurant on the second level."

"Neither did I. You have to see it to believe it. It's very nice."

"I have to check it out once I get below. See you shortly."

"All right."

The minutes were dwindling; I had fifteen more minutes left. I dropped a couple of ice cubes in the cup to cool down the piping hot solution. My thoughts were moments away from reliving a quick glimpse of the dream. It was so real. Since we had been in Atlanta, I hadn't thought much about it. I then set the cup down staring at the wavering fluid. Drifting, I couldn't help but wonder again, *What happened next?* I sure would have liked to have seen the outcome. Clearly, I could see Genesis laughing. Her sudden reaction shocked everyone, but eventually her blanket of cheer spread like wildfire. I never knew why we were asked to come other than to cheer her up. Sometimes, it was better not knowing. Just the fact that she came out of her shell and opened up was good enough. Emotionally, she had broken down on the side of the road. Uncle Madison would always say, as I could clearly envision his face, "Devin, my nephew, there is no street without a roadmap. Take the road that will get you to your next stop." Never really knew what he meant until later in life. As a young boy, he always inspired me to move forward, and somehow, I felt that Genesis was on the road to recovery—moving forward. Maybe, we were the catalyst to her next stop. From the way things were going, we were at the right place at the right time.

"Wow," Freddie the Teddy said observing, "this place is back off in the woods."

Looking out the window, Jarvis replied, "Sure is. It's secluded and quiet. It's amazing how you can drive right off the street into another world. I've been in Atlanta before, but it amazes me each visit. I wonder what cove I will wind up in next."

I was captured. "Look at all these trees surrounding this place," I thought out loud. "This is a beautiful city. I never would have pictured this. What a nice setting." The property was so large that it was big enough to include a miniature park on the premises.

Jarvis parked the black SUV. "We're here, gentlemen." He folded the map and put it on the dash.

"At last," I said.

He glanced at the clock. "Good timing. It's 4:30 p.m., *in ATL*." His humor was timely.

Unexpectedly, I saw an unusual site. "Man," I paused staring at a distance, "*look at that*." There's never been a time I could remember ever seeing a deer in real life.

"Where?" both Jarvis and Freddie asked.

"Straight ahead," they followed my gaze, "the big fella over there. *Rudolph*." I wondered if the zoo was nearby.

"Rudolph?" Jarvis mumbled, as they scanned the area for this person. The deer was so still, I guess they thought it was fake. They kept looking. "Who's Rudolph?"

"Right there in front of you. *Rudolph, the reindeer*."

Suddenly, it took off running like lightening. The deer startled them.

They chuckled.

"Ooh," Jarvis said, "*that Rudolph*."

My neck snapped to the left when I heard a crackle on the other side of the vehicle. "*What was that?*"

Their heads shifted in the same direction.

"Yeah," Freddie wondered, "what *was* that noise? I know I didn't imagine that. I heard it, too."

We heard it again when two squirrels shot up a tree.

Jarvis coolly laughed. "Those were dry leaves you heard crackle. The squirrels are having a ball around here."

Chuckling to myself, I said, "I need a camera."

Jarvis opened his door. "Right now, the snapshot I'm most interested in is finding out who has requested our presence."

"I know that's right," Freddie nodded.

Opening my door, I felt an urgency to know as well. "With a serious flash of the eye because my curiosity is burning, brutha. Let's get it over with. This has to be well worth framing."

Jarvis glanced at his watch. "I hope Carlton makes it on time. They fell a little behind schedule."

We got out of the vehicle.

Looking toward the street for signs of their arrival, I said, "They still have time, but not much. Knowing your uncle, they'll make it." I reached for my jacket and put it on.

Realizing how true that statement may be, he replied, "I'm sure he will. He's been to Atlanta many times before and knows this place well." Releasing that thought, he shut his door and so did we.

Soon after we begun to walk is when we noticed a black limousine driving up.

"That may be them," Jarvis said, getting another glimpse of the vehicle. "Although, it could very well be someone else coming besides our party." He wasn't for sure since the windows were tinted.

Someone waved out the window.

"Speaking of good timing," Freddie slightly smiled, "they caught us just in time."

The chauffeur stopped in front of the walkway and opened the back door. They all piled out, hurriedly, and we walked inside the facility to get the program rolling.

It was 4:50 by the time we were escorted to where the setup was. The place was larger than I thought. We were standing in a huge open-space area with partial light-grain hardwood flooring, surrounded by a sea of beige carpet. It was a bright and friendly atmosphere. Patients sat at tables lined with chairs around the platform. In the meantime, others sat on couches watching television. Nurses were at work getting ready to serve them dinner. I guess we were the treat.

Freddie and I glanced at each other. I had no problems singing to the crowd, but I had pictured a closed audience.

He nudged me. "Not a bad place. This facility is nice." Freddie analyzed the piano that he was about to explore at any moment. It was an older model that looked like it had miles left to sound off some more tunes. The dark-brown baby grand was set nicely in the middle of the floor.

We briefly took a moment to consider adjusting our routine since things were a little different.

After talking with a staff member who was in charge, Jarvis walked back to where we stood.

Standing beside the piano looking straight ahead, I whispered to him, "Did I miss something?" My lips barely moved.

He tapped the microphone. A thud came through loud and clear. The volume was just right. "Apparently, plans have changed again." Keeping a straight face, he played right along with me. Jarvis wasn't a bad actor himself.

"Did you ever find out who the mystery person was yet?"

"They wanted it to remain anonymous," he responded, lowly.

Making sure I heard him correctly, I asked, "Did you say anonymous?" This time I gazed at him.

"Yes," he smiled, "anonymous."

My eyes froze, trying to size it all up. *Who could that be?* Discreetly, my radar eyes were on the beat.

Freddie was in his own world, ready to go on display. He was humming something I couldn't quite make out. We were already in place waiting for the very moment to begin somewhat of a different journey.

Jarvis gave us the cue at 4:59 p.m. to begin.

I reached for the microphone to hold it in my hand for comfort. Turning toward Freddie, I introduced him, and then myself. I forgot all about who had summoned us here. My mind was on another plateau.

We were well received by the staff, patients, and visitors. Spotlights were not needed; there were plenty of eyes beaming on us that sparkled like starlights coming from every direction. We couldn't be missed. We were centerpieces, isolated in the center of the floor, formally dressed in chocolate-brown suits with all the matching accessories.

Jarvis slowly walked away and stood where Carlton and his family were. They were sitting in a row of chairs lined along the wall.

I slowly closed my eyes riding up an elevator of seclusion. Until it was time for the doors to open to make my grand entrance, I swayed as Freddie's fingers jaywalked along the keyboard. As I reopened my eyes, the elevator stopped and so did everything else. The microphone almost slipped out of my hand. Muscles in my face felt like they had flip-flopped. *Whaaaaaat, this can't be*, those words thundered inside my skull. Standing near Jarvis, was the same man I saw in Los Angeles at the restaurant—the ghost I was hunting down at LAX. And, I saw him again last night here in Atlanta at the airport getting into a vehicle. Then, *that lady* reappeared. *What is going on?* She was with him last night, too. It didn't stop there. The mystery guy joined her, walking alongside a nurse who was pushing someone so familiar that my mouth slid open.

By this time, Freddie grunted, trying to get my attention, but I couldn't move. He had to take another trip around the world to play his introduction again.

The lady in the wheelchair was smiling. To my disbelief, I mumbled, "*Ms. PeggyAnn.*"

My adrenaline increasingly shot up and I couldn't do anything but laugh, merrily. My expression had flipped sunny-side up.

The crowd of people laughed, as they looked in the same direction. Eyes shifted back and forth. By now, they probably had caught on from the shock on my face.

"*Umph, umph, umph,*" I heard myself say, quietly. She turned out to be the treat after all. This scene was developed in my mind and made a nice portrait to be framed in gold. It was a masterpiece.

The man and woman stood on both sides of her, but, *who were they?* One surprise after the other made me wonder, *Is this the cast, and if so, who are the actors?* How could that be—*IMPOSSIBLE.*

… this beat changed its rhythm,
EKG'n mysteriously…

ACTION

Action requires an act,
something done,
performed,
a deed,
an accomplishment,
a momentum to feed.

Roles to take action,
sets the tone,
loaded with attractions,
a world of its own,
an energy,
freed,
a regulated dial,
controlling its temperature,
actions that growl.

Events are orchestrated by many rhythms,
fast,
medium,
or,
slow,
a timing that flows,
what tunes of life brings,
unmasked,
as our actions sing.

… making the final cut.

Chapter 18

JARVIS

This was getting better and better. A chip of Devin's anticipation had rolled on me, and I would have given *just about* anything to witness this. The lady in the wheelchair, who was dressed in a soft pink suit and wore a fashionable hairdo, had to be Ms. PeggyAnn. Her motherly smile glowed from the cove of a warm heart. Expression and description of her was the clue, but I wasn't 100 percent sure. As a small-framed lady, she flourished in her spirit through youthful, kind, and caring warm eyes. It wasn't hard for me to figure out that her character was one to be admired. As she was wheeled in, I immediately saw the beauty of her life engraved in her countenance. She reminded me of a fluorescent light so bright that she couldn't be missed. Even though she was a senior citizen, sunshine still shined all around her—her entrance spoke volumes. She couldn't hide if she wanted to. No matter her age, she still had style and class, and her banner of rainbows sparkled. Whatever her setback was, from what I saw, interruptions in life did not change the beauty of who she is. Without knowing her personally, from Devin's brief description, he transcribed her perfectly. She appeared to be just that, a very special lady who possessed all those qualities. I smiled at the precious package. Without a doubt in my mind, she still had a chest full of treasures to share. Something about her made me even more eager to meet her.

One of the nurses came by. She stopped when she noticed I was standing. "Would you like a chair, sir?" she asked with a pleasant smile.

"Sure, I would like that."

She went into the next room behind her and brought out another chair. "Make yourself at home." She placed it next to uncle.

"Thank you," I smiled.

"Is there anything else I can get for you?"

"I'm fine. Thanks for asking."

"You're welcome."

Teddy kept playing the piano even though he had been startled with laughter, too.

Devin faced him and said a few words. I had guessed that he probably was ready to set sail now.

Teddy was good; he never did miss a beat. His fingers flowed as if nothing ever happened.

The onlookers were very quiet.

Uncle kept his eyes focused on Devin and Teddy, as he whispered, "This is something. Who is that lady in the wheelchair?"

Hard not to smile, I grinned and replied, "If I'm not mistaken, I think she's Ms. PeggyAnn."

A few seconds later, I noticed his eyebrows joining with question marks. "Could she possibly be the one who—" The bulb in his mind was flickering.

Quickly, I answered, leaning over for privacy, "Yes. I'm almost positive." I thought that would be his next question.

Glancing at the others, they were still as statues, looking straight ahead. Nothing could have broken their trance. And, as much as Correy, David, Jada and Joy loved watching Devin and Teddy perform, those two would always have an audience, even on a rainy day.

I was captivated in more ways than one. The sudden incline of Teddy's fingers crawling up the keys during his *final* grand introduction got my undivided attention. He played so magically but dramatically spiced. Even though Devin had not begun to sing, the heat in his beat alone were spoken words, and we all felt it. Then, Teddy played softly, gliding back down the scale. The stride in his rhythm was so catching that I could hear some of the audience drawing in their breath. *Better put*, a musical form of hypnosis and hypertension on the down low. His style, as usual, always came in big packages, a deliverance so unique and impeccable. When I gazed at him, he was absorbed in his masterpiece. I had heard him play on other occasions but, this was *the cruise* of all the cruises they sailed.

Concluding his melodrama, he paused, hitting one note. It became very quiet. If anyone could hear anything at this very moment, it would be Timex.

My eyes shifted to Devin.

He held the microphone with both hands. From his grip, I knew his first note would be a hook hanger. He held a long note stretching one arm.

Teddy starts slowly playing again, as both join roles, rolling up the anchor. They were creative, carrying us for the ride along with them. Like passengers on a cruise ship, we sailed away on course. They were exceptional.

After forty-five minutes of listening to one dynamic song after the other, they smoothly dropped the anchor of our course but at some other dock. Being tuned in, to the network of listeners, their mastery was a joyride, and it was addictive. They enjoyed injecting their audience with the miracle drug, a gift driven by the engine of the Man Upstairs.

Everyone clapped at the end of their performance.

Teddy stood and bowed with Devin.

All the visitors rose to their feet, too.

As I looked from left to right, Carlton leaned sideways toward me. "I believe Mr. Fairchild is trying to get your attention." He tilted his head in Devin's direction.

Devin glanced at me, then, at the lady in the wheelchair. His eyes rotated back toward me, giving me the signal.

I whispered to Carlton, "I'll be back."

"Take your time," he said. "We'll wait here. I'm enjoying this." He glanced at his watch. "We're in no hurry."

I walked toward the lady in the wheelchair and whispered to the nurse behind her, "Mr. Fairchild would like for her to join him." Smiling, I glanced at the lady who then looked up at me. Her eyes were humbling and glassy, set off by emotions. "May I have the honor of escorting her?"

The nurse unlocked the wheels. "*Sure*," she stepped aside. "What is your name, sir?"

I put my hands on both bars. "Brooks."

"Ms. Malone," the nurse got her attention, "Mr. Brooks is going to push you to where Mr. Fairchild is standing. Is that all right?" The nurse slightly bent over to get her approval first.

"That would be fine," she smiled.

Her response sealed my suspicion even more. There couldn't have been another Malone that fit her profile. Her voice was gentle as dew. Yet, hard to believe, the question rang in my head, *Is this really PeggyAnn?* The thought of standing this close to someone who held so much history was a rarity.

The other two, who were accompanying her, nodded with smiles that they had no objections. They were friendly, without any words spoken. I assumed they were family members, and if not, they were people who, definitely, were very close to her.

Slowly, I pushed her forward in front of Devin and Teddy and locked the wheelchair in place.

"Ms. PeggyAnn," Devin stretched out his arms, smiling, still surprised, "I can't believe it's you."

Teddy's eyes met mine. Confirmed, we were amazed, admiring this lady of many conversations. Seeing her in person was an honor.

"*Well, for heaven's sake, I can't believe it's you either!*" she said, as her eyes enlarged behind her sparkling glasses.

From her statement, I saw question marks forming on Devin's forehead and I wasn't far behind. *How could that be if she requested him? If it wasn't her, then, who could it be?*

Next, she said, "I'm so happy to see you again." She patted the back of his hand twice.

"I'm glad to see you, too," he kissed her on the cheek. "Excuse me a moment." He leaned toward me to say something.

I smiled at his request seeing that he still had ten minutes left to go. It was his choice since they had finished earlier than scheduled; they planned it that way. "Let me get a confirmation," I told him. "I'll be right back." With urgency, I walked across the floor and whispered to Carlton and Carla.

They smiled and approved by nodding.

Looking at Devin, I nodded yes.

Teddy sat at the piano, again, ready to sail on another journey.

Devin held the microphone. "I would like Little Angel to join me."

Eyes were zooming in on her as she stood up.

Surprised, she grinned, and so did Jada and her brothers. When she made it to the platform, the soles of her shoes tapped in rhythm and echoed against bear silence. The curls of her two ponytails bounced rhythmically. She was dressed in pink.

Devin bent forward, smiling, to say something to her in confidence as they turned to face Ms. PeggyAnn. They exchanged words seeming to be drawn into conversation like magnets.

A sudden glow shadowed Joy's face prompting her to whisper to Devin, again, in privacy.

He stepped aside to say a few words to Teddy and let her go for it.

Not only intriguing for everyone else, but I was waiting in suspense sitting on the edge of my seat. Uncle and his family had to wonder what role she would play since they had not rehearsed. This became so interesting that the pulse of anticipation swelled.

Carlton whispered, "I wonder what her part will be in all this?" He gazed at Carla who wondered, herself.

Slightly shrugging, I answered, "Uncle, I'm even in the dark on this one. It remains to be seen." Whatever they came up with, would be worth seeing. Somehow, I had a feeling they were about to feed us into their momentum.

That's just what happened after Joy unfolded a sheet of paper she had in her hand. It dawned on me that she had been holding on to that piece of paper ever since they arrived. She glanced at it for a second, and then gave it to Devin.

When he looked at it, soon after, his expression gave away that he had set eyes on something very familiar. His head slightly fell back, chuckling, as he laid it on the piano.

Teddy never moved. His eyes were steady on Joy. She was the target that would drive his next melody sending him spiraling up and down the ladder of keynotes. Nothing seemed to be too significant for him to handle.

"Hmmm," I mumbled to Carlton, "they have an interesting thing going on there." My eyes were glued on them. I didn't want to miss anything. Taking my eyes off them would have been risky. Whatever the plan was, could spark at any moment, and it looked as though the ball was in Joy's court.

Uncle leaned forward, clutching his hands together. "Apparently, whatever she's about to sing, it's no mystery to Mr. Fairchild."

Agreeing, I replied, "It appears that way." It felt as though we were on a roller coaster, stuck at the top of the tracks, waiting for, at anytime, an adrenaline rush to pump through our veins.

Joy's sparkling eyes strayed and fastened in midair, as if she had seen the most beautiful rainbow glistening above. Whatever was on that piece of paper had been transcribed in her photographic memory. Her smile said a thousand words. Slowly, her eyes fell on Ms. PeggyAnn.

Devin smiled at the pair, yet seemed to be in his own world.

Joy held the mic in position, and without music, she began to sing like a bird. She dipped from left to right, swaying, to a beat that reminded me of Walt Disney. The lyric was so moving…it stole my heart. It was so unusual until I really couldn't place it in any one specified category. The characteristics of that song carried weight—a sweet blend of inspiration and a canary fits this unique dual. The combo was striking. As soul stirring as it was, *how could anyone not latch on to every word?* She could have gone on and on, as far as I was concerned.

After a couple minutes of listening to her sing, Devin joined her. His expertise fit in anywhere. He had a show floor of his own, standing in position with his arms spreading like fans, harmonizing with the little one.

Even I started mumbling the words along with everyone else. Voices were humming like bees throughout the building following her lead, and some were swaying along with her. I guess all they needed were a pair of ice-skates.

"Looks like you're enjoying yourself, nephew."

"Big man, this is contagious."

He laughed discreetly and said, "*I see. You're not the only one. Take a look at my family.*"

We both leaned forward to capture a snapshot. They were photogenic, just as carried away as everyone else once they had gotten past being mesmerized.

And Teddy surprised me with a different spice of melody. The music was fitting, filling in where a harp would thumb its strings of glory. I envisioned violins on the stretch, orchestrating their blend of music too. Enjoying the onset, they were a dynamic trio.

Everyone clapped, and those who were able to stand, stood in an uproar.

Joy raised the mic. "Thank you." She turned and widely grinned at Devin and Teddy, who formally bowed. They looked as though they were honored to be a part of what burned within her. Then she turned toward Ms. PeggyAnn and slightly bowed, beaming with radiance. It was a chain reaction.

Overjoyed, Ms. PeggyAnn stretched out her arms and embraced her. She patted her on the back. Her joy, too, spilled over.

Joy has found herself a special friend, I thought. I'm sure the feeling was mutual.

"*What a performance*," I heard Uncle Carlton say.

"Outstanding!" were my exact words.

"I'm glad we came. Honestly, I can't think of any other place I'd rather be at this very moment." He shook his head in amazement, relishing the moment.

Shaking my head just the same, I replied "Neither can I." I had not expected this. All the riches in the world could not have paid a price for such a special occasion.

The applauding ceased when Devin began to speak, "In conclusion, I would like to say thank you. We hope you enjoyed the program during the last hour—" he paused, raising his wrist to glance at his watch. His eyes enlarged when he changed lanes and turned into a comedian, "*The last hour and five minutes over. Maybe we should pass around a collection plate since we've held you this long.*"

The audience laughed.

He chuckled. "Again, thank you, and good night."

Carla smiled. "Thank you for the invitation, Jarvis. This program was great." She glanced at the rest of her family who were supporting the three with another round of applause.

"My pleasure. I have to thank the one in charge here for allowing us to invite whomever we wanted."

Carlton said, "I'd like to join you when you do."

"Sure. You'll have the opportunity when I meet with them before leaving."

"Splendid!"

The handclaps ceased.

"Well, the program is over," I nodded to where the action was.

"Shall we join them?"

Jada and the others huddled around us as she chimed in, "That's not a bad idea."

Carlton stretched out his arms for them to follow my lead. Before we reached them, a swarm of people had already surrounded them.

Ms. PeggyAnn was occupied. A nurse wheeled her away.

During the perfect opportunity, Carlton put his arms around Joy with a bear hug and so did Carla.

She giggled.

"Joy, I have to ask," Carlton said. "Where did you get that song? *I've never heard you sing that before.*" A crease formed in the center of his forehead, looking down at her with wonder.

The rest of his family joined in with the same question.

She glanced at Devin. "It was *Faith.*"

Puzzled even more, he then said, "Excuse me?"

"*It was Faith,*" she repeated.

Now, we both were confused. No one could quite get a grip on her response, which came as no surprise to me. She was a natural but unique in her own innocent way.

"I think I can answer that question," Devin grinned.

Our heads shifted in his direction.

"Remember when you all met up with Faith and me at the restaurant this morning?"

"*Oh, Faith,*" we chorused. The joke was on us.

Joy laughed as if she were watching a cartoon.

"Yes," Devin chuckled, getting a kick out of hearing us chime like glee club members. "That was the song she sang."

"Ooooooo," Correy and David teased, sounding like owls, "I like *that one*."

"*That's what she was singing?*" I stared at Devin.

"Yep," he answered.

Impressed, I voiced, "*She's good*, bruh."

Carla smiled at Joy. "You brought Faith with you," she understood now.

She nodded. "Yes, I did."

Carlton put his hand on Joy's shoulder. "*Soooo*," the light came on, "*that's what you meant* when we were sitting at the table. Well, I'm glad you did…you were *great*." Then another thought hit him, "When did you have time to get with her and learn the song?"

"When she went with me to the ladies' room, I asked if she would sing that song she sang to Mr. Devin. When she finished," she giggled, again, "I auditioned for her, and she threw up two hands and gave me this sheet of paper." Joy held it up in her hand.

"I'm sure you entertained her well," Carlton smiled.

"I asked if I could sing it someday, and she said 'yes.'"

Carla glistened. "I have to thank her."

Minutes later, our attention was diverted by a soft voice. "Here's the little lady," Ms. PeggyAnn said, upon her return, extending her arms.

Joy met her at the path, shining like a light. "Ms. PeggyAnn, this is my family."

Uncle spoke up first and shook her hand. The others followed suit.

"And I know who this is," she looked up at Devin and added, "*OH MY, you have some voice*." Her eyes stretched with disbelief.

"Thank you."

"*Is this the same person I met in Phoenix?*" We were entertained by her sense of humor, as she scanned him from behind the microscope of her glasses. "*That was remarkable. I really enjoyed you.*"

"*Well, for heaven's sake,*" Devin responded, impersonating her.

She laughed and so did we. Her eyes were watery. She was holding her stomach with a handkerchief held to her mouth. Leave it to Devin, he could always shatter the ice.

"Ooooh, Lord," was all she could say. Each time she tried to speak and look at him, she went right back into orbit. "Umph, umph, umph. You certainly have a sense of humor."

"Sometimes, I can get a little happy," he told her, warning her a little too late.

She wiped her eyes and cleared her throat. "That's all right. They say that laughter is good for the soul."

"Yes, it is," Devin smiled, then said, "*What a surprise it is to be standing here talking to you, again.*"

She regained her composure. "I must say it is. We didn't have a chance to say very much earlier, but I'm having a hard time believing it's really you. For some reason, you look taller than before."

Smiling at the humble lady, he replied, "It's me…in the flesh."

"I'm glad our paths have met again."

"So am I. *You look great.*"

"You think so?" His compliment seemed to have grabbed her by surprise.

"Yes," the entire gang said, admiring this lady.

She chuckled. "Well, thank you."

"*Oh,*" he suddenly realized something, "I don't think you've officially met Jarvis and Teddy."

"No, we haven't. I remember the gentleman there," she glanced at Jarvis. "He pushed me up here during the program, but we haven't officially met."

They stepped forward and introduced themselves.

Her eyes fastened on Teddy. "Where did you learn to play like that, young man?" she shook her head, giving him ribbons to treasure.

He summed it up in one sentence, "The prayers went up and the blessings came down."

All heads slammed on brakes and stared at him.

Ms. PeggyAnn sat forward in her wheelchair and smiled. Obviously, what he said was no myth to her.

"*I'm feelin' that,*" Devin said. "Take us to *church, my brother.*" He spoke like he had just jumped up off the AMEN bench.

I put some words on the plate, too, "That's all right. Your gift came in a large package, my brutha. You have the magic touch and a lot to give. Your music will bring sunshine, even where the moon sets high and the earth sits low."

"Reach out and *touch someone,*" Devin added.

"I remember that poem," Teddy's fist tapped his. "How can I forget?"

Correy imitated Teddy by scrolling his fingers in the air and said, "You've already inspired me, Teddy. It's in action."

Teddy was surprised and so was I.

Devin chuckled. "It can be contagious."

"And, I'm jumping on board!" said Jada, as a bell seemed to be ringing inside David's head when his expression changed.

"Keep your hands open, maestro," Ms. PeggyAnn said, sharing a few words of advice. "When it rains, it pours. The palms of your hands are like suction cups; they are magnets. From what I've heard, your blessings dropped in puddles."

Teddy was intrigued. "In puddles?" It appeared hard for him not to smile.

"Yes," she confirmed and further said with clarity, "your gift came in an array of colors. You have the ability to inspire beyond measure."

"You certainly do," Carlton gave him a ribbon, too.

Carla nodded, agreeing.

"I'm trying to collect as many drops as I can," Teddy let her know, hanging his bows on the wall of his brain.

"Let it absorb, bruh," was my advice. "We'll see the rainbow."

"*That*, I will," he assured us.

With wonder in Devin's voice, he then said, "Although that I'm just as surprised to see you here, Ms. PeggyAnn, you're a long ways from Arizona. Can you believe we're chatting, again, in a different state?"

"One can never tell what tomorrow will bring."

"No, we can't. I can attest to that," he smiled, probably thinking back on the road of his yesterdays.

Her comment hit home. I had to smile at that myself remembering everything that had happened over the past two years. The attic where I stored my memories never got old. We were up to bat against a crisis numerous times but only made it to first, second, or third base. Eventually, we made a home run to recovery. Unemployment never sounded good because we made a comeback in a way that was beyond my imagination.

Devin then asked her, "Are you here to stay?" That was a question a few of us were interested in knowing. Seeing her in the wheelchair, he probably thought as I did, that it might not have been by choice.

She rubbed her hand across her knee. "Well, this leg gave out on me." There was disappointment in her voice. She shook her head seeming to not understand why her life had been suddenly disrupted. "It had to be operated on. I fell and broke it, but those things happen. I'm thankful because it could have been worse." It was elevated with a pillow underneath.

He said with sympathy, "I'm sorry to hear that."

"So are we," voices joined in, with concern.

"It will take time to heal, but I'm coming along." Under the circumstances, she was in good spirits.

"*Good*," Devin emphasized, "I'm glad to hear that."

Directing her attention toward me, she then asked, "Do you sing, too?" She was curious what my role was.

"No, madam," I chuckled, "I'm just the guy behind the curtains."

"Jarvis coordinated this event tonight," Devin informed her. "He's great, doing what he does best."

We glanced at Joy. In deep thought, she looked like she had traveled many miles away. The look on her face made my mind reel backwards, tracing that same look, soon, to drop bombs. Expressions on faces crashed, when she stepped in to say, "The pot is still hot."

The plate stopped right there.

The silence of the conversation was pierced with laughter and humming of others in the background.

Smiling, clutching Joy's hand, Ms. PeggyAnn was impressed with the little one. "Oh, my," she then turned her head as she tried to look over her shoulder. Because of her disability, Devin turned her wheelchair around.

"Thank you," she said, as she managed to get her visitors' attention to join us when they were free.

When Devin saw them, his eyes slanted in my direction to get my attention.

"I wish Faith could have been here; she loves gospel music," she thought out loud, diverting my attention, as if she was in a room all alone.

The others looked baffled.

Could she be referring to the same Faith we know? Hmmm, maybe not, was my thought. I let it rest, focusing on the lady and man who would soon join us.

Devin turned Ms. PeggyAnn's wheelchair back around to face us.

Jada and her brothers stepped forward with an interest to talk with her while they had the opportunity.

Joy approached her parents to give her other siblings some time with Ms. PeggyAnn. She gave the sheet of paper to Carla that she had been holding on to for hours, to protect and serve, I guess until the next time, or until she got home to put it in a special place.

Devin made his way to where I stood. I felt a nudge.

"Everything all right, bruh?" I asked him.

He sighed, lowly. "*Maaaaaan,*" he whispered, from the side of his mouth, "*that's the ghost I chased the other day in Los Angeles.*"

He threw me off. Forgetting what was going on, my head slid in his direction to get a glimpse of him. The whites of his eyeballs stood out more so than the pupils. I wanted to laugh badly, but couldn't, as I watched his eyes rotating on his targets.

Not to be rude, we politely stepped aside, for a moment, from the others.

"And, she's the one that was with him at the airport last night, as I watched them being briskly driven away. But, I've seen her before, *too. How bazaar is that?* This is like one of those nursery rhymes. There's something about them but, I can't put a finger on it."

"Maybe before the night is over, you'll remember." Before getting his mind off of any ghost, I said what zoomed across my mind, "*Did you pay your bills this month?*"

"*Huh?*" I heard him mumble under his breath. Shifting the conversation threw him for a loop.

"The only Casper that I know of, that makes people run is, a *bill collector.*"

He took a deep breath to keep from going into hysterics. After I realized how that sounded, I wasn't far behind. He mildly shook his head as we smoothly stepped back into the circle.

The timing was perfect. Ms. PeggyAnn's visitors were approaching.

"One last thing," Devin whispered.

"Um hm."

"When Ms. PeggyAnn mentioned the name 'Faith,' for a minute, she had me wondering."

"I know what you mean. So was I."

"But I doubt it," he dropped the subject.

The same ones, who were standing next to Ms. PeggyAnn when the program started, politely nodded and smiled. The elderly man and woman were dressed in navy blue suits, polished from head-to-toe. Their style was rich, and the gray in their hair was crisp, loaded with wealth. They appeared to have seen many days of success. From what Devin had told me, I was curious to know who they were.

"These have been my friends for many years," Ms. PeggyAnn said before she introduced them. When she said their names, the expression on Devin's face changed. He stared as if he heard a foghorn.

… this beat was dynamic and stunningly orchestrated…

ANTIQUE

Antiques are known for their beauty,
rarity,
quality,
a worthy keepsake.

Life consists of beautiful people,
glazed with gold,
a diamond heart,
surged as steeples,
polished in knowledge,
monumental in spirit,
a treasure of wealth.

An antique bleeds its beauty,
a special package,
folded with expensive baggage,
change opens as a flower,
into a glistening tower,
bleeding someone's history,
beautifully wrapped with victory,
when it unfolds,
with special bows.

… there is no measure for this treasure.

Chapter 19

DEVIN

I couldn't believe when Ms. PeggyAnn said her friends' names were Joshua and Josephine. *What a coincidence*, I stared.

"They're originally from my hometown," she continued, "Seminole County, Oklahoma."

I quickly shut the door of my mouth when I realized it had gaped even wider. *How could that be?* I thought, hearing the drumbeat of something mysterious echoing inside my head. I don't know which drummer was beating the fastest, my heart or my thoughts. Now, I was really confused.

The night did not end its chapter without another audience. Obviously, Jarvis and the others noticed the expression on my face. Eyes were shifting for answers wondering what could've been so baffling. *If they only knew.*

Handshakes were exchanged, as each person randomly rattled their names.

Being last, a throbbing question finally leaped from the tip of my brain, "Ms. PeggyAnn, since you weren't the one who requested my presence here, I wonder who did?"

Joshua admitted, "It was us who requested that you come here to sing for PeggyAnn."

"Yes, we're the ones who anonymously requested you. It was a surprise," Josephine said with honor.

Ms. PeggyAnn smiled, seeming to not know really what to say at the time.

"Umph," I couldn't seem to stop grinning seeing that some things were beginning to formulate from a trail of missing pieces. The most important piece of the puzzle was like trying to find a needle in a haystack. "You both *staged this*?" I had to ask for a second confirmation since this was an unusual request.

"Yes," answered Joshua, "with a lot of help. We can't do like we use to; we're up in age but still young at heart. These gray hairs are not here for nothing. We pulled it off with experience. PeggyAnn talked about meeting you in Arizona at an ice cream parlor some months ago. You were on a gospel tour at that time."

"Yes, I was," I confirmed.

"She expressed her desire to hear you sing, but she probably never thought it would be in real life."

Ms. PeggyAnn slightly chuckled. "No, I didn't. *What a surprise.*"

"Josephine and I wanted to make that happen, thanks to the one in charge here who helped to arrange it on our end. And, thanks to your manager, Mr. Brooks."

Jarvis cleared his throat. "You're welcome. It was my pleasure."

"We're delighted that we had the opportunity to be a part of this affair. You were superb," Josephine complimented.

"Thank you, ma'am," I nodded.

"And, the pianist," she then looked at Freddie, "we didn't expect this much orchestration. *Thank you*, I'm glad you came. You were captivating."

Freddie smoothly nodded to acknowledge her thanks with a smile.

"The young lady…I believe you called her 'Little Angel.' " Josephine shook her head numerous times admiring her.

"Yes," I said.

Joy was smiling at the lady who couldn't seem to believe that she sang the way she did.

Josephine placed her hand on the side of her face. "You are quite a young little lady. *I'm impressed.* You brought back memories. I loved every bit of it, Little Angel."

"Thank you," Joy's eyes shined. She charmed them with her character, an extraordinary girl, who was a pocketful of joy.

The next morning, Atlanta glistened with the sunshine of a new day. Gazing out the window, nature's salutation was rejuvenating. The sun made all the difference in the world, even when I was deprived of sleep. The rays were potent with all the necessary ingredients to help revive the mind, body, and soul.

Impressed by the character of this room, the atmosphere was a nice get-a-way. I was surrounded by a flavor of antique furniture and pictures with a coordination of floral arrangements on the fireplace and lamps to give that "*there's no place like home*" feel. Every piece of furniture shone like it had been freshly polished with Old English. On display, inside two antique etageres, were several books to choose from. This room, which is known as the living room, was setup for quiet time or to hold small gatherings like Sunday service. A piano sleeping in the far corner made the room complete. It looked like the same piano Freddie had played. If so, and after last night, I guess it needed to recuperate from the serious exercise. Freddie the Teddy had put some extra miles on it. As if in hibernation, it was resting until its next glory days of tunes to rang out from someone else's fingers hopping its strings.

Before our flight left for Los Angeles, I had to make a second trip to see Ms. PeggyAnn. She had so much wisdom and character. Reflecting on my conversation with her in

Arizona was interesting and, more so, educational. As a valuable antique with miles of history and knowledge, she possessed a treasure of wealth that money could not buy. Her heart sparkled like diamonds because she was precious, a lady who surged like a steeple. As special as she was, she was still glazing in gold just as I saw her last. The history of her life grew as a monument over time, and her spirit was just as monumental and never changed. Just as color adds beauty to nature, so does she, as I sat listening to her months ago bleed the beauty of her life. I considered her a special package with treasures of the past, which unfolded to be told from the basement of her mind. Those treasures were valuable, a story tagged with a price for keeps that would never leave the cellar of my heart. As I sat there, I thought of how her life opened like a flower. Over time through change, she had turned into a glistening tower. She did not have much growing up as many children have now in America, but as time passed, the wrappings of her victory unfolded to touch people with the special bows that she was blessed with from the Man Upstairs. I branded her like a plaque in my heart for keepsake.

Speaking of keepsake, I glanced at more of what gave this room character as I waited. It could leave a memorable impression on anyone's mind; it has a story of its own.

From around the corner, Ms. PeggyAnn was wheeled in. Her smile glowed just as the sunshine poured in. "Good morning," she said softly.

The nurse smiled, too, rolling her to a long antique table that was in the center of the floor. "Hello, Mr. Fairchild." She placed two mats on the tabletop with a saucer, cup, and spoon on top of each one.

I stood to walk toward them. "Good morning," I said. I looked down at Ms. PeggyAnn and handed her a gold box. "These are for you. I hope you like pink roses; they reminded me of you last night." As elegantly dressed in pink as she was yesterday, I would have been surprised if she didn't. Today, she wore a wine dress coordinated with gold jewelry. Even her nails were manicured, and her hair looked like it never touched a pillow last night. She didn't let any grass grow under her feet. Speaking of feet, they were colorful, as well. She had on a pair of wine fuzzy slippers matching from head-to-toe, which paraded her smooth, maple skin.

Her lips unlatched as her eyes widened with surprise. "Oh, for goodness sake, thank you so kindly." Apparently, I caught her off guard.

I chuckled. *"For goodness sake...you're welcome."* I enjoyed these moments; I had her down pat.

They laughed.

"It was my honor and pleasure," I further said.

She glimpsed at them. "Could you please put these in a vase for me?" she asked the nurse.

"Yes, I would love to," she smiled, reaching for them, and then glanced at me. "Did you come back to *sing* for us, Mr. Fairchild?" She softly laughed.

From the humor, all I could do for the moment was chuckle.

Leaving, she said, "You were great!"

Ms. PeggyAnn added, "Yes, he was."

"Thank you."

"Maybe, I should have asked first," Ms. PeggyAnn thought.

The nurse stopped.

"Devin, would you like some tea? Please join me," Ms. PeggyAnn's eyes pleaded.

Persuaded by her humbleness, I accepted the offer and sat next to her. It was time for another morning antidote, especially right before a good conversation.

"I'll be right back," said the nurse. She vanished into the hallway.

I sat back to relax. "This is a nice place, Ms. PeggyAnn. Quite different from what I would've expected." More and more jumped out at me the longer I stayed.

She nodded. "Yes, it is. I was surprised myself. The staff has been very nice."

"That's good."

"I am really enjoying the morning," she smiled, a little dazed. "Jessie and Ruth Young called and brightened my morning before a delightful breakfast. They are such good people, soon to be married 67-years and they thought of me. And now, you are here. I am so glad you were able to come back before catching your flight. We never know when we'll meet again."

"My trip would not have been complete if I hadn't spent some time with you alone to chat. I often think about our conversation in Arizona." That was the spark that took us back down memory lane to pick-up where we had left off.

After chatting a few minutes, the nurse returned with a small antique pitcher of hot water, a basket of teabags, and other side items. She left, and soon after, returned with the roses in a vase filled halfway with water and set it on top of the table.

"*Oh, thank you,*" Ms. PeggyAnn marveled, "*those are beautiful.*"

"And, so are you," my thought escaped. Certainly befitting for the person she was. She reminded me of my grandmother. Maybe that's why I was drawn to her.

"Oooh, you think so?" she said shyly, covering her mouth with a handkerchief that reminded me of a minister. They are prime suspects for carrying white flags.

Without a doubt, I nodded multiple times. "Yes, I do." Since she was on a cliffhanger, I then said, changing the subject, "I was very impressed by what your friends, Joshua and Josephine, did for you. Rarely do I see that."

Her eyes were getting glassy. "I did not expect that. They are such good friends. We have always kept in touch since growing up in Seminole County, Oklahoma." Her comment lit a match.

Beneath the bottom of the sea of my brain, it started bubbling. It was time for the settled particles of the deep to rise, which had been relaxed in a twilight sleep for the last couple of days. The conversation began to pour in the cup of my thoughts at half moon when I commented, "They are a nice couple and seem to work well together."

Before I could say anything else, she smoothly cut in to say, shaking her head, "Oh, no, no. They're not married."

I peeked at my cup of tea to see if steam was still rising. It was glowing like the moonlight. "Oh, I thought they were an item."

She was tickled. "They are a long ways from that."

My head tilted with curiosity.

She picked up her spoon. "They are brother and sister."

My eyes fastened on her. I couldn't believe my ears. So much for half moon—her comment just caused my cup to run over in my head with greater confusion.

She laid her spoon down. "Are you all right? You look spooked."

My eyes felt as though they had shifted a thousand times, as her voice faded. Staring down at my tea, my mind wondered into isolation, daydreaming, visualizing the two. Pieces of the dream floated from the surface of my crib, reliving reflections in my tea.

A hand touched my shoulder. "Devin, are you all right?" I heard Ms. PeggyAnn ask, again, in a motherly tone.

My name summoned me back into reality. Clearing my throat, I answered, "Yes, I'm all right."

Her concern had settled deep into her forehead. "You were in deep thought."

Playing it off, as if something amusing had occurred to me, I then said, "Didn't mean to be rude. This tea is *smooth as silk*, another dream tea, which I call smooth tea just like all the others."

Her eyes fluttered in bewilderment.

"Excuse me for drifting."

"That's quite all right," she smiled weakly.

I slightly grinned. "Back to the topic, they look so familiar." If I had mentioned anything about the dream, she would have probably thought I had escaped from some insanity ward.

"*And they should,*" her face lit up.

Even more baffled, my next question was, "Why is that?"

Now, she was confused. "*You don't know?*" She picked up her spoon, again, with her eyes steady on me. She was probably trying to read which page I was on.

Twisted, I had to surrender. "I can't say that I do. Are they musicians or in entertainment?" I rambled off the top of my head.

She nodded. "Yes, they are," she smiled.

My mouth almost dropped.

She stirred a little cream in her cup. "Well, I guess you wouldn't know about that. I'm talking as if they grew up in your generation. I forget sometimes."

"Don't feel bad, Ms. PeggyAnn. At some point, we all have senior moments."

We shared the moment of laughter.

"Isn't that the truth?" her eyes widened as verification. "In case you don't know, they were at one of your programs when you were in Arizona."

"*Is that right?*" my voice shot up.

"*Yes,* and according to Josephine, they were in the very first row."

Stung by that piece of information was vital. It had charged through my electrical system like lightening. I quickly remembered the two as their flashcards flickered before my eyes. "*That hat,*" I could visualize clearly. "That's it! *I knew I had seen them somewhere before.*"

"That hat has been around the world," Ms. PeggyAnn chuckled. "Wherever Joshua goes, that hat goes too. Even in their golden years, they follow talent and good music when they can. They're professionals."

I chuckled at the revelation of this news. "*They get around.*"

"Yes, they do. Not nearly as much as they used to, but they still get around, at times." Her eyelids swept upward. "*Oh my,*" she said with urgency, "*I almost forgot something.*" She turned her head and flagged down the same nurse who wheeled her in. She whispered to her whatever it was that stole her immediate attention.

The nurse gladly walked away with a glazed smile, as if honored to be of service.

"Excuse me, Devin. I needed her to get something for me."

"No need to explain."

"Where was I?" she pondered.

"You agreed that Joshua and Josephine still get around, but not as much."

"Oh yes, and if they could, they would be going just as strong as they were years ago."

Intrigued over the hot topic of discussion, I asked, "From your recollection, when did all this begin?"

She thought back, "I would say around the earlier part of 1900. They were good. I remember that so vividly."

The aroma of tea was prancing and dancing like music into my nostrils, and I was ready to sip the antidote with a listening ear. Picking up my spoon, too, I stirred in some sugar. The dream stalker would soon shake up my own memory bank even more, wondering could there be some connection. "I'm interested in hearing more about what happened back then," I said eagerly, and then glanced at my watch.

"Sure, if you have time."

"There is time left."

The eyes that sparkled through her mirrors were glistening as I waited for part two of her past to stir, to release what her mind wanted to sing. I was curious about what more would bubble from beneath, from what may have been buried at the bottom of the sea for some time. I was ready to listen for the sounds of history, as if I had just sat down to open up a good read.

"I know your time is limited, so I'll start around 1929. At about," she stumbled to remember, "hmmm, let me see now…I would say at age 15. Yes, that sounds about right. As young teenagers, Josephine and Joshua were friends that I saw almost daily. I had a horse named Mamie, and, *she was a pretty one…*"

I was in a state of shock. By the time she had gotten to the part about Joshua reading a poem at a high school, I traced that scene. The more she spoke, the more intrigued I became. "What was the name of Joshua's poem?"

She reached inside a little dainty purse and pulled out a sheet of paper that was folded. "I have carried this around with me for years," she said, as she unfolded it. "It's called 'Inspiration.'" She read it in its entirety.

By this time, I was coolly laughing in hysterics. *"I must be dreaming,"* I said. *How close on target is that?* The thought would not go away.

She softly laughed. "That tea was a little much for you, wouldn't you say?"

To keep the humor alive, I replied, "You're right! I'm hallucinating." Cackles deep inside my stomach were imprisoned. If I had reacted anything like how I felt right now, we probably would have been forced to zip-lock this conversation until another time. I had to wait and bust loose once I slid inside the vehicle—*outdoors.* It was hard to keep from busting out of all the stitches of my intelligence. For the most part, I caged my emotions for later.

Reaching for her cup, she sipped more tea. She doesn't know that what she was drinking was just as explosive. I don't know what tickled her, but she had no idea that we were on the same page. She reached inside her purse, again, and pulled out a picture. "A group of us took this picture together at that same high school." She placed the photo on the tabletop and pointed out everyone she knew by name. There was a group of kids in the picture, too.

Whew, the thought zoomed across my mind when I saw that I was not included. Even though I recognized the snapshot in the dream, it was just that—*a dream*.

As she continued, I remembered some things, but other details were vague. I don't know how I could ever forget with all the action and special effects. "And Mr. Jackson, a friend of the entire neighborhood."

Hmmm, I thought, *I don't remember anything resembling a neighborhood.* "Excuse me, Ms. PeggyAnn, but did you say neighborhood?" *Maybe a neighborhood did exist.*

"*Umph, did I say neighborhood?*" she tried to backtrack, smiling, and then said, "We lived in a rural area where neighbors were quite a ways away."

I nodded, waiting to hear more.

"Back to Mr. Jackson…he was a very kind man."

Ol' Mr. Jackson, I remembered, *I'll never forget the funny farm.* The dream stalker was on the loose, as more of the story bubbled to the surface.

When I was about to ask about him, she said, "Mr. Jackson and his brothers, who were triplets, got back together as a group and played music as they did when they were younger. From what I was told, in those days, they traveled a lot and had a large following. Years later, they never lost their touch; they were seasoned. After that program at Earlsmoth High School, they played locally with a different twist."

"How so?"

"Back then, I couldn't quite explain it. They played gospel in a way that I hadn't heard before. They recaptured their famous name, and took it to another height."

"Sounds like they made a change."

"Yes, they did, and changed the hearts of many people."

"What ever happened to Joshua and Josephine?" I forgot to ask.

"Oh, yes. They changed, too."

"I hope for the better."

She nodded. "I don't know what got into Joshua. Overnight, he was inspired to play music and *was good*. He played a saxophone like he had *twenty fingers*."

I snickered. "*Twenty fingers?*"

"*Yes*," her eyes inflated, again.

"He was good!" I blurted.

"Ruby, at a local restaurant, demanded that he play for their customers. That was his part-time job on the weekends."

Chuckling, my head fell back. "Umph." I couldn't say another word; my thought process went limp.

"And Josephine was very comical back then. If we wanted a good laugh, she was the one who could do it. *Oh my*, her character would tickle anyone. But, she really surprised me because that night at the high school, her brother had inspired her to sing and help children with learning disabilities."

I rose in my seat. "*She did?!*"

"Um hm."

I thought, *NOW THAT would've had a monkey scratching its head. The Josephine that I remember in the dream never gave me that impression—just a dream.*

"She was excellent with children and received many awards. Not only that, but," she shook her head in disbelief, "*Oooh, you talk about can sing.*" Ms. PeggyAnn's immediate expression was distorted with amazement for this lady.

I grinned. "Sounds like she could really blow the whistle."

My choice of words startled her with confusion.

For clarity, I said "What I meant is that she really must have some pipes."

Her face softened. "*Oh, I should say*; I could hardly believe it when she first opened her mouth. Josephine and Joshua joined the Electric Keynotes from time-to-time. They inspired each other and exploded. And I was so happy for Mr. Jackson because he was so determined to learn to speak English like the rest of us."

"Did he?" I almost shouted, but remained calm, once again.

She spoke until she finished. "Yes, he did. He had a rough time at first, but over time, he made progress. I made sure of that, and so did Genesis."

I batted my eyes as my brain came to a screeching halt. An instant snapshot of Genesis appeared and vanished as PeggyAnn continued her story.

"She was always a very quiet girl, but overnight, she blossomed. One day, Josephine, Joshua and I went to visit her. Never knew what troubled her. With some humor and creativity, she opened up. The imaginary show that we staged for her was a cure. Joshua's poem was her diamond ring because, years down the road they married and lived two fruitful lives as one. She grew up to be a doctor as a—" she paused, squinting her eyes, "a…Pedi—"

"Pediatrician?"

"Yes, that's it, a Pediatrician. She was wonderful with children. 'Inspiration' changed her life, which turned out to be the taxi to her success. And so it was for many others who were inspired."

"What about you, Ms. PeggyAnn?"

She smiled. "Besides being a country gal and a little farming in my young days?"

"Yes," I laughed at her humor, "I guess you can say that."

"Later, I got married, and had been for 59 years. We have a beautiful triangle of grandchildren."

"Triangle?"

"Yes," she smiled. "We have a wonderful host of grand, great-grand, and great-great-grandchildren."

"Oh," I understood now.

"Our family tree has *five bright stars*."

I was impressed as I listened to her paint a nice picture.

"We had five beautiful talented children—Catherine, Dean, Floyce, Ann, and Idella."

The cartwheel inside my head stopped. Those names were familiar but in a different order. When it registered, after scrambling the names around, I said, "*Oh…that's an interesting connection.*"

Tickled, she replied, "Many people get lost trying to remember my full name, just as you did."

I chuckled. "I have to admit, Ms. PeggyAnn, I have been up-and-down the alphabet tree, numerous times, trying to keep it straight. You have done well for such a long string of names."

"Young man," she glanced at me then sipped more tea, "all I can say is, I never *dipped, drank, smoked or chewed.*"

As humorous as that statement sounded, I had to laugh, again, and so did she.

"That's a good one," I said.

"That's an old saying, and I couldn't be but straight."

I snickered because I couldn't imagine her life any other way with the white flag nearby.

"For a 93-year-old," her eyes expanded, "I'm surprised I didn't stumble over my words."

Quickly, I said, "*Ninety-three?*"

"Yes," she nodded then chuckled.

"You're the most beautiful *93-year-old woman I've ever seen.*"

She blushed. "Well, thank you, dear."

"You have done well, Ms. PeggyAnn."

"I guess I have, Devin."

"Is there anything else you can tell me about your life growing up as a country gal?" I smiled and wanted to hear more.

"Oh, yes. I didn't finish telling you, did I?"

"I'm not certain," I told her.

"To finish answering your question, I was an ambitious person. Later, in life, I worked for a bank and graduated from school and became a minister."

My hands clapped together. "I knew it! A shining light. I'm glad we met."

"So am I, Devin. It has been delightful talking with you."

"Likewise. You are so graceful and full of wisdom. You are an antique, Ms. PeggyAnn, a rarity, with so much history."

"*Sho' nuff*?" she blushed.

I nodded, "*Sho' nuff*."

"Oh my," she smiled as an angel, "thank you."

"For many years, you have been a part of change and action to help make a difference by affecting other peoples' lives. You are a beautiful lady, ma'am."

She patted my arm. "You are so kind—"

"Is this what you're looking for, Ms. Malone?" the nurse asked, coming from around the corner.

"Yes, it is," Ms. PeggyAnn reached for it and thanked her. She faced me, reaching me the package. "This is for you. Joshua wanted you to have this."

"*Joshua, the poet and musician*." Excitement trailed in my voice.

"Yes," she chortled, "and he asked me to give you this note."

I laid the envelope down on the table to open the box first. When I opened it, there was that same hat that followed him around the globe. Smiling, I took it out the box and immediately stared at something so unique that I sucked in a quiet breath of unexpected air. Considering the mysteries, *No wonder it stood out.* I couldn't help but notice the beauty that looked like it never had a spec of dust on it. The detailing in the thick-black-velvet band around the crown had carved letters on both sides that spelled "Inspired," as if it had been engraved in stone, with two black leather tassels. Something else caught my eye. Smiling, I saw the dotted "i" staring at me, sparkling. It looked like a diamond. Instantly, my mind rolled backwards. Flashbacks came easy and so did a segment of the dream. My eyes were fixed in thin air, clearly seeing Joshua's face surrounded by a cloud of white smoke, evaporating into shining stars. He read

what surprised most, "...your inspirations are diamonds..."
Coolly, I laughed. Then, everything vanished like Liquid
Drano when I heard a faint voice.

Ms. PeggyAnn glanced at the hat then looked at
me with wonder. "Devin, it looks to me like that hat has
brought back memories." She picked up her tea cup, still
watching me.

For a moment, I couldn't speak. The film on the reel
was still flapping in my head.

She put the cup down. "Are you all right, dear?"

Finally, I nodded. "Yes," I grinned. "If you *only knew*,
Ms. PeggyAnn." Clearing my throat to speak above the
whisper, I added, "This hat says a trillion words."

A smile spread across her face. "For sure."

Still admiring the showcase, I raised it up on display,
spinning it around my hand. "Looks like it never left the
shelf. *The hat with twenty fingers.*"

PeggyAnn laughed. "It certainly is. You will always
have something to remember him by."

"I sure will." Shocked that he even thought to give
me what he had treasured, brought me joy. "This is quite a
surprise." I was honored to receive this gift.

After I read the note, all I could do was laugh. "This
is something. So, this was originally Mr. Jackson's hat; he
passed it on down to Joshua. Umph, umph, umph, *Good ol'
Mr. Jackson.*"

"Mysteriously, years ago, Mr. Jackson found money
in his cellar one day and," Ms. PeggyAnn remembered, "he
said there were coins and bills spread out everywhere. He
joked about how the hogs' heads guarded the money. That
was the strangest thing."

My mouth was wide open. The thoughts that went
through my mind...*I let it rest.*

She went on about this hat that had me on a mystery
hunt for the past few days and said, "One day, he used the
money to have that hat specially made and later handed it

down to Joshua. I agree that the hat says a trillion words. You deserve it, young man."

"Thank you, Ms. PeggyAnn. This hat will always be noted in my records of Historic Hall of Fame," I pointed toward my head.

"I can understand why," she smiled. Reaching in her purse again, she pulled out something else. "And here are a few newspaper clippings to read about him, including some about Josephine and the Electric Keynotes."

Something about the last clipping got my attention. As I strained to get a closer look, I noticed a man who resembled the mystery man standing with James and the others. "Umph," Ms. PeggyAnn heard me, "I wonder who he is?" My eyes became keen as a magnifying glass.

"Who? Mr. James?" she pointed at the wrong guy.

"The other one," I pointed out. Never knew what his role was. He looked like the man in the dream but I was not certain. Maybe he was someone else.

"Oh, Mr. Alexander. Mr. James knew him quite well and called him the 'grandfather clock.' "

"Interesting. Why did he call him that?"

Ms. PeggyAnn gleamed. "Back in those days, the young man had an unusual talent. He had a style of his own when it came to music. Later, I understood what Mr. James meant when I heard him for myself. Back then, I never heard anything quite like it. He was *magnificent*."

"Was he?" I asked.

"Yes. Whenever he came into town, the Electric Keynotes would request that he join them."

"That's probably why they played with a different twist. They were inspired by what he could do."

"I believe you're right, Devin. I agree with Mr. James. He said Mr. Alexander was the pendulum of music and he chimed right on time."

I softly laughed as my head fell back. His description of Mr. Alexander was well put, which gave me a very clear picture of just how dynamic he was. To be called the "grandfather clock" was significant. Clearly, the man could reach any altitude of music. The magnitude of his style apparently lit up the torch of tunes. He had to be diverse. *Amazing.*

"You can hold on to those articles," I heard Ms. PeggyAnn say.

I refocused and said gratefully, "Thank you."

"You're welcome. I held on to those from the paper Mr. James gave me. He owned a small newspaper company. That's how I kept up with what was going on. He was a very important man since we didn't have a television."

As she reminisced, I asked question after question, absorbed with every bit of information I could get.

Looking ahead dazed, Ms. PeggyAnn finally confirmed, concluding what I had been thinking all along, reliving memories, "...one change led to another, and Seminole County was never the same."

Listening, while seeing through the vision of her eyes, put the icing on the cake. We both had experienced special effects from our own memories, which ended on a good note. And...*that was good enough for me.*

As I almost dashed into the hallway to leave to meet the others to catch our flight, Ms. PeggyAnn called out, "*OH, YES, DEVIN.*"

I stopped and turned, pushing the hat with twenty fingers above my brow.

She beamed. "*How is Jordache?*"

HUH? she changed gears on me, *HOW DID SHE KNOW THAT?*

There was no more film left; the reel stopped. I guess I'll never know.

The plane took off across the sky. It was clear, sunny, and blue, just as my thoughts were. They beat, as I smiled.

Chuckling, I could feel the spirit of their dance. Their ribbon waved high in the sky of my mind, displaying melodies of life. *Colors of events that had been waiting to play tunes developed with change, which can only be unmasked as action sings. Accomplishments were activated by action. The sounds of chimes were ringing a beautiful song—a purple melody. Gray lenses were defects, manufactured to dismantle the mind. Deactivation was its friend. One inspiration injected another and made an impact. Their progression occurred with new sets of glasses that had color, something that would show them the rainbow. Otherwise, they probably would have never seen the radiance of opportunity. Above all, as Jarvis would say, they followed Him, the Purple Ribbon of trophies.*

Finally, this chapter has ended, I realized, staring out the window, *and I guess I was a part of the cast of my own imagination. Lessons learned can be taught through performances brought to life that sometimes lead to change in our lives and to even affect others. Fascinating, how the horizon of growth glows as cobblestones of our footsteps from behind the backstage of our minds. The question is…how will it be put into action? The dial of time increased its orchestration in rhythm from energies of the rising of change, clearly seeing that curfew time had ended, playing unknown drum rolls before entering into a rendition of a new song of life. Released from the walls of my crib, dynamics thundered in the cerebellum, showing me the dance of liberty and the lyrics were as royal as purple melodies. Hmmm,* a beat in my mind was EKG'n, *what's next, as time delivers more beautiful songs?...*

*WHAT TIME IS IT?!...*The ballerina bowed, gracefully.

…this beat is a classic…

CURTAINS

Reflections in My Tea

A cup of tea,
hot as can be,
a miniature body of water flowing free,
resembling the substance of the sea,
settled with particles of the deep,
relaxed in a twilight sleep.

Tea cups are hollow,
outlined to hold as a container,
receives the rich tinted substance,
waiting to meet its claimer,
just as history was affected by change.

Tea comes in many flavors poured at half moon,
colors of events just waiting to play tunes,
counterparts are the saucer and spoon,
forming its shape below the brim,
silky and fluidly trimmed,
sparkling bright as the starlight,
glowing like the moonlight.

The aroma prances dancing like music,
wavering a glory to awaken,
shaking memories that were forsaken,
alerting reflectors through eyes of sparkling mirrors,
adding sugar – the dream stalker,
the spoon to stir – stirring up the past,
listening for the sound of history,
and maybe some added marshmallows and cream,
an added antidote,
to release what the mind held to sing,
bubbling up from beneath,
what's buried at the bottom of the sea.

Staring down in my tea,
daydreaming of what the mind sees,
floating to the surface from its crib,
reliving,
Reflections in My Tea.

About the Author

*R*eflections in My Tea is Sandra Porter's second novel of The Brooks Series. She is also known as Camey Brooks for writing her first novel *Whistling in the Wind*. She is a former resident of Phoenix, Arizona and currently resides in the state of Georgia.

Printed in the United States
205826BV00001B/1-102/P